MW00466476

Bug Out! Texas Book 6

Citizen Vengeance

Robert Boren

South Bay Press

Copyright © 2017 by Robert Boren.

All rights reserved. No part of this publication may be reproduced, distributed or transmitted in any form or by any means, including photocopying, recording, or other electronic or mechanical methods, without the prior written permission of the publisher, except in the case of brief quotations embodied in critical reviews and certain other noncommercial uses permitted by copyright law. For permission requests, write to the publisher, addressed "Attention: Permissions Coordinator," at the address below.

Author/Publishing South Bay Press

Publisher's Note: This is a work of fiction. Names, characters, places, and incidents are a product of the author's imagination. Locales and public names are sometimes used for atmospheric purposes. Any resemblance to actual people, living or dead, or to businesses, companies, events, institutions, or locales is completely coincidental.

Book Layout ©2017 BookDesignTemplates.com
Cover design: SelfPubBookCovers.com/Fantasyart
Bug Out! Texas Book 6– Citizen Vengeance/ Robert Boren. – 3rd ed.
ISBN 9781973212300

For Aaron

I must say as to what I have seen of Texas, it is the garden spot of the world. The best land & best prospects for health I ever saw is here, and I do believe it is a fortune to any man to come here. There is a world of country to settle.

–David Crockett

Contents

Previously – in Bug Out! Texas Book 5

Governor Nelson traveled to Fort Stockton and held a meeting with several resistance groups, including the one led by Simon Orr, which led to controversy. The groups formed a loose plan to integrate themselves. During his visit, the Governor's Mansion in Austin was bombed, and an attempt was made on the Capitol Building.

Nelson moved his office to the bunker below Kip Hendrix's house, and ordered other officials to take refuge in bunkers too. A wave of attacks began on bunker locations, and Kip's house was destroyed, leaving the bunker intact. Maria learned from her mother that her sister Celia had escaped from the mental institution. The Governor's team suspected Major General Landry of being a spy for the enemy and took steps to expose him. Nelson developed a new strategy to get out of reactive mode: Stop concentrating on protecting the cities. Move their resources to protect the Gulf Coast port and refinery infrastructure. Attack enemy supply lines through Southwest Texas and New Mexico.

Curt had previously given Nelson a program he'd developed that allowed the Patriots the ability to track enemy cellphones. Because of this, Landry was exposed and relieved of his command of the Air National Guard. Simon Orr called Landry while he was in custody and said he was planning on attacking Fort Stockton. DPS Commissioner Wallis and Austin Police Chief Ramsey told the Patriots in Fort Stockton, who attempted to flush out Orr at his base. They walked right into a trap. It was a terrible loss of good men including Earl, Jackson, Nate and Gray. Simon Orr later tricked Landry into committing suicide with a cyanide capsule hidden in his shoe.

Supplied with additional 3D printers and arms by Governor Nelson's team, the Fort Stockton Patriots manufactured more vehicle armaments. Ramsey contacted them and told them to expect a major assault on Fort Stockton, and that the Islamists had formed an alliance with Militia groups, including Simon Orr's. The Patriots made tremendous progress on weapons overnight and were told the next day about the strength of the enemy – over a thousand troops to their north and another large group to their south. The Governor's team suggested they flee, but Junior suggested instead that they enlist the citizens through social media. Don and Sydney began a campaign, resulting in many thousands of ordinary citizens committing to the battle.

As night fell, the Fort Stockton group engaged the enemy north of I-20, doing tremendous damage, but there were too many enemy fighters, so the Patriots retreated south. As they did so, thousands of citizens showed up to join the fight. The Patriots defeated the enemy, taking no prisoners.

On the Gulf Coast, the DPS boats repelled a massive attack. Richardson, Brendan and Juan Carlos participated and when it was over, returned to their trailer park to find their homes destroyed and their women missing. They found them at the local emergency room; Madison had cut her foot badly and needed stitches. The men received word that they were being moved to Houston and would be protecting Galveston. DPS command suspected a mole in their organization as their residences had been hit. The group was cautioned not to reveal their movements to the DPS office. Richardson moved the group to Loyola Beach to rest and recuperate. They fled from their hiding place when Islamists attacked the area, escaping to San Antonio. There, they hoped they were safe, even venturing out to dinner at the Riverwalk, only to be forced into another battle with terrorists, this time with hundreds of armed citizen Patriots on their side.

{ 1 }

San Antonio Terror

Richardson froze as the gunfight intensified on the Riverwalk below.

"You saw some Islamists enter the restaurant?" he asked.

"Yeah, dude," Juan Carlos said. "We'd better go get them. The girls are safe up here if they stay down."

"I'm on it," Brendan said, slipping into the restaurant, rushing past shocked patrons hiding under their tables.

"Stay here, Juan Carlos," Richardson said. "Guard the women." He raced into the restaurant after Brendan.

"They're down there, by the door," Brendan whispered as Richardson caught up to him by the stairs.

"They aren't coming up, they're hiding," Richardson whispered back. "See them by the window? They don't have guns on any of the patrons. Probably afraid of that old coot with the hog leg."

"Yeah, that guy was the bomb," Brendan whispered, flashing a grin. "Let's waste those creeps."

"They've got AKs," Richardson said.

Suddenly there were several quick blasts downstairs.

"Shotgun!" Brendan said.

Richardson peeked his head down. "Probably the owner. Those Islamists are toast. Bad cleanup job down there."

"What now?" Brendan asked.

“Back to the balcony,” Richardson said.

They rushed out, getting down and crawling to the edge of the balcony. Citizen gunfire continued, the Islamists fleeing.

“The people have this, dude,” Juan Carlos said, sitting under a table with the women, gun at the ready. “Don’t mess with Texas.”

“Yeah, the Islamists are running away,” Brendan said, moving back from the edge. Hannah shot him a terrified glance. He moved over to her, pulling her into his arms.

“What about the men downstairs?” Lita whispered to Richardson.

“Somebody used a shotgun on them,” he said. “It’s a mess.”

“They weren’t in there to attack the patrons,” Brendan said. “They were hiding from the citizens.”

“The Islamists had the citizens out-gunned,” Juan Carlos said.

“There’s at least a hundred armed citizens down there,” Richardson said. “I saw maybe twenty-five Islamists. Better weapons can’t fix that kind of ratio.”

“Can we go?” Madison asked, tears streaming down her cheeks.

“Wait till the gunfire stops,” Richardson said.

“So much for our nice quiet dinner,” Lita said.

“Why do we keep running into this stuff?” Hannah asked, clinging to Brendan.

“I don’t know, sweetie,” Brendan said softly.

“Look, there’s a group of Islamists running away,” Juan Carlos said, rushing to the edge. He opened fire, killing three of them, Richardson joining him and dropping two. The others got away, out of view of the balcony.

“We’d better save the rest of our ammo,” Juan Carlos said. “We still have to get back to the hotel.”

“I have another magazine,” Brendan said.

“Not me,” Juan Carlos said. “I’ve only got four rounds left.”

The gunfire finally stopped.

“Is it over?” Madison asked.

"Sounds like it," Juan Carlos said, coming back over to her.

"You don't think they came here looking for us, do you?" she asked.

Juan Carlos petted her cheek, brushing the blonde hair out of her eyes. "No, sweetie, this was a random attack."

"Yeah, if they knew we were here, they would've come after us quietly," Richardson said. "They wouldn't have rushed right down the middle of the Riverwalk."

"This was like those attacks in Europe," Brendan said. "Pure terror on soft targets. No strategic value other than the terror itself. Most of them probably assumed they'd die in this."

"Most of them did die," Juan Carlos said.

The manager rushed onto the balcony, shotgun still in his hand, dropping to his knees next to the dead waitress.

"Oh, no," he cried, sobbing.

"That poor man," Madison whispered.

"That was probably his daughter," Juan Carlos said. "They look alike."

"Oh God," Lita said, breaking down. "Can we go?"

"Yes, let's go to the hotel," Richardson said. "We'll just order room service."

"They might not be doing room service after this mess," Brendan said.

"I don't care, let's go," Hannah said.

"Okay," Richardson said, "but keep your eyes open and your guns at the ready. Stay near cover."

Richardson put some bills on their table under a pitcher, and they left, Juan Carlos protecting Madison as she hobbled along on her crutches.

"My God, look at all the dead Islamists," Hannah said, eyes darting around.

"Lots of dead citizens too," Brendan said. "This was a bad attack."

"Crap, the back gate is closed," Lita said.

"There's a card reader next to it," Richardson said. "Let's try a room key." He stuck his into the slot and the gate clicked.

"Thank God," Lita said as Richardson pushed the heavy gate open. He held it until everybody was through, then closed it again.

"So much for the city being safer," Madison said.

"It *is* safer," Juan Carlos said. "We were in a big gathering point. Perfect target for terror attacks like this."

"Sorry," Richardson said. "That was my idea."

"You had no way of knowing," Lita said.

"Yeah," Madison said. "It wasn't your fault."

They went through the lobby to the elevator. Richardson pushed the button for their floor. Nothing happened.

"You think they're down?" Hannah asked.

Madison's brow furrowed. "Oh, God, I can't go up the stairs with these damn crutches."

"Use your room key," Lita said. "They might have turned up the security."

Richardson inserted it and then hit the button again. The elevator doors opened.

"*Thank you*," Madison whispered.

"I'm glad they did that," Richardson said.

"Yeah, me too," Lita said.

They arrived on their floor and walked to their rooms.

"Want to eat together?" Lita asked.

Juan Carlos looked at Madison. She shook her head yes.

"Okay," Juan Carlos said.

Hannah shook her head yes too. "I'd rather be with the group now."

"Sure, honey," Brendan said.

They went into Richardson and Lita's room.

"You notice that the police never showed up?" Brendan asked.

"Yeah, I noticed," Richardson said. "The citizens did a good job on their own." He picked up the TV remote and clicked it on. There was video of the battle running.

"Well, it made the news," Lita said, setting down the room service menu.

"Look at the banner on the bottom of the screen," Juan Carlos said. "San Antonio Police stations hit by terror attacks."

"That explains it," Brendan said. "Geez, between those two stations, we lost almost fifty cops."

"No," Hannah said.

"Could you imagine if this happened somewhere like Chicago, where people can't carry guns?" Juan Carlos said. "It would've been a blood bath."

"Seriously," Brendan said. "It'd probably still be going on now."

"Ready to order something?" Lita asked. She moved to the others, holding the menu open.

"I'm so hungry now that I'd eat almost anything," Juan Carlos said.

Richardson walked over to the window, deep in thought, staring out into the city. The heavy traffic they drove through to the hotel was gone now. People scurried nervously around below.

"Honey, come away from the window," Lita said.

He nodded and walked to her, his face grim.

"What's wrong?" she asked.

"The city is terrorized," Richardson said. "The enemy got what they wanted."

{ 2 }

Imagery

Don and Sydney watched as their team hammered on keyboards, still keeping up the pace, focusing more on the enemy fighters south of the RV Park, down around Big Bend National Park. Sydney's phone rang.

"Amanda," Sydney said. "I'll put it on speaker." She set it on the stage and punched the speaker button.

"Sis, you okay?" she asked.

"Hell yeah," Amanda said. "This is a rout."

"Really?" Don asked.

"Really," Amanda said. "The citizens came in from the east and the west, right down I-20. Flooded the whole area. Must be more than ten thousand people. We're chasing what's left of the enemy now."

"Anybody get hurt?" Sydney asked.

"Yeah. Lost one of the tanks. Lost several of Gray's bikers. Lost somebody in one of the off-roaders. Not sure who it was."

"Not Curt," Sydney asked.

"No, he's fine," Amanda said. "He's been back for more ammo twice now. I had to move up, finally. Before the citizens showed up we were getting ready to flee. They had us pushed back all the way to I-20."

"Geez," Don said.

"What's going on down south?" Amanda asked.

"Don't know," Don said. "In the last satellite picture, there were enemy troops showing up. We sent that out. Last check we had about ten thousand volunteers headed that way."

"That's what they said, anyway," Sydney said.

"After what we saw here, I believe it," Amanda said. "Here comes Curt again. I think this thing is almost over. Gotta go."

Sydney ended the call and grabbed her phone.

"Well, sounds positive," Sydney said. "Thank God. I was so worried."

"I'll feel better when we get the next satellite picture," Don said. "The last one was almost an hour ago. Ought to be any minute."

"Hey, Dad," Alyssa said, rushing over.

"What, sweetie?" Don asked.

"Just heard from some people down south. The Air National Guard just attacked the enemy down there."

"Good. Hope they don't hit any of our folks."

"Doesn't sound like they got there yet," Alyssa said. "They're going in to mop up."

"Good," Don said.

"What's going on with our guys? I saw you two on the phone."

"We're winning," Don said. "At least it sounds like we are. I want to see the next picture."

"Yeah, it's about time, isn't it? People are asking for it."

Don's phone rang. "Gallagher. I'll put it on speaker."

"Don?" Gallagher asked.

"Yeah. Got that new photo for us?"

"Just sent it to your inbox," Gallagher said. "My God."

"Is that a good *My God* or a bad *My God*?" Sydney asked.

"Bad for the enemy," Gallagher said. "Our analyst said we had more than twenty thousand citizens join the battle up north, and almost ten thousand heading towards the south. We just nailed the enemy down south with air power. They're trying to get back across the river into Mexico as we speak."

"We gonna chase them?" Don asked.

"The planes are. Tell the citizens not to, okay? We don't want to lose a bunch of them."

"You heard that, Alyssa," Don said. "Pass the word, okay?"

"You got it, Dad," she said, rushing back to her team.

"Heard from your people?" Gallagher asked.

"Yeah, my sister," Sydney said. "About five minutes ago. She said it was a rout."

"That's an understatement," Gallagher said. "I'd better get off. Got to contact the Governor and tell him the good news."

"Thanks," Don said. "Talk to you later."

"Take care," Gallagher said. Don ended the call.

"Let's go check out that picture and get it uploaded," Don said. He and Sydney rushed over to Don's laptop and clicked on the file.

"Good Lord," Don said, looking at the picture. "This is insane." He sent the file to the drop area, then stood up and turned towards the team. "The satellite picture is out there. Distribute it far and wide."

There were murmurs in the room.

"Holy shit," Chloe said, covering her mouth after the words came out. Alyssa laughed.

"Language," Don said. Half the room cracked up.

"Okay, *Dad*," Sydney said, sly smile on her face.

He chuckled. "Maybe we should crank up some more coffee."

"I'll help," Sydney said. They walked to the kitchen together.

Don took the top off the big coffee maker and sniffed.

"Bad?" she asked.

"A little burned," Don said, "and almost gone. It's time." He got to work.

"Do you think this makes us safe?" Sydney asked.

“Safer, maybe,” Don said. “This is a long way from over. I keep hearing that there are half a million enemy fighters in the southwest. If that’s really true, we’ll need to get better at recruiting. Thirty thousand won’t be enough if they mount an attack with anywhere near that many people.”

“Comforting thought,” Sydney said, taking the rinsed coffee basket from Don. She dried it with a paper towel and loaded it with scoops of coffee.

“Wonder how late it’s gonna be when our people get home?” Don asked. He filled the coffee pot with water and set it on the counter as Sydney thought about it.

“Late,” Sydney said. “We’ve probably got another wake coming. People got killed.”

“I know,” Don said. “The last one was hard.”

“It was,” Sydney said. She set the coffee basket into the pot and put on the top. “Ready.”

Don plugged it in, then looked at her. “You decide yet?”

“Decide what?”

Don rolled his eyes, and she giggled. “Oh, that.”

“Yeah, that,” Don said. “I want you with me.”

“Are you sure?” she asked. “What about your daughter and Chloe?”

“I talked to Sherry. She wants them to stay in their trailer. Francis agreed.”

“You sure they aren’t just being polite?”

“Pretty sure,” Don said.

“Okay, then I’ll give you my answer tonight,” she said.

{ 3 }

X-Rays

Kip Hendrix and Governor Nelson were in the bunker living room, watching TV coverage of the attacks in San Antonio.

"The terrorists did worse against the citizens than they did against the police," Hendrix said.

"The citizens are unpredictable," Nelson said. "I'll bet the terrorists didn't expect the resistance they got at the Riverwalk."

Maria walked in and sat next to Hendrix. "Did we get more news about Fort Stockton?"

"Not yet, and it scares me," Nelson said. "I hope Junior's plan worked."

"You and me both," Hendrix said.

"I wish we would've been able to keep Landry alive longer," Nelson said. "Somebody might have called him over this."

"Maybe," Hendrix said.

There was a beep from the console. "That's probably Gallagher," Maria said, getting up. She rushed into the console room, Hendrix and Nelson hot on her heels.

"It's Gallagher all right," Maria said, clicking accept. She turned up the sound volume.

"Hello, Major General Gallagher," she said.

Gallagher chuckled. "Always so businesslike. Hi, Maria."

"Hi," she said. "Got news for us?"

"Yeah, and I just sent the satellite picture."

"Did our people survive?" Nelson asked.

Gallagher chuckled. "Remember when I said this could be a *Little Big Horn* event?"

"It went that well?" Nelson asked.

"Yeah, it went that well," Gallagher said. "We got nearly twenty thousand people on the northern front, and another ten thousand down south."

"Casualties?" Hendrix asked.

"We won't know that for hours," Gallagher said. "Not good numbers, anyway."

"We talk to anybody on the scene?" Hendrix asked.

"Second hand, from a woman whose sister is at the battle. Sounds like they lost one of the M-1 tanks and one of their off roaders."

"There has to be more than that," Nelson said.

"Probably," Gallagher said. "We pounded the group down south with air power. They fled across the river into Mexico. I told Fort Stockton to pass the word not to follow them down there."

"Good," Nelson said.

"Gotta run," Gallagher said. "We're still chasing down what happened to the police in San Antonio. Talk to you later."

"Thanks," Nelson said.

Maria shut down the call and printed the satellite picture.

"I'll get it," Hendrix said, rushing to the printer as it came out. He handed it to Nelson.

"Good Lord," he said, looking closely at it. "All those people."

"Is this going to be a turning point?" Maria asked.

"We need to remember Little Big Horn," Hendrix said. "They won a battle but lost the war. We don't want to have the same problem. There are a lot of enemy fighters in the southwest. We've got a long, nasty fight ahead of us, and we still can't trust our Army National Guard."

"We might have another problem," Nelson said.

"What's that?" Hendrix asked.

"They may figure out that we have satellite imagery now. It'll make them more careful with their troop buildups."

"Oh," Hendrix said. "Shit."

"How could they be more careful?" Maria asked.

"I'd be surprised if they build up a large force on open ground again like they did," Nelson said. "They might infiltrate a target area slowly instead."

"That's easier said than done," Hendrix said. "We give up a little in the way of surprise if they know we can watch, but it also restricts their movement. That in itself is a big advantage for us."

"That's a good point," Nelson said.

"So what's next?" Maria asked.

"Assess what happened on the battle field, discuss it, meet with the people involved, and try to motivate the citizen participants into organizing," Hendrix said. "I miss anything?"

"Redouble our efforts to weed out the bad guys in our state military," Nelson said.

"We've done pretty well in the Air National Guard," Hendrix said.

"True, but we're only using about a third of our available choppers because of the shortage of pilots," Nelson said. "We have work to do there."

"Check the chopper pilots for RFID chips," Hendrix said.

Nelson froze, then grinned at him. "There you go again. Maria, get Wallis on the line, please."

"Yes sir," she said, going back to the console. She had Wallis on the line in a few seconds.

"Hello, Governor," Wallis said. "Great news about the battle today."

"Yeah, and nasty news about San Antonio," Nelson said. "You see that?"

"Yes," he said. "We've got Dallas and Fort Worth locked down tighter than a drum. All the major civilian gathering spots are under surveillance."

"Good," Nelson said. "Don't keep armed civilians out. That's counter-productive."

"How do we know which are the good civilians and which are the bad?" Wallis asked.

"Profile," Nelson said. "You know what I mean."

Wallis chuckled. "Well, it is wartime, isn't it? What else is on your mind?"

"Another good idea from Kip. We need to x-ray all of those chopper pilots for RFID chips."

There was silence on the line for a moment. "Dammit. Want a job, Kip?"

"Busy with the one I have," Hendrix said. "C'mon, one of us would've figured that out."

"I suggest doing this carefully," Nelson said. "Bring in a few at a time, and tell them not to pass it along. Arrest anybody with a chip, of course."

"Okay, we can do that," Wallis said. "I'll get that started in the morning."

"Oh, and nice job down by Big Bend National Park," Nelson said.

"Nice to be in the fight," Wallis said. "One of the officers that I do trust made a suggestion."

"What's that?"

"Contact the Israelis and see if they'll sell us some drones on the QT. They manufacture them, you know. We could use the tactical reconnaissance."

"That's a good idea," Nelson said. "I'll get on that personally. I have a relationship with the Prime Minister, and he knows what President Simpson is up to. He'll probably go for it."

"Good," Wallis said. "Anything else?"

"Let me know right away if you find any RFID chips," Nelson said. "If this works, we need to use it with the Army National Guard."

"Roger that," Wallis said. "Talk to you guys later."

Maria ended the call.

"This calls for a drink," Nelson said.

"And some ice cream?" Maria asked.

Nelson grinned. "Don't tempt me."

{ 4 }

Aftermath

Amanda watched as several vehicles approached her bobtail, Curt leading.

"More ammo already?" she asked as Curt pulled up.

"It's over," Curt said, getting out of his Barracuda.

Junior and Rachel pulled up in their off-roader, followed by Cindy in hers, then Jason and Francis in the Jeep.

"We lose anybody else?" Amanda asked.

"Not since the citizens arrived," Curt said. "Not that I saw anyway."

"Where are the citizens?" Amanda asked.

"Burning bodies," Junior said.

"No prisoners?" Amanda asked.

"Nope, we killed all the bad guys," Jason said. "I was against it for about two seconds."

"I wasn't," Curt said. "We need to be a terror to these guys. It's what they understand. We ought to put the bodies on display."

There was a whoosh about five hundred yards away, and a bright glow as the bonfire started.

"Wow," Cindy said, still sitting in her off-roader. "Glad the wind isn't blowing this way."

Kelly drove up with Brenda in their truck. “Looks like the barbeque is starting.”

“Sick, man,” Junior said. Brenda rolled her eyes.

Kyle and Kate rolled up in their truck, followed by Moe in his Jeep and Clancy in his truck.

“Seen Eric and Kim?” Jason asked.

“They’ll be along,” Kelly said. “They were chasing down stragglers. Eric was looking at some of the bodies before we burned them.”

“I’ll bet he wants to see if they have RFID chips,” Jason said.

“Yeah,” Curt said. “I was thinking the same thing.”

“What’s that going to tell us?” Rachel asked.

“It’ll tell us if they’ve put these chips in all of their forces,” Curt said.

“Oh,” Rachel said.

“We need to crack those,” Junior said. “Think you can do that, Curt?”

“I have no idea,” Curt said. “Not really my cup of tea. The phones weren’t too difficult because I could use the phone’s operating system to figure it out. RFID chips don’t run programs. They just transmit codes.”

“Do we need to stick around?” Amanda asked.

“Let’s wait until the rest of our folks show up,” Curt said.

“Here come the tanks,” Clancy said.

“Wonder if they’re low on fuel yet?” Amanda asked. “I’m at least a week from real production of fuel for them. We need to buy some holding tanks.”

“We should talk to Ramsey about that,” Jason said. “I’ll ask him if they can send fuel tankers for now. Maybe he can help us with holding tanks too.”

“Him or Gallagher,” Kyle said.

“Can we go?” Kate asked. “I don’t feel so hot.”

"She's pregnant," Brenda said. "Take her home."

"Okay, sweetie," Kyle said, worried look on his face. "We'll go home right now. See you guys back at camp."

They drove away in their truck.

"I hope she doesn't have a problem," Brenda said. "Too much stress early in a pregnancy can be bad."

Rachel shot a glance at Junior. "Maybe we ought to go back too."

"Wait, you aren't, are you?" Amanda asked.

"Probably not," Rachel said.

"You're *late,*" Brenda said. "Yeah, let's get you back home."

Junior nodded. "Let's hook this thing up to your truck, okay?"

"Yeah," Kelly said, walking over to it. Junior pulled the off-roader up against the back and helped Kelly hitch it up. They were done in a couple of minutes, and took off for home.

Eric and Kim rode up in their Bronco. "Everybody survive?"

"We lost a few people," Jason said. "Plus one tank and one off-roader."

"Could've been worse," Francis said. "A whole lot worse."

Dirk and Chance drove up, parking the truck and trotting over.

"We kicked their ass," Dirk said.

"Yeah, seriously," Chance said. "What were you doing with the bodies, Eric?"

"Checking on something," Eric said.

"The RFID chips," Jason said. "Right?"

Eric nodded yes.

"Any have them?"

"Yeah, brother," Eric said. "All of them. He picked up a white cloth on his dashboard and held it up. "I've got six of them right here."

"Wonder if they're still transmitting?" Chance asked.

"That's a good question," Jason said. "Maybe we shouldn't take them back home."

"Yeah, might not be a good idea," Kim said.

"I'd take them. Possible that we can use them to our advantage," Curt said.

"I suggest we stash them someplace," Jason said. "Use them for a trap."

"Should have brought some mines," Chance said. "We could bury them on top of one. The enemy comes to investigate and boom."

"I think it's wise to hide the fact that we know about them," Dirk said. "At least for now."

"I've got an idea," Eric said. "I'll hide these off the road a ways. Take the GPS coordinates. We'll come back and look for them later."

"What will that tell us?" Kim asked.

"It'll tell us if they're using this to track their people on the run, or if they just use them to check people in and out of their bases," Eric said.

"You think the enemy will come for them?" Jason asked. "With all of the dead they have here, they're going to check out six signals?"

"You're forgetting something, pencil neck," Curt said. "We're burning all of the bodies. That destroys the chips. They'll see only six and wonder if they've got a few fighters who escaped. If they're really using them the way we suspect, anyway."

"If the chips are just sitting stationary, won't the enemy figure out they're no longer in living people?" Jason asked.

Moe laughed. "Let me see one of those."

Eric opened the white cloth and pulled one out as Moe walked over.

"Ewww, gross," Kim said. "Bloody with pieces of flesh."

"I cut them out kinda fast," Eric said.

"Hell, these are small," Moe said. "We've got those goats, in a pen behind the RV park about sixty yards. Maybe we ought to let the goats be *stand-in Islamists.*"

"That works on so many levels," Chance said.

Clancy cracked up. "Yeah, let's do that and watch. See if a rescue squad shows up. Nab them."

"What if they send a larger force and attack the park?" Kim asked.

"We'll see that coming in the satellite pictures," Dirk said.

"Maybe we would," Curt said. "The enemy leaders aren't stupid. They have to know we saw their forces coming into the area. They'll trickle in next time if they can get away with it. Hide their numbers."

"Or they'll have enough vehicles to drive in fast," Dirk said. "If they would've done that this time, we'd be dead right now."

"He's right," Eric said. "If we don't consider that they'll learn from their mistakes, they'll nail us good."

"Need I remind you guys that none of us got buzzed by any cell phones?" Curt asked. "Or that none of us saw them coming using the tracking app? They figured out what we knew and adjusted."

"Yep. I checked my phone more than once," Jason said. "They learned that we could track those."

"Damn straight," Curt said.

"So what are we gonna do?" Dirk asked. "Enlist the goats?"

"I think it's a good idea," Curt said. "We could use a chance to interrogate some of these guys."

"We need to tell Ramsey what we're doing first," Jason said. "Agreed?"

"Yeah," Curt said. "Call him up."

"I'll call on the way to camp," Jason said. "We should go."

"Yeah, let's," Amanda said.

{ 5 }

Casualty

Jason walked over to Francis, who was helping Curt hitch the Barracuda to the truck.

"Francis, can you drive, so I can make the call to Ramsey?" he asked.

"Yeah, sure"

"You pencil necks ready?" Curt asked.

"Hey, do you have to ride back on that thing?" Amanda asked. "I'd rather have you in the bobtail with me."

"Sure, I can ride with you," Curt said.

"Good, then let's go, honey," Amanda said.

"Honey?" Francis asked, grinning.

Curt chuckled. "Not you too." Amanda took his hand and they went back to her truck.

"He's in for a wild night, I suspect," Jason said.

"Seriously," Francis said. "You ready to go?"

"Yeah." They got in, and Francis drove them towards camp. The others followed.

Jason hit Ramsey's contact. It rang twice.

"Jason! So good to hear from you. I heard the battle went well."

"We slaughtered them," Jason said. "Thanks to all those citizens who showed up. If not for that, we'd all be dead right now."

"What's on your mind?"

"Eric looked at some of the enemy bodies before they got burned," Jason said. "They all had those RFID chips in them."

"Where?"

"Shoot, I didn't ask," Jason said. "I'll get back to you on that."

"I'll need to chat with Wallis and Gallagher on this," Ramsey said. "We were just discussing it a little while ago."

"We had an idea," Jason said.

"Go ahead."

"We want to attach the RFID chips to a herd of goats that Moe has in a corral about sixty yards behind the RV Park."

Ramsey chuckled. "Bait, huh? Sure that's a good idea?"

"Maybe it's slightly risky, but it'll be hard for the enemy to sneak in enough people to attack the RV Park, now that we have the Satellite imagery."

"We might lose access at any time," Ramsey said. "Keep that in mind."

"Shit," Jason said. "Really? How much chance is there of that?"

"Unknown," Ramsey said. "Nelson is working on an alternative. I can't talk about it over the phone."

"Good," Jason said. "You have any objection to us baiting these guys?"

"No, but I'll run it past Gallagher and Wallis after I get off the line. Go ahead unless I call you back on it."

"Thanks," Jason said. "Talk to you later."

Jason ended the call.

"Well?" Francis asked.

"He said to go ahead unless we hear differently. He's gonna talk to Wallis and Gallagher."

"We should talk to him about getting another tank," Francis said. "We won't have all four corners of the park covered now."

"Yes," Jason said. "Maybe we can use one of the off-roaders instead, for now. Those M19s have pretty decent range."

"True," Francis said.

They rode silently for a while, both deep in their own thoughts. Jason was worried. This was a great victory, but what would the follow-up be from the enemy?

"We're getting close to route 18," Francis said. "See it ahead?"

"Barely," Jason said.

"Think they would've marched all the way to the RV Park?"

Jason thought about it for a moment. "That's hard to say. If they'd defeated us, they might have turned around and gone back to New Mexico. Their main concern is keeping the supply lines open."

"What about our weapons?" Francis asked.

"We had most of the good stuff with us," Jason said. "Of course they didn't know that. Wonder what happened to Simon Orr?"

"Maybe he's burning up in that bonfire," Francis said.

"Possible," Jason said. "I'd be surprised if nobody noticed him, though. He doesn't look like an Islamist."

"Were there militia people in that battle?" Francis asked.

Jason froze for a moment. "You know, I didn't look. When the battle was over I went back to our lines pretty fast."

"We should use our social media contacts to ask," Francis said.

"Yeah, we need to do that."

"There's the tanks," Francis said as they rolled by them.

"Yep," Jason said. "You know who was in the tank that we lost?"

"No," Francis said. "Probably Gray's guys. They trained hard on the tanks. I think about 70% of our tank crews are from that group."

"They've given a lot," Jason said. "We need to go out of our way to acknowledge that."

"Agreed. You think this was a turning point?"

"No, I think this was just the beginning, and it's going to get harder now," Jason said.

"Why?" Francis asked.

"Because they know we're more than just a nuisance to them," Jason said. "We're a threat to their mission. Big time. We'll need to prepare, to get smarter, to lock in our support from the surrounding areas."

They were silent for a while as they raced down route 18, headlights behind them. Jason's phone rang. He answered it.

"Jason, its Chief Ramsey."

"Hi, Chief. You get an answer?"

"Yeah, use the goats. We're very interested to see what happens. Keep your eyes open, though, okay? If they send a small detail to check out the signals, they might also send a group of assassins in. We don't want any of your key folks there to get killed or captured. Understand?"

"Yeah, we'll put a 24-hour guard on this," Jason said. "Thanks."

"Don't mention it," Ramsey said.

"Hey, one other thing," Jason said. "No, a *couple* other things. Any chance we can get another tank, to replace the one we lost? It leaves a hole in our defenses."

"I'll check," Ramsey said. "I can't promise anything, but I'll push for it. What else?"

"We need some storage tanks so we can store fuel from the still operation. Think you can help us with that?"

"I'll give that a shot too," Ramsey said. "There has been some discussion about sending a tanker out there to refuel you guys. Gallagher figured you'd need it after the battle."

"Perfect, that would be helpful. Thanks."

"No problem," Ramsey said. "Be careful. Talk to you soon."

Jason ended the call.

"He go for it?" Francis asked.

"On the RFID chips, yes. He'll check into the tank stuff."

"Great," Francis said. "We're almost home."

"Good, I'm beat," Jason said.

They covered the remaining road in less than ten minutes.

"I'll get out here, if that's okay," Francis said, pulling over a few yards inside of the park.

"Okay, thanks for driving," Jason said. "Thanks for fighting with me too."

"It was a pleasure," Francis said as he got out. Other vehicles were flooding through the gate now. Jason got behind the wheel and drove back to his site. Carrie was sitting on the picnic table next to their rig, head in her hands.

"Hi, sweetie," Jason said.

She ran into his arms, hugging him tight, sobbing.

"It's okay," Jason said. "I'm safe. All our friends are safe too."

"Kate had a miscarriage," Carrie whispered.

"Oh, God no," Jason said.

{ 6 }

Justice of the Peace

Hannah woke up next to Brendan as the sun was coming up. She got out of bed and walked to the window, looking out over the bustle of the city.

"Hey," Brendan said.

"Oh, you're awake," Hannah said, turning towards him.

"Come here," Brendan said. She smiled and got back on the bed, snuggling against him. "What's it look like out there?"

"It looks like normal," she said. "As if nothing happened."

He turned face to face with her, looking into her eyes. "You aren't buying it, are you?"

"Those enemy fighters slipped into the middle of the city unseen," Hannah said. "They were probably hiding out nearby. They might be within a few hundred yards of us right now."

Brendan brushed hair out of her eyes. "If you think like that, you'll be nervous all the time. They probably got into a vehicle and split. If they left on foot, somebody would've seen where they went. I saw a couple guys following the survivors of that group we fired on at the end."

"Well, I hope you're right," Hannah said. "Hope they're far away from here."

"So what do you want to do today?" Brendon asked. Hannah punched him on the arm.

"Stop that," she said. "You know what we're doing today."

"I do?" He did a fake yawn.

She giggled. "You're gonna mess with me until we're married, aren't you?"

"I'll mess with you even more afterwards," he said, pulling her close. They kissed passionately.

"I love you so much," Hannah said, arms around him tight. There was a knock on the door.

"Shit," Brendan said. "Probably Juan Carlos already. Or Richardson." He got up and checked out the peep hole. "Richardson."

He opened the door a crack.

"Oh, you guys aren't up yet?" Richardson asked.

"What time is it?"

"Almost ten," Richardson said. "Can you guys be ready for breakfast in half an hour?"

"Where, in the hotel?"

"Yeah," Richardson said. "We'll go to the courthouse after that, if you're still interested."

"Oh, I don't know," Brendan said.

"Shut up," Hannah said. "We'll be there, Richardson."

"Yeah, I'll bet you will," Richardson said. "See you two in a little while."

Brendan shut the door and then ran towards the bed, leaping, coming down on his belly next to Hannah.

She giggled. "You *are* excited. Don't deny it."

"Okay, you found me out," he said. "Shall we get dressed?"

"Yeah," she said, getting up, turning her back to him and wiggling her butt.

"Wait, on second thought, come back here," Brendan said.

"Nope," she said. "After the wedding. Comprende?"

Brendan laughed and watched her get dressed. He joined her. They went out into the hallway. Juan Carlos and Madison were out there waiting.

"It's about time, girlfriend," Madison said. "What were you two doing in there?"

"Waiting until after the wedding," Brendan said, rolling his eyes.

"Damn, dude, you too?" Juan Carlos said with mock indignation.

"Get a load of these two," Hannah said. Richardson and Lita came out into the hallway.

"They're finally up," Lita said.

"Kids," Richardson said.

"I'm hungry," Juan Carlos said. "Hope they have good food in this dump."

Madison rolled her eyes. "Let's get going."

The restaurant was crowded for a weekday morning. It took a few minutes to get a table. Richardson insisted on a table away from the windows.

"How far is the courthouse again?" Madison asked.

"A little too far to walk, with you on crutches," Lita said.

"Sorry," Madison said.

"It's not a problem," Richardson said.

The waitress came over and took their orders.

"So I almost hate to bring this up," Juan Carlos said. "Is it safe to be in public spaces like the courthouse?"

"I've been thinking about that, believe me," Lita said.

"Me too," Richardson said. "The courthouse is a harder target than a mall or the Riverwalk. We should be fine."

"Maybe we should take a cab so we don't have to park our car in the open," Brendan whispered. "We've got guns in there, remember?"

"Yeah, I remember," Richardson said. "I'm okay with doing that. Might even be able to take the hotel shuttle."

“Good, let’s ask them,” Lita said. “After we’re done here, unless any of you needs to go upstairs again.”

“My, aren’t we anxious?” Hannah cracked.

“As a matter of fact, we are,” Madison said. “Geez, listen to me.”

The waitress brought their breakfasts, and they attacked the food, eating quickly.

“That was pretty good,” Juan Carlos said.

“Let’s go check on that shuttle,” Richardson said, getting up. He put bills on the table and they walked out of the dining room.

The hotel lobby was busier now, people rushing around, talking and laughing.

“This is a good sign,” Brendan said.

“A Good sign of what?” Hannah asked.

“Good sign that the terror attack didn’t work.”

“I agree,” Richardson said as they got to the concierge station. A middle-aged woman with short gray hair sat behind the desk.

“Can I help you?” she asked.

“Yeah, we were wondering if we could get a shuttle ride to the Courthouse on South Main Avenue,” Lita said.

The concierge punched on her computer keyboard, looking at the screen.

“Which one? The Bexar County Justice Center, or the County Marriage License Office?”

“The Marriage License Office,” Lita said. “That’s where you can get married, right?”

The woman grinned. “Yes. Congratulations. Which couple is getting married?”

Lita smiled. “All three.”

“My my,” the woman said. “I’m seeing this a lot. Kinda like what happened during World War II, from what I’ve read.”

“Can we get a ride there, and a ride back?” Juan Carlos asked.

"Yes, of course. Free of charge, since it's so close. When you're ready to come back, just call me." She handed a card to Lita.

"Thank you," Lita said, taking the card from her.

"I'll have the shuttle brought around. Should be less than ten minutes. You can sit over there." She pointed to couches and chairs in the middle of the lobby.

"Thanks so much," Lita said. They sat down.

"That was easy," Richardson said.

"Yes," Lita said, snuggling up to him on the couch. "I'm so happy."

"Me too," Richardson said.

The three couples sat waiting for about five minutes. Then the concierge person raised her hand. "It's right outside. Enjoy!"

"Thanks," Lita said. They headed out to the driveway. The shuttle was waiting.

"Are you the couples getting married?" the driver asked.

"Yep," Madison said.

"Very good, please get in and take a seat. I'll have you there in a couple minutes."

"Thanks," Richardson said. They got in.

"I can't believe it's really going to happen," Madison whispered to Hannah. She smiled back.

"I know," she said, taking Brendan's hand into hers. The shuttle took off, turning right on College Street and then left on North St. Mary's Street.

"Too bad one of you is on crutches," the driver said. "It's a nice, short walk."

"What's a good place to have a reception dinner?" Richardson asked.

"For how many people?" the driver asked.

"Just us," Richardson said.

"On the Riverwalk?" he asked.

"No!" Madison said quickly.

"Yeah, not after what happened yesterday," Lita said. "How about something nearby that's not in such a busy area?"

"Hmm," the driver said. "Restaurant Gwendolyn is nice. It's north of the Riverwalk, a little out of the main tourist area. There are other upscale restaurants in that area too. On Pecan Street."

"Maybe that'll be a good place to go," Lita said. "We won't go right after, though. We just had a huge breakfast."

"Yeah, we might want to go back to our rooms for a while," Brendan said. Hannah punched him in the arm.

"I'd be okay with that," Madison whispered.

The driver turned left on East Commerce Street. "We're almost there."

"Good," Madison said. She squeezed Juan Carlos's hand tighter.

The driver made another left, this time on Military Plaza, went one block, then turned left on Dolorosa, pulling to the curb. "Here we are."

"Wow, that *was* fast," Richardson said. He fished some bills for a tip out of his wallet, handing them to the driver as they left.

"You have to walk past the first building to get to the Marriage Center, I'm afraid. Just call Rebecca at the concierge desk when you're ready to come back."

"Will do," Lita said.

They got out and walked onto the Courthouse plaza, then made their way to the second building.

"This should be quick, since we got our license paperwork filled out already," Hannah said.

"Shoot, the door is on the far side of this building," Lita said. "Sorry, Madison."

"I'm fine," Madison said, shooting a smile at her. "I'm the happiest girl on earth."

They finally made it to the doors and went into the lobby. A sign directed them to the marriage license desk. There was no line, so they walked up to the window.

"My, this is quite a crowd," the young clerk said behind the window, wearing a name tag that said Ricardo.

"Hi, Ricardo," Lita said. "We've got marriage license paperwork filled out. We'd like to get it processed, and get married."

"Well, you've come to the right place," Ricardo said. The three license applications were slid into the window to him. He looked at Lita and chuckled. "All three of you are getting hitched, huh? Cool. IDs please?"

All of them slid their licenses in.

"By the way, the grooms are all DPS employees," Lita said. "We'd like to get married today."

"Great," Ricardo said. "We can waive the waiting period. No problem." He arranged the papers and driver's licenses in front of him, then started typing on his computer. "This will take a few minutes."

The group stood, waiting silently. Juan Carlos saw a bench a few feet away. "C'mon, sweetie, let's sit so you can rest."

"Okay," she said. He helped her sit down. "Happy, Juan Carlos?"

"Are you kidding?"

She sighed and leaned against him.

"Okay, Richardson and Lita, you're ready to go," Ricardo said.

Richardson slipped some bills to Ricardo. "This should cover all three."

"Thanks," Ricardo said. "The chapel is down the hall. You might want to put all the names in. Sometimes the line gets a little long."

"Great, thanks," Richardson said. He took the document and walked to the door, hand in hand with Lita. "See you guys down there."

"You know I'll want to have a ceremony eventually," Hannah said to Brendan. "With a dress and a cake and all."

"Love to," Brendan said.

"I like that idea too," Madison said. "When I'm off these damn crutches."

"You're healing up pretty well," Juan Carlos said. "It looked better today when I changed your dressing."

"I know, it doesn't hurt much anymore," Madison said. "I hardly have to take any pain meds now. That means I can have a little Champagne tonight."

"Brendan and Hannah," Ricardo said. "All set."

"Great," Brendan said, rushing over to the window. He took the document and thanked him, then came to the bench and sat next to Hannah.

"You aren't going down there?" Madison asked.

"We'll wait," Hannah said. "No sense going over before you guys."

"Madison and Juan Carlos," Ricardo said.

"There we go," Juan Carlos said, smiling. He rushed up to the window and picked up the document. "Thanks, dude."

"Good luck," Ricardo said. "She's gorgeous, man."

"Thanks," Juan Carlos said. He helped Madison up, and the four of them went to the door.

"What'd he say to you?" Madison asked.

"He said good luck, and that you're gorgeous," Juan Carlos said. "He's right."

She smiled at him as she hobbled along.

"I don't see any line," Brendan said.

"Not out in the hallway, at least," Hannah said.

"What are we gonna do for rings?" Juan Carlos asked.

"Don't worry about it," Madison said. "We'll get rings when we can."

"Yeah," Brendan said.

Hannah nodded in agreement. "Another thing to look forward to."

They went in the door. Richardson and Lita were sitting on chairs which were lined up against the wall.

"Great, you're here," Lita said. "We're lucky, there's only one couple in front of us, and they should be almost done."

"Perfect," Hannah said. "How're we gonna do this?"

"One at a time, and we can witness each other," Lita said. "We don't have rings yet."

"Yeah, we were just talking about that on the way over here," Hannah said. "We'll get them soon enough."

"Yes," Madison said.

A couple, all smiles, burst out of the double doors and hurried out into the hallway.

"Lita and Richardson?" asked the Justice of the Peace.

"That's us," Richardson said, standing up.

"Right this way."

"C'mon, guys," Lita said. She took Richardson's arm and they went inside. The others followed, sitting down in the front row.

"Up here," the Justice of the Peace said. "In front of the lectern. Do you have rings?"

"Not yet," Lita said.

"Okay, not a problem. I'll just cut that part out."

Richardson and Lita stood side by side as he spoke the words, saying their *I dos*, both of them misting up. They kissed, then turned around to face their friends.

"We have two spaces for witnesses to sign on the Marriage Certificate. It's not required in this state, but many couples want it. Who would like to sign?"

"I'll do it," Hannah said, getting up.

"Me too," Brendan said.

"Sounds good," Lita said.

"Fine." The Justice of the Peace watched as Brendan and Hannah got up and signed the document on the lectern. "Okay, who's next?"

"Go ahead you two," Madison said. "You're already up there."

"Okay, thanks," Hannah said, looking up at Brendan. He nodded yes, and they took the spot in front of the lectern, as Richardson and Lita sat next to Madison and Juan Carlos. The ceremony was over in a couple of minutes, their kiss lasting almost too long.

"Can I sign this one?" Madison asked.

"Of course," Hannah said.

"Yeah, you too, bro," Brendan said to Juan Carlos.

Madison got on her crutches with a little help from Juan Carlos. They went to the lectern and signed, then took Hannah and Brendan's place and did their ceremony, Madison crying through most of it. They kissed tenderly. Hannah and Brendan signed for them.

"Good luck to you all," the Justice of the Peace said.

The three couples went into the hallway.

"We did it," Madison said softly, staring into Juan Carlos's eyes.

"Yes we did," he said, eyes brimming with tears. "You're everything to me."

Hannah and Brendan went by the windows and kissed again. Lita watched them for a moment, but then Richardson pulled her into his arms and kissed her.

"Let's go home," Madison said. "Okay? We need some *us* time."

Richardson smiled at her, and pulled out the concierge's card.

"This is the happiest day of my life," Juan Carlos whispered to Madison.

"You don't have to whisper anymore," Madison said, pulling him in for another kiss, almost losing her balance on the crutches.

"Be careful you two," Lita said, laughing.

They walked slowly back to Dolorosa street. The shuttle was already waiting for them.

{ 7 }

Picnic Table

Amanda drove the bobtail into its parking spot next to the still, Curt watching her in the dark cab. She stopped the engine and put on the brake, then noticed him looking.

"What?" she asked.

"Oh, nothing," he said. "Sorry."

"You were checking me out," she said, a self-satisfied look on her face. "Weren't you?"

He chuckled. "Does that offend you?"

She smiled and slid close to him on the bench seat, getting onto his lap, her arms around his neck. "What do you think?" They kissed passionately.

"I guess you're not offended at all," he said.

"I'll be offended if I can't get you out of those clothes in a hurry," she said as she came in for another kiss, longer this time.

"Well, why are we hanging out here, then?" he asked.

"Good question," she said. "C'mon."

Curt opened his door and lifted Amanda off his lap, sliding out and then pulling her into his arms outside. They walked towards the toy hauler.

"Uh oh, what's everybody doing there?" Curt asked.

"What?" Amanda asked.

"Look, some of my friends are sitting on the picnic bench next to Jason's rig. They don't look happy. Maybe we'd better go find out what happened."

"Yeah, I think you're right, honey," Amanda said. They walked over hand in hand.

"Everything okay?" Curt asked. Eric, Kim, and Carrie looked up at him and shook their heads no.

Jason looked up at him, grim look on his face. "Kate lost the baby."

"Oh, no," Amanda said, eyes welling with tears.

"No," Curt said. "The battle?"

"Probably," Carrie said, "but it happens for no reason at all sometimes. Especially when it's this early."

Kyle came out of his trailer, closing the door slowly to be quiet. He walked over.

"I'm so sorry, man," Jason said.

"So sorry, Kyle," Curt said, on the verge of tears. Amanda pulled him close and nodded in agreement, not knowing what to say.

"Yeah, we all are," Carrie said. "How's she doing?"

"The sedative the doctor gave her knocked her out pretty good. I've been watching her sleep for a while. Needed to come out and get some air."

"You'll have to give her a lot of support," Carrie said. "This happened to me once. Your hormones go nuts for a few days."

"Yeah, my sister went through it too," Kim said. "It's hard."

"Yes, I know," Kyle said. "Don't worry, I'll be there for her. I feel so stupid."

"Don't blame yourself," Carrie said. "Sometimes it happens in the best of circumstances. This wasn't either of your faults."

Kyle sighed, tears running down his cheeks. "It doesn't feel that way now. I should have protected her better."

"She wasn't going to let you go into battle alone," Jason said. "She made that pretty clear to all of us."

"I know," Kyle said. "Still bothers me. We'll need some time to work through this."

"Yes, and see that you take it," Kim said. "She's got to be your priority for a while."

"I feel like somebody hollowed me out," Kyle said. "I've never been in love with somebody so much before. Maybe I've never *really* been in love."

"It's easy to see how you feel about her," Kim said. "I saw it from the first day I met you guys."

"Seriously," Eric said.

"You want to talk for a while, man?" Jason asked.

"No, I'm going back in a sec. I don't want to leave her alone for more than a few minutes."

"Okay," Jason said. "You know where I am. Anything you need."

"Yeah," Carrie said. "You know that. We love both of you so much."

"I know," Kyle said. "You know how we feel. I'm gonna go back. Try to get some sleep. Tomorrow is gonna be crazy again."

"Forget about it," Carrie said. "We have this. Be with your woman. She needs you more than anybody else does."

Kyle nodded, his eyes like a hurt little boy's. He went back to the trailer.

"He's taking this hard," Curt said.

"I know, but he'll be all right," Carrie said. "So will she. This happens."

"We're going back," Eric said. "See you in the morning."

The others nodded as he and Kim walked away.

"We should be getting inside too," Carrie said. "Chelsea will be up bright and early, I'm sure."

Curt and Amanda watched as they got up and went into their rig.

"Let's go to bed, honey," Amanda said. "It'll be okay."

Curt nodded to her, and they went to the toy hauler hand in hand.

Amanda turned on the lights. "Want a quick bite to eat?"

"I don't know," he said. "You?"

"I don't care," she said. "I just want to be close to you. Even if we don't do anything."

"Me too," he said.

Curt shut off the light and they went into the bedroom, Amanda sliding the door shut behind them. She switched on a small lamp, then turned towards him, pulling him to her. "I'm so sorry about your friend."

"I can't believe that happened," Curt said. "I'll never forget the look on Kyle's face before he walked away."

"I know, honey," Amanda said. "Get undressed, and let's get into bed."

"You sure?" he asked. "We haven't even seen each other naked yet."

"No, we haven't," Amanda said. "I want the comfort. I need you next to me. Like I said, I don't care if we do anything or not. Let's just let nature take its course. If we just sleep, it's okay, but I want to be close."

"Okay," Curt said. He pulled his dirty shirt over his head and tossed it aside, and slipped out of his pants. When he looked up she was before him, a curvy Viking Princess.

"Don't worry about it," she said. "Get into bed."

He nodded, unable to take his eyes off of her. She shot him a soft loving smile and got under the covers, reaching for him, their naked bodies touching for the first time.

"Oh, God," Curt said. He kissed her gently as they tried to mold their bodies together.

Amanda broke the kiss, breath coming fast. "I can feel you. You want me." She kissed him again, more passionate this time, Curt rolling on top of her. It was time. They both knew it, and they wouldn't be denied, bringing each other up to a fever pitch and down again.

"That was better than I could have dreamed," she said.

"It's never been like that for me," Curt said softly.

{ 8 }

Social Media Warriors

Don and Sydney were exhausted, watching their even more exhausted crew as they continued online chatting with the citizens.

Alyssa walked over. "You two look beat."

"You find out anything?" Sydney asked.

"There were militia and Islamists in the battle," she said. "Mostly Islamists."

"I figured," Don said. "Wonder if this Simon Orr character was with them?"

"Nobody knows what he looks like," Alyssa said. "He'll come after us again if he lived, won't he?"

"Impossible to say, honey," Don said. "Don't drive yourself crazy worrying about it."

"Okay," she said. "The good news is that we won, and maybe we woke up the people."

"You're wise beyond your years," Sydney said.

"I'm just scared most of the time," Alyssa said. "How much longer should we keep going?"

"Not long," Don said. "You still seeing a lot of traffic?"

"Yeah, and it's expanding outwards from this area," Alyssa said. "Lots of interest in the Dallas area, and even in Austin and San Antonio."

"Good," Don said. He looked over at Sydney, who was fighting back a yawn. "You're done, aren't you?"

"I'm pretty tired," she said. "It's been a good day, for the most part."

"Did something bad happen?" Alyssa asked.

"I heard that Kate lost her baby," Sydney said quietly. "That's why the doc was here earlier. Well, that and a couple minor injuries."

"Some people got killed, though, right?" Alyssa asked.

"Three of Gray's people in the tank, plus a local and one of the rednecks in an off-roader," Sydney said. "I'm sure some citizens got killed or wounded too. We probably won't know about those right away."

"Not good," Don said. "It'll be like this for a while, I'm afraid."

"Battles?" Sydney asked.

"Losing people," Don said. "I was so relieved when I heard that Dirk, Chance, and Francis lived through this."

Chloe walked up. "People are finally signing off. Maybe we ought to stop for the night."

"Yes," Don said. "Everybody's tired."

"Let's end it, then," Sydney said.

Don went on stage and turned on the microphone. "Everybody, listen up. Great job tonight. We're going to shut down. Go get some sleep. Thanks so much. You turned the tide."

There were sighs of relief in the room, as people started shutting down.

"We're going to Francis and Sherry's trailer," Alyssa said.

"Okay," Don said. "See you tomorrow."

"Sleep in, dad, all right? You look beat."

"Okay, sweetie," he said, watching her walk away with Chloe.

Don shut down his laptop, Sydney doing the same with hers.

"Did you decide?" Don asked softly.

"Decide what?" Sydney asked, trying to hide her smile.

"C'mon," he said.

Sydney sighed. "I'll spend the night in the trailer, but no promises. You gonna be okay with that?"

"Yes, of course," Don said.

"Good," she said as she closed her laptop. "I'm ready."

They watched as the rest of the team slipped out the door. "I'll get the lights," Don said.

Sydney nodded, picking up her laptop. They walked to the door together, Don taking one more look before he shut down the lights. They walked out into the cool darkness.

"Do you think things will settle down for a while after this battle?" Sydney asked.

"I doubt it," Don said. "I think things will get worse. We should brainstorm ways to keep the local citizens engaged, and how to win over people from other areas too."

They walked silently for a moment.

"You okay?" Don asked.

"I'm scared," she said. "I'm afraid something's gonna happen to us before we get together."

"We can't worry about that, honey," Don said. "We just have to go along at the pace we're both comfortable with. If it's meant to be, we'll have each other. If not, there's nothing we can do about it."

"I'm still afraid," Sydney said as they got to the trailer.

Don unlocked the door and held it open for her. She went up, him following.

"The light switch is right here," Don said, reaching for the switch above the kitchen counter, right inside the door. He flipped it and several lights came on around the coach.

"Everything working?" she asked.

"Can't get the TV antenna switch to work," Don said. "I'll mess with it when we have some down time. That's the only thing I've had problems with so far. I suspect the house batteries will need replacement before too long. They took a long time to charge up."

"We don't need them if we're plugged in, do we?"

"No, but it'll matter if we have to move," Don said, sitting on the couch. "I want to get them fixed before something happens."

"Something happens?"

"You know, like we have to evacuate in a hurry," Don said. "We need a hitch on the SUV. That's my top priority."

Sydney sat down next to him on the sofa. "The walk woke me up a little."

"Me too, but the sleepiness will be back with a vengeance," Don said. "Trust me on that."

"I know," she said, leaning against him.

"Want something to drink, or a snack?"

"I'm still full from that food the women brought over earlier," Sydney said. "Rather not have a drink. I'd rather stay clear-headed."

"Fine, honey," he said. "Want to just go to bed?"

"Yeah," she said.

"I'll make up the bed out here," Don said. "You can take the bedroom."

"No, you take the bedroom and I'll sleep out here," she said. "It's your place, after all."

Don searched her face. She looked tired and scared. "Of course, whatever you're comfortable with."

"You disappointed that I'm not going to bed with you?"

"No," Don said. "Really. I'll go as fast as you want to go. It's okay."

His look calmed and warmed her. When she locked eyes with him, feelings came in a rush.

"You look like you're in love with me already," she said.

"Don't worry about it. We go at our own pace."

"Are you?"

He was silent for a moment. "I don't think we should talk about it tonight. You all right with that?"

She nodded yes. "You don't want to know how I feel?"

"Not until you're ready to tell me," he said. "I'm not going anywhere unless you send me away."

She chuckled softly, then looked him in the eyes. "That's the last thing I want to do. We'll just leave it at that. How does this bed work?"

Don got up and folded the front bed out, pulling sheets and a blanket out of the overhead cabinet above it.

"I can make it," she said, smiling. "You go ahead and get your bed set up."

"It already is," he said, watching her.

"Then give me a goodnight kiss," she said.

He moved to her, taking her into his arms, kissing her softly but with passion. "Good night."

He turned and walked into the bedroom, her eyes on him every step, body buzzing with desire and love. *Stop it. Go slow.* When he slid the door shut, she finished making the bed, got undressed, and got in, asleep within minutes.

"They're coming," somebody shouted.

The tanks began firing. I ran, not sure where Don was. Suddenly there were barbarians at the gates, in Islamic attire, weapons in their hands, shooting anybody they saw as the group struggled to fight back. Chloe and Alyssa ran, only to be swept up by Islamists on horseback, kicking and screaming as they were carried away. Somebody grabbed me from behind. I tried to pull free, and saw Don rushing towards me. Then he froze, his mouth opening, blood flowing out as he collapsed. "Don!" I cried as I was dragged away, more of them on me now, pulling at my clothes, hitting me all over, laying me down naked on the hard dirt, pebbles and rocks digging into my back, several rifle barrels just inches from my face as my remaining clothes were torn away. "No!"

Sydney woke up in a cold sweat, panting, covers laying on the floor next to the bed, her naked body clammy, her mind still in a panic. She staggered towards the bedroom door, sliding it open, Don's soft breath calming her in an instant. She slipped into bed next to him, her naked body against his back. He stirred, waking up, turning his head towards her.

"Whaa…" he said, groggy.

"I had a bad dream," she whispered. "Go back to sleep. I just want to be next to you."

He turned his head back, and was asleep again within seconds as she clung to him. She drifted off.

Don woke up sweaty as the sun rose, peeling back his blankets. Then he felt the warm body against his back, and the arm over his torso. He was instantly overcome by feelings of love and lust, vaguely remembering when she came in, too tired to process it then. He turned onto his back, Sydney getting closer, her soft breasts against the side of his chest, her breath hitting his face, her black hair spilling over the pillow. He was watching her pretty face when her eyes fluttered open.

"Oh," she said. "Sorry. I had a nightmare."

He chuckled, his hand going to her side. "I'm glad you're here."

She sighed, getting closer, leg going over his middle, the contact making him groan.

"Oh," she said. "Sorry. Wow."

"I'll settle down," he said. "Can't help it. Maybe I'd better go to the bathroom. That's part of the problem."

"Go ahead, but then come back, okay?"

"Okay," he said, getting up, trying to keep his back to her as he rushed into the bathroom. He could hear her giggle as he shut the bathroom door.

He was done after a couple minutes, and cracked open the door. She was still laying on her back, facing away from the door. He rushed in and got under the covers, getting his first glimpse of her naked body as he lifted them.

"Get a good look?" she asked.

"Sorry."

She smiled and pulled the covers down, revealing herself to him. "There, now we don't have to worry about this part." She sat up and pulled the blankets away from him, taking a long look. Then she laid back down and moved against him again, her leg coming back up on his torso, not avoiding his condition this time.

"You're driving me crazy," he whispered.

"You want me, don't you?"

He looked into her eyes, silent, moving in for a kiss, which she returned with passion. They broke it and continued staring.

"You're something else," he said.

"So are you. I think we can sleep in the same bed from now on."

He smiled, not knowing what to say, his heart pounding, all of him feeling electric.

"You're pretty worked up," she said, petting his hair. "You'd take me right now if I asked, wouldn't you?"

"I'm only human," he said.

"We'll get up now," she said. "If you don't mind."

He chuckled, then was silent for a moment. "No, I don't mind."

She kissed him again, moving over him, both of them moaning. "We'll do a little more tonight. Not everything, but a little more. I promise."

"Like I said, at your pace, honey," he said, sitting up.

She smiled at him, still lying down, letting the covers fall again, watching his eyes on her. He noticed her watching, his face turning red.

"You're having yourself a time, aren't you?" he asked.

"You aren't upset, are you?" she asked. "I'm not trying to tease you. It's all I can do to hold back."

"I know that," he said. "Haven't been looked at like that for years. I know what it means."

"Oh, really?" she teased.

"Yeah, really," he said softly. "We don't need to say anything. We understand each other."

Her eyes welled up with tears as she looked at him.

"I'll see about breakfast," Don said, getting out of bed, not hiding his nakedness now, feeling her eyes on him. It gave him a thrill. He slipped on a robe and went into the kitchen.

"There anything to eat out there?" Sydney asked as she got out of bed.

"I got a few eggs from Moe's store yesterday," he said. "I'll try the stove. How do you like yours?"

"Over easy," she said, walking through the salon naked.

"What are you doing?" he asked, trembling.

"My clothes are out here, silly, remember?"

"Oh, yeah," he said, face turning red. He got out the eggs and frying pan as she dressed. "I'll go get my other clothes later. They're in the cabinet over by the still, along with some of my other stuff."

"I'll help you," Don said. "We'll bring the SUV over."

"Good," she said, coming up behind him as he stood at the stove, arms going around his waist. "I didn't give you quite enough this morning."

"It was fine," he said. "Best morning I've had in a long, long time."

"But still," she said, turning him towards her. She got on her tiptoes and kissed him, arms going around his neck. He hugged her tight. They broke the kiss after a couple of minutes.

"Wow," he said. "I'd say that's enough."

"That wasn't what I was going to give you," she said.

"No?"

"No," she said, hugging him. "I love you."

They kissed again, long and passionate. Then she broke it and sat on the dinette bench. "So what are we doing today?"

He chuckled. "Something that will make the day go quickly, I hope."

{ 9 }

Screening

Nelson walked into the kitchen, where Maria and Hendrix were sitting, sipping their first cups of coffee.

"Ready to be rid of me?" he asked.

"You're leaving?" Maria asked.

"Is it safe yet?" Hendrix asked.

"Yeah," Nelson said. "They've got the large bunker under the Capitol building set up as a new Governor's residence and office space. I'll get picked up later today, in an armored personnel carrier."

"We going too, or staying here?" Hendrix asked.

"Staying here for now, just in case," Nelson said. "We've got a new strategy."

"Really?" Hendrix said. "What?"

"We're installing airport scanners to monitor everyone coming into the Capitol building," Nelson said.

"You mean you're checking for weapons?" Maria asked. "Like we do in the criminal court buildings?"

"We'll be telling everybody that's what we're checking for, and that's part of it," Nelson said. "We've got the scanners fine-tuned to look for RFID chips."

Hendrix chuckled. "Perfect. Hear anything about the chopper pilots?"

"I'm still waiting for Wallis to call," Nelson said. "We ought to hear from him any time now."

Nelson's phone rang. He looked at it. "Brian. Excuse me a minute."

Nelson went into the console room. Maria smiled at Hendrix.

"We get to be alone again."

"Sounds like it," he said. "It'll be nice, but I'll miss my friend."

"I will to," she said, "I can see how close you two are."

Nelson walked back in. Hendrix eyed him.

"Nothing important," Nelson said. "Details about office set up."

"Oh," Hendrix said. "Good. You looked worried about something."

"San Antonio," Nelson said. "They still haven't found the cell responsible for the attacks yesterday."

"Maybe they left the city," Hendrix said.

"Maybe," Nelson said. "We've legalized open carry for all citizens there. No permit required."

"Might be a tad risky," Hendrix said.

"Yeah," Nelson said. "Ought to shorten any new terror attacks, though. Probably worth it for now."

The console beeped.

"Call coming in," Maria said, getting up from the table. She rushed to it and looked. "It's Director Wallis."

"Great," Nelson said. He rushed into the console room with Hendrix just as the call started.

"Hi, Director Wallis," Maria said.

"Good morning, Maria," Wallis said. "Nelson in there with you?"

"Yes," she said.

"Hi, Wallis," Nelson said. "Hendrix is in here too."

"Perfect," Wallis said.

"You sound chipper," Nelson said.

"The RFID check has paid off big time," he said. "There were 47 plants. We've got them under arrest now."

"Out of how many?" Hendrix asked.

"Just over two hundred," Wallis said. "This is a game changer. We can use our choppers now, full strength, if we keep the retired guys on the job."

"Don't push them too hard," Nelson said.

Wallis chuckled. "Hell, they don't want to stop. They're loving this."

"Okay, but if they change their mind, I'd let them off the hook," Nelson said.

"Understand," Wallis said.

"Can we tell when these people were compromised?" Hendrix asked.

"We're still working on that," Wallis said. "Some of them have been in the Air National Guard for more than five years."

"Geez," Nelson said.

"We still have Landry's body?" Hendrix asked.

There was silence on the line for a moment. Nelson looked over at Hendrix.

"Dammit," Nelson said. "If we do, check him for a chip."

"You think they'd put them in somebody up that high?" Wallis asked.

"They might," Hendrix said. "We don't have a full understanding of what they're doing yet."

"I think Landry's still in the morgue," Wallis said. "We haven't released news of his death yet. His family doesn't even know."

"I wonder how much of his family is still alive?" Hendrix asked. "We know they iced his daughter."

"I'll put somebody on this right away," Wallis said. "Get the sensors set up at the Capitol yet?"

"A team is working on it now," Nelson said. "As soon as they're up and running, I'll be moving into the bunker under the building. The big one. I'll have most of my team there too."

"You think that will give us enough security there?" Wallis asked.

"We'll see," Nelson said. "I'm not bringing my family down there until I feel comfortable with it."

"Don't blame you," Wallis said. "I'm gonna run. I'll work the Landry thing."

"Good, thanks," Nelson said.

The call ended, and Maria shut down the console.

"Well, that was good news, for the most part," Hendrix said.

"Yeah," Nelson said. "We need to figure out how to deal with those RFID chips."

"General Walker has somebody working it, right?" Hendrix asked.

"Walker didn't start that. It's General Hogan. His asset is working it on his own."

"They aren't giving up the name, are they?" Hendrix asked.

"Nope, and I'm not asking."

{ 10 }

Overflow

Madison and Juan Carlos lay next to each other, spent, breathing hard.

"Happy?" she asked.

"So happy," Juan Carlos said, petting her blonde hair. "Your foot didn't get hurt, did it?"

"No, honey, I'm fine," she said. "It only hurts when I stand on it."

"Good," he said. "Getting hungry?"

"I'd be happy just to stay in here with you," she said.

There was a boom outside, and the sound of breaking glass.

"What the hell?" Juan Carlos asked, getting up and rushing to the window. He saw a rocket fly off a roof on the other side of the river, slamming into a high-rise hotel half a block down. "Oh shit!"

"What's happening?" Madison cried.

"Somebody's shooting an RPG at hotels on the Riverwalk."

"No!" she cried.

"Get dressed," Juan Carlos said, picking her clothes off the floor and handing them to her. There was a knock on the door. He rushed to it, pulling up his boxers.

"Look out the peep hole first!" Madison said as she struggled with her pants.

"Richardson," he said, opening the door a crack. "Madison is getting dressed."

"Get her out of here. We need to move the women to the other side of the building."

"Roger that, dude," he said. "Then what?"

"Then we get the long guns and the SMAW out of the car," Richardson said. "Let's take these creeps on."

"I'm dressed, honey," Madison said, hobbling over to the door.

"Go with Hannah and Lita," Juan Carlos said.

"I heard," she said. "Don't get killed."

Juan Carlos finished dressing as two more rockets were launched. The building shuddered, and glass fell down in front of his window, covering the balcony with debris.

"Shit, man, get out of there!" Brendan shouted. The women ran to the hallway and moved to the far side of the building as Richardson, Juan Carlos, and Brendan rushed to the elevator, taking it to the parking garage.

"People are gonna see us with the weapons," Brendan said.

"Don't care," Richardson said as they rushed from the elevator to the car.

"What are we taking?" Juan Carlos asked.

"As much as we can carry," Richardson said. "I could see the shooter up on the roof."

"There was more than one," Brendan said.

They heard another couple rockets hit.

Richardson opened the back of the SUV, and handed their rifles and the SMAW out to them.

"C'mon, let's get back up there," Juan Carlos said.

They got into the elevator and rode it back up, holding their breath most of the way. The women were near the elevator.

"If they get a bead on you, get away from the window," Lita shouted. "Hear me?"

"Yeah," Richardson said as he ran after Juan Carlos and Brendan.

"Should we go to the lobby?" Madison asked.

"No, stay up here," Richardson said. "We don't know what this is yet. They might send fighters in."

"Okay," Madison said.

"Get away from the elevators," Brendan shouted, watching Juan Carlos unlock his door. They rushed in, Brendan loading the SMAW.

"That thing is gonna jam again," Richardson said.

"I can get out the old round," Brendan said. "Don't worry." He rushed out to the balcony and got down on one knee, SMAW on his shoulder. "Think they're in range?"

"Oh, yeah, they're in range, but if they see where that comes from they're liable to fire right into this room," Richardson shouted.

"There he is," Juan Carlos said, bringing his rifle up. "See him?"

"Let Brendan fire first," Richardson said. Another rocket flashed off the roof, hitting the building next door with a loud rumble.

"Take this, suckers," Brendan said, firing the SMAW. The grenade blew up its target, the enemy fighter flipping over the edge and falling. Then machine gun fire peppered their window from the same area.

"Get back," Richardson said. They rushed out of the room as Brendan struggled to get another round loaded into the SMAW.

"Got it," Brendan said. "Let's go in another room."

"Yeah," Richardson said, rushing to his door. He opened it and they ran to the balcony.

"I'll be ready to fire this time," Juan Carlos said. "As soon as you take out the next guy, we'll surprise them."

"Yeah," Richardson said, aiming his rifle too. Another rocket flew towards the hotel, hitting the room they just left, exploding inside. One of the women in the hallway screamed as the building shuddered.

"Shit, dude," Juan Carlos said.

"Eye on the target," Brendan said as he fired again, the grenade exploding in the midst of several Islamists. Rifles came out, pointed at them.

"Got them," Juan Carlos said, pulling the trigger on his M-16, cutting down a fighter. Richardson joined him, hitting another bad guy. The rest ran for cover.

"Time to leave this room," Richardson said. They got up and ran to the door as another round broke through the window, going off as Brendan slipped out.

"Shit, dude, that was too close," Juan Carlos said. "You okay?"

"Yeah," Brendan said. "We wasted five of them with that salvo."

"So where do we go now?" Juan Carlos asked.

"The roof," Richardson said. "Let's take the stairs."

"Good idea," Brendan said. They rushed to them and started the climb, going five stories.

"Roof access," Juan Carlos said, pointing at the door. He tried it. "Shit, locked."

"Move," Richardson said. Juan Carlos jumped back, watching him shoot the lock and kick open the door.

"Good," a large man yelled, running towards them. He had a long case, and was sporting long hair and a beard.

"What's that?" Richardson asked.

"BMG .50 cal," the man said. "I'm Max. Let's go get those punks."

"Now you're talking," Brendan said, reloading the SMAW.

"Oh, that's what that was," Max said. "Haven't seen one of those since the service."

"We're DPS," Richardson said.

They went to the roof and watched several more rockets fly, hitting more buildings to their right.

"This isn't strategic," Max said. "What the hell are they doing?" He had the tripod set up, and pulled the caps off the scope, then aimed. He pulled the trigger, the sound of the gun ear-splitting. "Scratch one."

"They'll return fire in a minute," Brendan said, aiming the SMAW. He pulled the trigger, the grenade flying, hitting a man about to fire another RPG, the explosion expanding when it went off.

"You just got their ammo," Max said, laughing. He got a bead on another person, on a roof half a block down, and fired, dropping the man.

"Nice amount of range," Richardson said, aiming his M-16 at closer buildings and firing away, trying to draw somebody out. Then a rocket headed towards them.

"Look out!" Juan Carlos said, diving behind the wall. Brendan and Richardson got there a split second before the rocket blew up, knocking Max backwards, his face and chest blown to bits.

"Dammit!" Richardson shouted. "Son of a bitch."

"Get on that .50 cal," Juan Carlos said.

"Yeah," Brendan said as he reloaded the SMAW.

The wall they were hiding behind got peppered with machine gun fire. Richardson got on the .50 cal, aiming and firing, bullets going right through the sheet metal the Islamists were hiding behind, killing them.

"Yeah, dude," Juan Carlos said, firing his M-16 at the two men who survived, dropping one of them. Then another round from the SMAW flew into the midst of the Islamists and blew up. After that there was silence.

"Let's get downstairs and find the girls," Brendan said.

"Yeah, and we're taking this," Richardson said, folding the tripod back up under the barrel. "Max won't be needing it anymore." He put the gun back in the case and latched it.

"He should've gotten down," Brendan said. "Dammit."

"Let's go," Juan Carlos said. They rushed back to the stairs, flying down to their floor and rushing to the far side. The women were huddled with some other civilians, trembling with fear.

"Is it over?" Lita asked.

"We think so," Richardson said.

"We need to leave now," Madison said.

Juan Carlos gave her a hand up. "You read my mind. We need to be someplace off the beaten path."

"Why are they doing this?" Hannah asked. "What good is it doing them?"

"They're trying to terrorize the population," Brendan said. "Wonder if they have something big planned?"

"Where'd you get that thing?" Lita asked, looking at the BMG case.

"Some guy named Max, who joined us on the roof," Richardson said.

"Where is he?"

"He died up there," Richardson said. "Hit by a rocket."

"Shit," Madison said. "Let's go."

"Okay," Richardson said. "Wonder if the elevator is working?"

"Good question," Juan Carlos said. He rushed to it and punched the button. The doors opened. "Yeah, it's working. Let's go straight down to the car."

"What about our stuff?"

"Our rooms are blown up," Brendan said.

"Yeah, we don't want to go back there," Juan Carlos said. "I'm sorry, sweetie."

"We're all alive," Lita said. "Let's get the hell out of here."

They rode the elevator down to the parking structure and rushed to the car, stashing the weapons into the back.

"At least the car next to us is gone now," Madison said, opening the door. She got in. "Same as last time, right?"

"Yeah, Brendan next to the door with the SMAW," Richardson said, getting behind the wheel. The rest got in and he backed out. There was a line at the exit gate. The car in the front was fumbling, looking for a ticket. Then he got pissed and drove forward, snapping the gate off. The rest of the cars followed.

"Thank God," Lita said.

"Stay sharp and keep your eyes open," Richardson said. "We're still in the middle of the tourist area. They might be anywhere."

"Yeah," Juan Carlos said, hand on his M-16, looking out the back window.

"Where are we going?" Madison asked.

"Good question," Richardson said. "Suburbs. Get on that, okay honey?"

Lita nodded, looking at her phone. "Shit, my phone charger is in the room."

"And my purse, with the marriage certificate and my driver's license," Hannah said. "Dammit."

Brendan laughed.

"What's so funny?" she asked.

"We just can't win," he said, shaking his head.

"Yes we can," Lita said forcefully. "We're still alive."

They were silent for a few minutes, eyes out the windows, watching for more danger.

"College Street dead ends into Losoya Street," Lita said. "Turn left, get on East Houston. That'll take us to I-37."

"Shit, dude, that will take us right by the Alamo," Juan Carlos said. "Nice place for a fire fight."

"Well, we need to get out of this area," Richardson said. "Look, the street is blocked up ahead."

"There's no other way out of here, with these damn one-way streets," Lita cried.

Machine gun fire erupted from above, hitting a car three spots in front of them.

"Out of the car," Richardson yelled. He rushed to the back, getting out his M-16, shooting at the rooftop where the fire was coming from.

"Juan Carlos, help Madison get to the sidewalk. Brendan, help me with the guns. Lita and Hannah, go with Juan Carlos and Madison."

"Look out!" Brendan shouted, pointing at the roof on the other side of the street. He aimed the SMAW and fired, hitting the façade of the old building, the man with a machine gun tumbling down to the sidewalk with a blood-curdling scream.

Lita and Hannah got to the sidewalk next to Madison as Juan Carlos raced to get his M-16 from Richardson. He saw somebody coming out of the corner of his eye.

"Fighters on the ground!" he cried, turning and spraying fire in that direction. Then there was a shotgun blast, and several more rifle shots. Juan Carlos turned to see a group of citizens running in his direction.

"Yes!" Juan Carlos shouted, aiming at the approaching Islamists. He opened fire, cutting down several as more fire came from the roof. Brendon aimed the SMAW again, firing, a grenade blowing out the machine gun nest. Suddenly a hail of gunfire hit the side of the building, right by the edge, taking out more of the Islamists.

"The citizens have had enough!" Brendon shouted as he struggled to reload the SMAW.

"Look out, Brendan," Juan Carlos said, aiming his M-16 at another roof. He fired, forcing the Islamists to duck behind the façade. Brendan aimed the SMAW and fired, blowing up that part of the roof.

"Yes!" a citizen yelled as debris and bodies fell down the front of the building.

"Nice shot, dude!" Juan Carlos said, covering him as he reloaded.

"I'd better check on the women," Richardson yelled, running towards the sidewalk. They were down on the ground, Lita seeing him as he ran up.

"Give us some guns, dammit," Lita said.

Richardson nodded, handing her his M-16.

"Now you don't have a gun," she said.

"Wanna bet?" he asked, opening the case he carried. He pulled out the BMG .50 cal and turned back to the street. There were more Islamists gathering on one of the roofs, getting ready to pour fire down on the citizens, who had all but slaughtered the Islamists on the ground. Richardson dropped the tripod on the .50 cal, ripped off the lens caps on the scope, and took aim, firing as fast as he could pull the trigger, the bullets smashing right through the cheap façade the enemy fighters were hiding behind.

Brendan and Juan Carlos focused on another roof, watching for movement.

"Look, there," Juan Carlos said, pointing. "They're setting up."

"On it," Brendan said, firing the SMAW, the top of the building crumbling as it exploded. The dust settled, Juan Carlos aiming his M-16 at the area when he saw a face pop up. He fired, hitting the man between the eyes, just as Brendan shot another round from the SMAW. The whole top of the building exploded in flames.

"Torched something up there," Juan Carlos said.

"I've only got a few more rounds," Brendan said.

"Yeah, I'm running out of ammo too," Juan Carlos said.

More citizens were coming into the area, aiming guns of all types up at the rooftops, waiting for more fighters. Nobody came.

"We knocked them out!" yelled a citizen holding a bolt-action hunting rifle. "I nailed eight of them!"

"You think it's over?" Brendan asked.

"It's not," Richardson said, aiming further down the street with the .50 cal resting on the top of a car. "I can see them in my scope. They're setting up down there."

"I'll go get in range," Brendan said.

“No, save your ammo,” Richardson said. “I’ve got this.” He fired several times, men screaming. Then the citizens saw where he was aiming and rushed up, sending a hail of lead at the position.

Richardson rushed over to Brendan and Juan Carlos. “Let’s go check on the girls. They aren’t safe where they are.”

“Yeah,” Juan Carlos said. They ran over to the sidewalk. The women were gone.

“Dammit, where’d they go?” Brendan asked.

“They helped a wounded woman into the drug store,” an old man said, his eyes on the roof tops, hands on his Winchester.

“Thanks,” Richardson said. He rushed in the door, Brendan and Juan Carlos following.

“Oh, thank God,” Lita said when she saw them coming.

“Is it over?” Madison asked.

“I don’t know,” Juan Carlos said. “It’s over on this section of the street.”

“This has awakened the citizens,” Richardson said. “There’s nearly a hundred armed civilians out there.”

“Are we bringing this stuff with us?” Hannah asked, face grim. “San Antonio was quiet for a while before we arrived.”

“Coincidence,” Richardson said. “They don’t know we’re here.”

“What now?” Lita asked.

“How’s the person you helped in here?” Richardson asked.

“She’s gonna be okay,” Lita said. “Flesh wound. Her husband came and got her.”

“We’re stuck in the city, aren’t we?” Madison asked.

“We might be,” Richardson said. “And we’re getting low on ammo.”

More automatic gunfire erupted, but it was further down the street, followed by the thunder of hundreds of rifles.

“Hear that?” Brendan asked, grin on his face.

“You think that was the citizens fighting back?” Hannah asked.

"Yeah," Brendan said.

"Did the car get hit?" Lita asked.

"I don't know, honey," Richardson said. "Even if it's not, we're locked in for a while."

"Stay in here as long as you want," and old woman behind the counter said. "There's a gun shop two doors down. They got plenty of ammo."

Richardson looked over at her. "Thanks."

"Go around the back, through the alley," she said. "I'll call them and say you're coming to the back door. You guys are military, right?"

"DPS," Juan Carlos said.

"No uniforms?"

"Long story, miss," Brendan said.

"Carol," she said as she picked up the phone. She had a hushed conversation, then hung up. "Knock on the back door. Two doors to the left."

Richardson smiled. "Thanks, Carol, you're a life-saver."

She smiled as Brendan and Richardson rushed towards the back.

"Juan Carlos, stay here and guard the women," Richardson said as they left.

"You got it, dude," Juan Carlos said. He got up and went to the windows, rifle in hand.

"They're gone, aren't they?" Madison asked, hobbling over to him.

"Looks like it," he said. "We should get back from the windows."

"I'll go back if you will," she said.

He smiled and helped her back.

"They're trying to lock everything down in this city," Lita said. "I hope they aren't going to try another invasion."

"That's what I'm afraid of," Carol said. "It won't go any better than last time. The citizens are ready now. Chuck's been selling ammo by the bucketful."

"Chuck?" Lita asked.

"He runs the gun shop that your men are at," she said. "He's also my boyfriend." She smiled with pride, her eyes tearing up as she pushed the gray hair out of her eyes.

The back door opened, Richardson and Brendan rushing in with a shopping cart.

"What'd you do, buy the whole store?" Lita asked.

"He has an account with the DPS," Richardson said. "They're charging the department. I got Jefferson on the phone and he gave Chuck the codes."

"Wish he had ammo for the SMAW," Brendan said, setting it down on the floor next to the cart.

"What is that, a little bazooka?" Carol asked.

"Yeah, basically," Brendan said. "Wasted a lot of cretins with this thing."

"That's more than ammo," Madison said.

"Yeah," Juan Carlos said. "More rifles and pistols, plus three shotguns."

"Why?" Hannah asked.

"Because you women need weapons too," Richardson said. "We're on the ground in hostile territory, and Jefferson said they've seen massive troop movements coming this way."

"Oh, crap," Madison said. "What are we gonna do?"

"Chuck's putting us in touch with the civilian forces," Richardson said. "We're gonna fight with them. We need every gun we can get here."

"What about Houston?" Madison asked.

"We'll get there," Richardson said. "After this is over. Jefferson said to stay and help. We have to protect the city."

Brendan chuckled. "Let's be honest. The city is surrounded. We aren't getting out of here either way."

The back door opened again, a huge middle-aged man with black and gray hair rushing over to Carol.

"You okay, honey?" he asked.

"Sure," she said. "What are you doing here? Who's minding the store?"

"Terry," Chuck said. "Hey, Richardson, I got a line on more SMAW ammo. Interested?"

"Hell yeah," Richardson said.

"We need a new part," Brendan said. "The extractor is busted. Takes three or four times longer to reload."

"Let's see that," Chuck said. Brendan handed the SMAW to him.

"It's this thing," Brendan said, pointing to the broken piece of spring steel.

"I can improvise a fix for this," Chuck said. "I think I can adapt a Mauser piece to fit. Probably take me half an hour. Come with me to my shop. I've got a good gunsmith setup over there."

"Okay, boss?" Brendan asked.

Richardson nodded his head yes.

"I'm going too," Hannah said. "I'll take a weapon."

"Remember how to load these?" Brendan asked, pulling an AR-15 out of the shopping cart.

"Yes," she said, pulling the magazine off. She loaded it and put it back on.

"Safety, remember?" Brendan asked.

"Yeah," she said. "Let's go."

"Be careful," Madison said.

Brendan and Hannah took off with Chuck through the back door.

Juan Carlos sat down on the floor next to Madison. "How's your foot?"

"Fine," she said. "It's getting better fast. Of course dealing with this now sucks."

"I know, honey," Juan Carlos said.

"When are we meeting the citizen forces?" she asked.

"Yeah, we need to be involved too," Lita said.

"Don't know yet," Richardson said.

"They have a meeting tonight," Carol said. "We're going. It's just down the street. You can go with us if you want to."

"That'd be great," Richardson said. "Hey, Juan Carlos, let's get all the weapons loaded."

"You got it, dude," he said. They worked on an aisle between the cold medicine and the dental supplies. Suddenly there was a low rumble. The building creaked.

"Oh, crap, what was that?" Madison asked.

Carol rushed to the window and looked outside. "Don't see anything."

More gunfire erupted outside, down the street a few blocks. Automatic weapons fire, answered by hundreds of shots from hunting rifles.

"Whoa, dude," Juan Carlos said. "That's a lot of rifles."

Richardson ran outside, looking down the street. "My God!"

Carol rushed over. "What do you see?"

"Several hundred citizens with guns," Richardson said. They watched as more citizens were running down the street past the drug store, with weapons of every imaginable type.

"Holy shit," Lita said, joining them, looking down the street in awe.

"What's going on?" Madison shouted.

"Hundreds and hundreds of armed civilians joining the fight," Lita said as she came back over. "Need some help?"

"Sure, you can load these extra mags with the .223 ammo," Juan Carlos said.

Richardson came back over. "This is some crazy shit." His phone rang. "It's Jefferson."

He put it on speaker and set it on the floor next to the ammo boxes.

"Richardson?" Jefferson asked.

"Yeah, boss. Got you on speaker. Need my hands free to reload."

"We just got satellite imagery of the San Antonio area."

"Uh oh," Richardson said. Carol moved closer.

"There's about twelve thousand fighters coming in from the north and south. We're pounding them with air support, but they're using buildings and people in the suburbs for cover."

"Oh no," Carol said. Madison flashed a look at Juan Carlos.

"What do we do?" Richardson asked.

"Find a safe place to fight from," Jefferson said. "Use that BMG. I'd suggest finding a roof."

"There was a huge explosion a few minutes ago," Madison said. "You know what that was?"

"No, haven't heard anything. I'll check on it."

Brendan and Hannah rushed in through the back door. "That guy's a genius."

"He fixed the SMAW?" Richardson asked.

"Yeah," he said. "What's wrong? You guys look scared shitless."

"There's about twelve thousand enemy fighters closing on the city," Jefferson said over the phone speaker.

"Oh, crap, I didn't know you were on a call," Brendan said. "What are we gonna do?"

"You guys want to use the roof on this building?" Carol asked. "It's got masonry facades. Good cover."

"You have access?" Richardson asked.

"I have a key to the stairwell. There's no lock at the top door."

"Perfect," Richardson said.

"Yeah, I'd get up there," Jefferson said. "You can control the whole damn area with a BMG if you have some good sight lines."

"How many floors up?" Madison asked.

"Only seven," Carol said. "It's doable."

"On crutches?" Madison asked.

"Maybe you should stay here," Juan Carlos said.

"With thousands of fighters coming this way?" she asked. "No, I'll take it slow, but I'm going where you go."

"We got a problem," Lita said, nodding towards the floor. Water was flooding up through a drain hole.

"Oh, crap," Carol said, looking at it, then looking out the front windows. The street was filling with water. "That's what the explosion was. They blocked the river. It's dumping into the storm drain system, and running down the roads."

"Get the guns off the floor, now!" Richardson shouted.

{ 11 }

Only Two Thirds

Hendrix paced around the living room, nervous as hell. Governor Nelson had just left ten minutes ago, in a convoy of military vehicles.

Maria came out from the kitchen. "Lunch?" she asked.

Hendrix stopped for a moment, then smiled at her. "Yeah, I need to take my mind off this stuff. I won't settle down completely until Nelson calls me from the new capitol bunker."

"Understand. I'm worried too," she said. "I'll be back in a second."

She rushed through the hallway to the bedrooms as Hendrix continued to pace.

"Kip!"

Hendrix looked at the hallway, then rushed inside. "Something the matter?" He went through the door, and she was laying naked on the bed before him. "Oh."

"Yeah, oh," she said, smiling. "Come here. It's been too long."

Hendrix walked towards the bed, shedding his clothes as he went, then ravishing her with abandon. They were lost to all but each other.

"I needed that," Hendrix said softly, petting her cheek as she stared into his eyes.

"I know, me too," she said. They stayed on the bed together for a while, chatting and caressing each other, cherishing the break. Then the console beeped.

"Uh oh," Hendrix said.

"Want to take it out there or in here?" Maria asked, getting off the bed.

"Out there," Hendrix said. "Just in case it's something bad."

"Okay, honey," she said, pulling her sweat pants on and rushing out the door, zipping up her hoodie. He put on his pants and shirt, then joined her in front of the console.

"Ready?" she asked.

"Yeah," Hendrix said. She clicked accept. Video of a conference room came up. Brian was sitting at his laptop, next to the head of the table.

"Ah, Kip, glad you could make it," Brian said. "The Governor will be here in a second."

"Good, he made it there safely," Hendrix said.

"Yeah," Brian said. "Gallagher is here too."

"How about Wallis?"

"Still in the Dallas area," Brian said, "but he'll be on this call."

"Ramsey?" Hendrix asked.

"He'll be here too," Brian said. "He's with the Governor right now."

Nelson walked in and sat at the head of the table, Ramsey following him in, then Gallagher.

"Who's on?" Nelson asked.

"Kip Hendrix," Brian said. "Wallis should be on any minute."

"How about our asset in Fort Stockton?"

"Don will be on in a moment, and he has his social media team assembled again."

"Good," Nelson said.

There was a beep on the screen, and a new window opened, showing Wallis's smiling face. "Sorry I'm late, folks."

"We're just starting," Nelson said. "Good to see you all."

"What's going on?" Hendrix asked.

"Big series of attacks in San Antonio," Nelson said. "There's over ten thousand enemy fighters entering the city, and several thousand more are already there."

"What are they doing?" Hendrix asked.

"General mayhem," Gallagher said. "This morning they were shooting RPGs at hotels along the Riverwalk. Citizens responded again, and eventually chased them away from the area, but then gunfire started up on College Street, down by the Alamo, and in several other spots."

"They blew up part of the river channel after everybody fled the Riverwalk area," Ramsey said. "It's overflowing into the city now. Too much water for the flood control system to handle in such a small area."

"Dammit," Hendrix said. "How many people we lose?"

"A lot less than we would have if the citizens didn't show up," Gallagher said. "Fort Stockton on yet?"

"Not yet, sir," Brian said. "Should be any second."

"They're kinda far away from San Antonio, aren't they?" Hendrix asked.

"We want them to do their social media recruiting again, like they did for the big battle last night," Gallagher said. "We need all the help we can get. We've got many hundreds of civilians in that battle right now, but we need many thousands."

There was a beep. A third window came up, showing a middle-aged man and a very attractive dark haired woman. There were rows of people in front of them, laptops open.

"Hello, Governor," Don said. "We've already gotten started, based on what Ramsey told us to do."

"Excellent," Gallagher said. "Tell people to go south of the city along I-37, and also north of the city, just south of Boerne on I-10. That's where the satellite pictures show most of the incoming forces. We're trying to pound them from the air, but they've got a lot of cover. Human shields, buildings, housing tracks, and so on. We'll have to hit them on the ground."

"Also tell people that there are hundreds of sleeper cells activating inside the city, especially downtown and in the tourist areas," Ramsey said. "We're going to need a lot of help down there."

"What about the Army National Guard?" Don asked.

"We're rushing as many as we can in that direction," Gallagher said, "but we weren't quite ready to mount a large assault. We're still screening for RFID chips."

"How's it going?" Nelson asked.

"Way worse than we expected," Gallagher said. "We're running about a third with chips. Damn President Simpson and his *service for green cards* BS."

"You're saying most of the bad people are foreigners?" Hendrix asked.

"Yeah," Gallagher said, "most but not all. We have a lot of militia folks joining in too. There were more *Simon Orr* types in the state than we thought."

"Wonderful," Hendrix said.

Brian held up his hands, looking at his laptop screen.

"What's going on?" Nelson asked.

"We sent a team to unblock the river. Enemy forces attacked. Killed our whole team."

"Son of a bitch," Nelson said. "How many Army National Guard guys do we have ready to field right now?"

"Just a sec," Gallagher said. He got up from the table and walked away with the phone to his ear.

"How badly can San Antonio be flooded?" Maria asked.

"Bad enough to tie up traffic," Ramsey said. "It'll be hard to get fighters in there. We could lose all of downtown to the enemy if we aren't careful."

"My God," Nelson said. "If they can take that part of town, they'll expand outwards from there. They might take the whole damn city."

"We're getting a pretty big response from people in the San Antonio city center," Don said. "A lot of them are already in the fight."

"He's right about that," Wallis said. "We've got some eyes and ears right in the middle of it."

"Really? Who?" Nelson asked.

"One of our key Patrol Boat crews," Wallis said. "They were on their way from Riviera Beach to Houston."

"Kinda out of the way, isn't it?" Gallagher asked.

"They got chased out when the enemy landed on the gulf coast," Wallis said. "They barely got out of Loyola Beach ahead of the enemy. I've got one of my best guys talking with them. He told them to stay in the city and help. Now we'll use them for spotters and intel."

Gallagher came back in. "We could field about fifteen thousand troops right now," he said.

"Wallis, can you get them airlifted to San Antonio?"

"Yes sir," Wallis said. "Where are they now?"

"Camp Bowie, in Fort Worth," Gallagher said.

"Okay, let's rush them down there," Nelson said. "I'll let you guys figure out how and where to use them."

"Can't we divert the river from someplace outside of the city?" Hendrix asked.

"It's spring fed from inside city limits," Nelson said. "No shutting that off, I'm afraid."

"Shoot, that's right," Hendrix said. "Should have remembered that."

"What about all the choppers we have at our disposal now?" Nelson asked.

"We still need to patrol the roads, especially around Fort Stockton and El Paso," Wallis said. "We'll have more civilian casualties if we send them in, too. I suggest we wait a little and see what the citizens and those Army National Guard folks can do."

"Okay," Nelson said. "What else?"

"We've had a hard time getting patrol boat crews to the Galveston area," Wallis said. "You already know about one of the teams. Two more got killed in action in Riviera Beach when the invasion happened."

"On their boats?" Nelson asked.

"No, they were hiding out, waiting to leave the area like the team that's in San Antonio. Other crews are trickling in slowly, but the roads are a mess down there. Lots of enemy fighters attacking and then disappearing."

"What happened to the boats?" Hendrix asked.

"We paid contractors to take them to Galveston," Wallis said. "Captain Jefferson led that operation. He's the guy talking to the crew in San Antonio. The boats got to the base safely, but we only have three crews right now. Jefferson wanted to man one with a couple of officers, but I told him no."

"Good call. How many boats do we have down there?" Nelson asked.

"Sixteen," Wallis said. "More than enough to protect the infrastructure down there, especially since we wiped out their aircraft carrier and their other large boats."

"So we bought ourselves some time," Nelson said. "But they'll recover. We'd better start looking for alternatives on the crew problem."

"Yeah," Gallagher said. "We can't afford to lose any more infrastructure."

"Especially oil refineries," Wallis said. "At least we got the one in Corpus Christi up and running again."

"How much danger is it in?" Hendrix asked.

"A lot, but it'll take the enemy a little while to recover from the pounding we gave them down there, and we're bringing their two aircraft carriers up."

"We need choppers for that, don't we?" Nelson asked. "And pilots."

"Working on that," Wallis said. "We'd be further along if we didn't have to deal with this mess in San Antonio. We need to be careful. They're trying to get us back into reactive mode after the slaughter up by Fort Stockton. They've probably figured out our strategy already."

"What strategy?" Don asked.

"Sorry, can't talk about that right now," Nelson said. "How's the social media action going?"

"People were out there waiting for the information," Sydney said. "We're getting pledges on a huge scale. Forty thousand people in the San Antonio area and the surrounding suburbs."

"Excellent," Nelson said. "Stay on it. After we get past this, I want you guys to work with some other groups. Spread your knowledge and experience."

"You got it," Don said.

"I need to get going," Wallis said. "Anything else for this call?"

"I don't have anything else," Nelson said. "Anybody have anything more?"

There was silence.

"Okay, I'll take that as a no. Talk to you later. Godspeed."

Brian ended the call. Maria clicked off the meeting, then leaned back in her chair and took a deep breath.

"You okay, honey?" Hendrix asked.

"This is a long way from over, isn't it?"

"Yes," Hendrix said.

{ 12 }

Mixing the Mash

Curt woke up next to Amanda, the prior night rushing back into his head. She stirred.

"Good morning," she said.

"Good morning," Curt said, searching her eyes.

"I did what I wanted to do last night, all right?" she said softly. "I have no regrets. Do you?"

"No," Curt said, caressing her face.

"You want to go again now?" she asked.

"No, let's save it for later," Curt said. "We've got stuff going on today."

"More weapons production?" she asked.

"We're out of vehicles," he said. "I was thinking more about your operation, just in case we have a hard time getting more fuel for the tanks." He got up and looked out the window. "Lot of activity down at the clubhouse. Wonder what's going on?"

"Maybe we should get dressed and go check it out."

"I need a shower pretty bad," Curt said.

"Maybe I should join you."

He smiled. "I could live with that, but it'll be pretty tight."

"I don't care," Amanda said, getting out of bed. Curt moaned as he took her in.

"You are so beautiful," he said.

"Sure you don't want to play a little before we get moving?" she asked, getting next to him.

"Dammit," he said, pulling her towards him, their naked bodies touching as they kissed. They fell back onto the bed, making frantic love, then lying on their backs. Curt chuckled.

"What?" Amanda asked.

"I don't want to do anything but that," he said. "I could stay in here all day with you."

"No you couldn't," she said. "Let's go get that shower, and then we'll get busy, okay?"

"Oh, all right," he frowned, faking disappointment.

They squeezed into the little shower and cleaned off, then got dressed and left their coach. Don drove up with Sydney, and they parked by the still.

"Good morning," Sydney said as she got out of the SUV, Don joining her.

"Yes, it is, isn't it?" Amanda grinned.

"Shit, you did it, didn't you?" Sydney whispered.

Amanda just looked back at her with an embarrassed smile.

"What's going on at the clubhouse?" Curt asked, walking up to Don.

"Ramsey called this morning. There's an attack going on in central San Antonio. He asked us to get our social media warriors back on line to gin up some citizen support."

"How bad?" Curt asked, brow furrowed.

"Lots of sleeper cells in the center of town were activated," Don said. "Satellite imagery is showing about twelve thousand enemy fighters making their way into town from the north and the south."

"Dammit," Curt said. "Where the hell is the Army National Guard?"

"On their way, from the sound of it," Don said, "but they found about a third of their troops had RFID chips."

"Shit. A third?" Curt said.

"What's wrong, honey?" Amanda asked.

"Infiltration on a much bigger scale than I expected," Curt said.

"Oh, almost forgot. Moe and Clancy were asking about you," Don said.

"They need me?"

"They wanted to chat about the RFID chips in the goats," Don said.

"Go," Amanda said. "I'll get the still fired up. Don't need help on that."

"I'll stick around and help you," Sydney said. "Just need to grab my stuff out of the cabinet next to the still and load it into the SUV."

"Oh, really now?" Amanda asked.

"Shut up," Sydney said as she walked towards the cabinet. "Want to help me, sweetie?"

"Sure," Don said, rushing over. "You can ride with me if you want, Curt."

"Yeah, I'll go," Curt said.

He watched as Don and Sydney grabbed plastic containers of clothes and other possessions, sliding them into the back of the SUV.

"That all of it?" Don asked.

"Yeah," Sydney said. "I'll have clean clothes for tomorrow, finally."

Don chuckled. "Okay. Sure you don't want to come back?"

"No," she said. "You can just leave my stuff in the back of the wagon. We'll deal with it tonight."

"Oh, you will, eh?" Amanda asked, twinkle in her eye.

Sydney rolled her eyes. "Whatever. What do you need help with?"

"Mixing up some mash," Amanda said. "We'll need more raw materials pretty soon. Maybe after we get this batch going you can use your skills to find us a source nearby."

"Sounds like a plan," she said.

"We're gonna take off," Don said. "See you later, honey."

"Bye bye," Sydney said, blowing him a kiss. Then she looked at Amanda and snickered.

Both women watched as Don and Curt drove back to the clubhouse.

"Okay, tell me what really happened last night," Amanda asked.

Sydney smiled. "Let's talk about something else." She rolled out the large steel vessel. "We got a water spigot nearby?"

"Yeah, right over there," Amanda said, pointing as she was looking through another cabinet sitting next to the still. "Wish we could've left this stuff in the bobtail."

"We should buy some of those sheet-metal sheds when we're in town," Sydney said.

"Good idea," Amanda said, as she watched her fill the vessel with water.

"So tell me what went on between you two last night," Sydney said.

Amanda glanced over at her, face turning red. "Only if you tell me what's going on with you, dearie."

"Nothing to tell," Sydney said. "Well, almost nothing, anyway."

"Come on," Amanda said.

"Okay, okay," Sydney said. "I slept in the trailer last night. I started out on the couch bed in the front of the rig. He slept in the bedroom."

"That doesn't sound very exciting," Amanda said. "No fair."

Sydney sighed. "I had a nightmare. I snuck into bed with him at about three."

"Now we're talking. Naked?"

"Yes," she said quietly, looking around to make sure nobody was listening.

"I knew it," Amanda said. "So you two did it?"

"Nope," Sydney said. "We cuddled, and I let him look at me. That's all."

"That's all? No way."

"We kissed," Sydney said.

"Why are you holding back? I know you're on fire for this guy. You told me, remember?"

"He's more conservative than my usual boyfriends," Sydney said. "I like it. We're going slow."

"Well, I'll bet that's fun."

"Oh, it's all I can do to hold back," Sydney said. "He'll get me soon enough… or rather I'll get him."

"I'm glad," Amanda said. "Teasing on the side, you two deserve each other."

"I think so," she said. "How about you? Did you two really do it?"

"Yeah," she said softly. "I don't think he planned on it yet, but as soon as I got into his bed naked, it was over."

"Really?" Sydney asked. "How was it?"

"Oh, God," Amanda sighed, "better than I imagined."

"I'm glad, sis, especially after Casey," Sydney said.

"Shut up about him," Amanda said.

"Sorry. I just think it's good that you're finally getting over him, that's all."

"It's okay," Amanda said. "Curt's twice the man anyway. I could see a real long-term future with him. Kids, even."

"I think that's great," Sydney said.

"If we manage to survive this war, we stand a good chance of having a nice life," she said.

"You're worried," Sydney said.

"Aren't you? Look at this place. If a force a twentieth the size of the one we fought last night attacked here, we'd be dead meat."

"That's what my nightmare was about," Sydney said.

{ 13 }

Migration?

Kelly, Junior, Moe, Clancy, Jason, Eric, and Dirk were sitting on the office porch chatting. They watched Don's SUV roll up.

"About time you got up," Jason said, watching Curt and Don walk over.

"Shut up, pencil neck," Curt said. "How's Kyle?"

"Taking the day off," Jason said. "Spending it with Kate."

"That's right where he should be," Kelly said.

"Damn straight," Dirk said.

"What's going on?" Curt asked, walking up to Moe. "Heard you were looking for me."

"We put those RFID chips on the goats. Probably won't be there for long, though. You know how they are. They'll chew them right off each other."

Curt laughed. "How'd you attach them?"

"Belts around their middles," Moe said. "I didn't want to risk infection by stuffing them under the skin. They've got nasty rancid blood all over them, and I don't know how to clean them well enough without causing damage."

"They're where the goats can't reach themselves, but other goats can," Clancy said.

"We got a team watching?" Curt asked.

"Yeah, we got a couple snipers set up, about forty yards away. They're hidden pretty well."

"So what'd you want to talk to me about?" Curt asked.

"We saved one," he said. "It was Eric's idea. Thought you might want to mess with them a little. Try to figure out what makes them tick."

"Oh," Curt said. "Those things might lead somebody to their location. Where did you stash it?"

"It's in my office right now, in the safe. Think that will block the signal?"

"That's a good question," Curt said, brow furrowed. "You obviously think it's a good idea, Eric."

"Hey, they already know exactly where we are," Eric said. "We aren't giving them any new info. If there's really a danger, they'll hit the goats first. There's more of them, and they're not right in the middle of enemy territory."

"Well, not quite, anyway," Curt said. "I don't know much about RFID. We need a manufacturing guy for that. Somebody who's been in the IT department of a company that uses them to track inventory. I don't know anybody like that."

"Shit, neither do I," Moe said. "Maybe we ought to send the idea up through Ramsey."

"Yeah, maybe," Curt said.

"I'll call Ramsey right now," Jason said, pulling his phone out of his pocket. He hit the contact and listened.

"Jason," Ramsey said.

"Hey, Chief."

"I'm kinda busy right now. What's up?"

"Question about the chips. We can talk later if you're busy."

"Just a second," Ramsey said.

Eric saw the worried look on Jason's face and walked closer. "What?"

Jason shrugged and shook his head no.

"Jason, is Curt around?" Ramsey asked.

"He's with me, along with Kelly, Junior, Eric, Don, Moe, and Clancy."

"Got somewhere nearby that you can put this on speaker? We need to have a confidential chat."

"The guys I mentioned okay?" Jason asked.

"Yeah, they're desired," Ramsey said.

"Moe, can we use your office?"

"Sure," Moe said. "All of us?"

"Yeah," Jason said.

Moe nodded and led them inside. Jason came in last and shut the door, then put his phone on speaker and set it on the counter.

"Okay, we're alone in Moe's office. What's up? Something about San Antonio?"

"I wish," Ramsey said. "I've got Gallagher and Governor Nelson with me."

"Oh," Jason said. "Sorry."

"No, I'm glad you called," Nelson said. "We would have been calling you anyway."

"What happened?" Moe asked. "We got another invasion coming at us?"

"General Walker was killed last night," Gallagher said, lump in his throat. "He's on the internet. His head, anyway."

"Oh, shit," Curt said.

"No!" Jason said. "How?"

"He was at the RV Park of another group like yours. It was overrun."

"Is that where the chip guy was?" Curt asked.

"Yeah, but he and his people escaped," Gallagher said. "Just in the nick of time, too."

"There's more, isn't there?" Eric asked.

There was silence on the line for a moment.

"Guys, this is top secret," Nelson said. "Don't tell the rest of your group yet. It'll put people in danger."

"Understand," Jason said.

"Good," Nelson said. "There's a coup in progress right now, in Washington DC."

"Good guys or bad guys?" Curt asked.

"Good guys, *we think,*" Nelson said. "They investigated after that photo of Simpson and Saladin came out. His administration is behind this whole mess. People are being arrested now. President Simpson is already in custody."

"You're kidding," Eric said.

"I knew it," Moe said. "That bastard."

"So what do we do?" Clancy asked. "Does this mean the war is over?"

"We really don't know yet," Gallagher said. "There might be a lot of blowback on this, given the number of Islamists and Militia who are in the fight right now."

"Dammit," Jason said.

"What about the RFID chips?" Curt asked.

"Oh, yeah, that's why we wanted to talk," Jason said. "We need an expert in manufacturing to look into them. We saved one. It's in Moe's safe."

"Oh, that's right, you put the other ones on the goats," Gallagher said, chuckling.

"I know this is gonna sound bad," Nelson said, "but I'm going to ask you to stand down on the chips. We don't want the enemy to have any idea what we know about them. In fact, I suggest we remove them from the goats and burn them with the one you have in the safe."

"Shit," Curt said. "Really?"

"Yeah," Nelson said. "That was a request from General Hogan. He's managing the effort to break the chips. We were going to get with you on that within the hour."

"We'll get them off the goats as soon as we get off the line," Moe said.

"I'm still not getting why you're worried about us looking at them," Curt said.

"This enemy is smart," Gallagher said. "If they see you or people related to you search the internet about RFID chips, it might spook them into deactivating their system. We don't want that."

"Why not?" Eric asked.

"They're putting these chips into very high-ranking people," Nelson said. "We verified that Landry had a chip about two hours ago."

"You're shitting me," Kelly said.

"I get it," Junior said. "We'll have to weed a lot of bad guys out of the government and the military. We might be able to use those RFID chips to do that."

"You got it," Gallagher said. "Understand, everybody?"

Jason looked at the others, all of whom nodded in agreement. "We all get it."

"One other thing," Nelson said. "Simon Orr had a chip."

"He's dead?" Kelly asked.

"Yeah, he's dead. General Hogan killed him this morning."

"What?" Kelly asked. "How?"

"He's been out of Texas longer than we thought. We think he planned the attack that you guys beat back last night, but he did it from Utah."

"Son of a bitch," Junior said. "Remind me to buy Hogan a beer."

"It was actually a guy named Jeb who took him down," Gallagher said. "Jeb shot Orr with a bow and arrow while he was holding a gun on others in that group. Came really close to killing him. They locked him and the surviving Islamists in a cell."

"Okay, I'll buy him a beer too," Junior said. "Sounds like our kind of folks."

"How did Hogan kill him?" Jason asked.

"He tossed a grenade into the cell," Gallagher said.

"Why?" Moe asked.

"Hogan wasn't sure if the main enemy force knew where this new base was," Gallagher said. "The chips don't survive fire."

"Simon Orr figured it out," Junior said.

"True," Gallagher said, "but Orr was a tracker. We've figured that much out. We don't know how much communication he did with his superiors while on a hunt."

"If I was him I would've been telling them exactly where things were as soon as I found them," Eric said. "The enemy probably already knows about the new base. Hope the group is being careful."

"I agree, Orr probably told his superiors," Gallagher said. "This isn't a cut and dried situation, though. The location is somewhere with very restricted cell coverage, which protects the group somewhat. It's also got some topography advantages. That's all I can say."

"I think we get it," Junior said. "So what now?"

"We've been looking at Satellite Imagery of the depot we wanted you guys to attack," Gallagher said. "It appears they've moved. We're trying to verify."

"Moved to where?" Curt asked.

"South of Santa Fe," Gallagher said. "Close to I-25."

Junior pulled out his phone and brought up the map application.

"What're you looking at?" Kelly asked.

"Keep your panties dry," Junior said.

Gallagher and Nelson chuckled.

"This is gonna be good," Ramsey said.

"Shit," Junior said. "Anything bad going on in Colorado?"

There was silence on the line for a moment.

"I'll take that as a yes," Junior said. Kelly shook his head.

"What are you seeing?" Eric asked.

"I-25 is a perfect pipeline from Mexico to Colorado Springs, Denver, and Fort Collins," Junior said. "New Mexico is still the wild west, isn't it?"

"Yeah," Gallagher said. "It's still the number one problem in the Southwest. It's being used to pump enemy fighters and materiel from Mexico and Southwest Texas into Arizona, Utah, and Colorado."

"Well isn't that special," Curt said. "Santa Fe isn't just a hop, skip, and jump from here, you know."

"We'll have to stage you guys up north to do this job," Gallagher said. "Amarillo would be the best place."

"What do you mean by *stage*?" Moe asked. "Do you mean move everybody up there?"

"I think that would be better than cutting your force in half," Gallagher said. "You know anybody with a big RV Park up there?"

"Yeah," Moe said. "How sure are we about this?"

"Pretty sure, but not a hundred percent yet," Gallagher said. "We'll need a few more days."

"You might want to have a meeting," Nelson said. "Tell your people what may be coming."

"How about the tanks?" Gallagher asked.

"We have the three flatbeds," Moe said. "Of course we're down by one tank now. It'd be nice to get a replacement."

"We're working on that," Ramsey said. "Same with the fuel tanks you requested."

"You guys running the still yet?" Gallagher asked.

"Just getting it fired up this morning, as a matter of fact," Curt said.

"Good," Gallagher said. "How about the weapons systems?"

"We're fresh outta vehicles, I'm afraid," Curt said. "I still have the remote control machine guns. Deployed almost all of the M19s already."

"You want more off-roaders?" Nelson asked. "That could be arranged."

"That would be good, but we need more Jeeps or four-wheel drive trucks, too," Jason said. "We'll need to tow the off-roaders. If we have to relocate, some of our people will have to drag their trailers with vehicles we were using to tow off-roaders for the last battle."

"Understand," Nelson said. "Start planning for that, and let us know what you need."

"Whoa," Gallagher said. "You seeing this?"

"Shit," Nelson said. "Guys, we need to go. Something big is going on in San Antonio. Talk to you later."

"Okay, good luck," Jason said.

The call ended abruptly.

"That's a little scary," Moe said.

"No shit," Kelly said. "Wonder what's going on in San Antonio?"

"I'm more worried about us having to pack up and go," Eric said. "That's going to be a huge undertaking."

"We'd better set up a meeting," Moe said. "When do you want to do it?"

"Couple of hours," Jason said.

"Everybody agree?" Moe asked. Everybody nodded in agreement.

"Remember, nobody mentions what's going on in Washington DC, all right?" Jason asked.

"We got it," Junior said.

They left the office.

{ 14 }

Water World

Juan Carlos helped Madison in the stairwell.

"Last flight, sweetie," he said. The others were already upstairs with the weapons.

"You made it," Hannah said, rushing over.

"Yeah," Madison said. "Hope we don't have to go down soon."

"Hey, Juan Carlos, come over here," Richardson said.

"What's up, boss?" he asked, standing behind a waist-high façade.

"Shit, dude, get down," Brendan said.

"Oh," Juan Carlos said, getting down onto his knees next to him. "There are snipers?"

"Yeah, they tagged a citizen on that roof half way down the street," Richardson said. "Surprised you didn't hear it."

"Holy shit, dude, look at the water down there. It's up to the tops of cars."

"Yeah," Richardson said. "I think they broke the channel in a few more places. This is just too damn much water."

"Look to the west," Brendan said. "It's deep all the way down there."

"Yeah, I know," Richardson said. "Probably has City Hall flooded out. It's in that direction. Really bad to the east, too."

"Shit, the Alamo," Brendan said, eyes tearing up.

"Don't worry, it'll be okay as long as they don't blow it up," Richardson said. "This river used to go over its banks a lot. That's why they put the channel in there in the first place. The Riverwalk was an afterthought."

"What's going on?" Lita asked, coming over, scooting on the dirty roof. Hannah followed, helping Madison along.

"Flooding's gotten a lot worse," Richardson said. "Be careful up here, though. Stay outta sight as much as possible. We're still hearing shots from snipers pretty often."

The door from the stairs opened. Chuck came up, rifle slung on his shoulder, carrying a large box in both hands. Carol followed him with a smaller box and two more rifles.

"Damn, that was heavier than I expected," Chuck said, setting the box down carefully.

"What's that?" Brendan asked.

"My buddy brought over six hundred grenades for your SMAW," he said.

"Holy shit, really? Fantastic!"

"You charged it to the DPS, right?" Richardson asked.

"Yeah," Chuck said.

"What else you got there?" Juan Carlos asked, eyeing the box that Carol had brought up.

"Night vision goggles," she said. "Don't know how easy they are to use with rifles. Hopefully they'll help after it gets dark."

"Look," Juan Carlos said, pointing to the west. "Vans lining up. See?"

"What street is that?" Richardson asked.

Chuck came over and looked through the binoculars he had hanging from his neck. "Looks like North Flores. Dammit. Islamists. You can see in the side door of this one. Looks like they got it lined with Kevlar."

"Let me see that," Richardson said. Chuck handed the binoculars to. "Son of a bitch, looks like they're setting up a defensive line on the far side of the flooding. Whoa."

"What?" Chuck asked.

"They're setting up mortars, pointing out from the center of town. They're gonna try to lock down the city center."

"Shit," Madison said.

"I see some to the east too," Brendan said. "Not as far. Commerce street."

Richardson handed the binoculars to Chuck, and he took a look.

"Yep," Chuck said. "Same thing. Dammit."

"I'm calling Jefferson," Richardson said, backing away from the front and pulling out his phone. He punched the contact and put the phone to his ear.

"Richardson? Where are you?" Jefferson asked.

"We're on a seven-story building, on College street. The flooding around here is up to the tops of cars."

"No, it's over that now," Juan Carlos said from the wall. "It's coming up fast."

"Scratch that, over the tops of the cars and rising," he said.

"It's gonna stay that way for a while," Jefferson said. "I just saw some really disturbing satellite photos. They're attempting to take the center of the city with sleeper cells, while the larger forces to the north and south push inward. We can't even evacuate at this point. They've got people all over the roads, shooting anything that moves."

"What should we do?" Richardson asked.

"Hey, boss, there's enough room to run our old boats down there," Juan Carlos said. "They can bring them in on choppers, can't they?"

Richardson laughed. "That sounds a little far-fetched, man."

"What?" Jefferson asked.

"Oh, nothing. Juan Carlos just suggested that you guys drop some of the old-style boats down here with choppers."

"Hey, worked in Apocalypse Now, remember?" Brendan asked.

Richardson laughed, but Jefferson was quiet. "Wait a minute, you don't really think this is doable, do you?" he asked.

"I'm gonna talk to Wallis. Those small patrol boats are built not far from there. And yes, we can sling them under choppers. We'd need to bring in more crews and drop them too. One boat isn't going to do enough good."

"He's really thinking about it, isn't he?" Juan Carlos asked.

Richardson shook his head yes.

"It'll work, dude," Juan Carlos said. "They won't be able to shut off the flood they started, and they aren't gonna have boats. At least not boats like ours. We'll be able to blast the hell out of them from down there."

"What's he saying?" Jefferson asked.

"He's saying that this will work," Richardson said, taking a moment to relay the whole statement.

Jefferson laughed. "Yeah, he's right, you guys would have them by the balls. I'm gonna call Wallis. Get back with you in a little while. Keep your fingers crossed."

Richardson shut down the call and slipped the phone back in his pocket. "He's calling Wallis right now."

"DPS Director Wallis?" Chuck asked. "Holy shit. You guys really think you can pull something like this off? Won't they just shoot holes in your boats?"

"They're armor plated," Richardson said. "The old ones are vulnerable in the back, because of their outboards, but we'll have a lot of firepower in a place they won't expect."

Richardson's phone rang again. "That was fast." He answered it.

"Put it on speaker," Jefferson said.

Richardson did that, motioning for everybody to gather around.

"Hear us okay?" Richardson asked.

"Perfect, except for some wind noise. You guys hear me?"

"Yeah," Richardson said. "Go ahead."

"It's a go, but we're doing it after dark. I'll let you know when. Think you can lay down cover fire?"

"Yeah, but it's only us," Richardson said. "We'd need a lot more guns to be effective."

"You remember that citizens group I was talking about earlier?" Carol asked.

"Yeah," Lita said.

Chuck laughed. "I was just thinking about that. I can get almost four hundred men on the roofs around here in a hurry."

"Wait until dark," Richardson said. "If the enemy sees them, they'll turn those mortars around and pound the crap out of this area."

"Yeah, wait until dark," Jefferson said. "Oh, and one other thing. You guys won't have to fight on your own for long. We have fifteen thousand Army National Guard troops on the way. Some of them have already landed. Half of them are going to San Antonio International, and the rest to Lackland Airforce Base."

"Whoa, dude," Juan Carlos said. He shot a smile to Madison, who still looked scared to death.

"They won't all be there until morning," Jefferson said. "We're using C130s, but they only hold 92 men."

"How many planes we got?" Chuck asked.

"Just twenty-five," Jefferson said. "We did send some by truck, along with some armored vehicles. They're coming from Fort Worth, though. That's over four hours to drive."

"How long ago did you send them?" Lita asked.

"The first group left three hours ago. We ought to have most of them on site by mid-morning tomorrow."

"Sounds like a blast," Brendan said.

"Sounds scary to me," Hannah said.

"I'm gonna get off and work on coordination. Stay out of sight, even if the enemy comes close in a row boat or something. Got it?"

"Got it, Captain," Richardson said. "Talk to you later."

Richardson ended the call.

"I'll get a text message out to the citizens group," Chuck said.

"Make sure they don't show up before dark," Richardson said.

"Roger that," Chuck said. "Some of them are gonna have to walk."

"There's still so many people here," Lita said, pointing at building windows. "Look at the other tall buildings. There's people in almost every window, and lots on the roof."

"Haven't been any sniper shots for a while," Brendan said.

"Yeah, some of our guys are already here," Chuck said. "I've been getting texts. Those last few shots we heard weren't snipers firing. They were snipers dying."

{ 15 }

Life Goes On

Don and Curt got into the SUV.

"How's Amanda going to take this?"

"Bad, probably," Curt said. "She just got that still set up. If she has to tear it all down again in a few days, she won't be a happy camper."

"Maybe that ought to be set up permanently in the bobtail," Don said. "Or better yet, in one of those three toy-haulers."

Curt looked over at him, grinning. "Damn, that's a good idea," he said. "Need another tow vehicle for that third toy-hauler, though. I think we need to get that inventory done in a hurry, so Nelson can get us the stuff."

"Yeah, that ought to be a big topic in the meeting."

They pulled up next to the still.

"Well, here goes nothing," Curt said, getting out of the SUV. He strode over to Amanda, who was working on the vessel with Sydney. Don joined them.

"Uh oh, you've got something to say," Amanda said.

"We're probably moving soon," Curt said. "Just talked to Nelson."

"You mean we'll have to pack this damn thing back up again?" she asked.

"Yeah, but Don had an idea. Maybe we can use that third toy hauler to make a permanent mobile installation."

Sydney and Amanda looked at each other.

"That means we'd have water, power, and a stove right there," she said. "Could we use the whole rig?"

"All but the counter that we have the two 3D printers on," Curt said. "What do you think?"

"Oh, hell yes," Amanda said, hugging him. "We're having problems with our stuff here. Too much blowing dust."

"We better make sure we're flush with fire extinguishers in that toy hauler," Don said.

"True that," Sydney said. "Why are we leaving?"

"The next target is outside Santa Fe," Curt said.

"Santa Fe? New Mexico?" Amanda asked. "Why so far?"

"The enemy moved their depot," Curt said.

"This is important," Don said. "The enemy is pumping men and materiel right up I-25 from the El Paso area with very little resistance."

"Is it coming to Texas?" Sydney asked.

"Sounds like it's feeding enemy operations in Colorado, Utah, and parts of Arizona," Curt said. "New Mexico is still the wild west. No state government left at all, and the enemy is free to move through there. We've got to put a stop to that or we'll lose everything west of the Mississippi River."

"My God," Amanda said. "How'd they get so many people in the country so fast?"

"Combination of tactics," Curt said. "A lot of them snuck in during that refugee migration that President Simpson pushed. A lot of them have flowed over the border, which he left wide open for them."

Don shot a warning glance. Curt nodded.

"We're having a meeting in a little while," Don said. "We should start working up an inventory of things we need. Vehicles, for example."

"Yeah," Curt said. "We'll need something to tow that third toy-hauler, and more vehicles to tow off-roaders too, since people will be towing their trailers for this trip."

"Where we gonna stay?" Sydney asked.

"Moe's looking for an RV Park up in Amarillo."

"Amarillo? That's a long way," Amanda said.

"Yeah, it is," Sydney said. "It's not a short drive from there to Santa Fe, either, you know."

"I know," Curt said. "It's going to be insane."

"What about the tanks?" Sydney asked.

"We've got three of the flatbed trucks that they were brought in on," Curt said. "Moe and Clancy fixed them up. New tires, mainly."

"Sydney, let's stop this batch and start setting up the still in the toy hauler now."

"Yeah, I think you're right," Sydney said. "You guys want to help us?"

"Yes, let's do it," Curt said. Don nodded in agreement. "I'll go get her opened up. We can put the wettest stuff in the garage."

"Sounds great," Amanda said.

Jason and Carrie came out of their coach with Chelsea. "What are you guys doing?" Jason asked.

"We're using that third toy hauler for the still, so we don't have to take it apart every time we move," Curt said.

"Good idea," Jason said.

Dingo whined from behind the screen door. Jason went over and got her on the leash.

"I'm almost going to miss this place," Carrie said.

"We'll probably be back," Jason said as he walked Dingo over. They watched Curt and Don carrying the heavier objects into the back of the third toy hauler. Kyle came out of his trailer with a pale, tired looking Kate.

"What's going on?" Kyle asked.

"We're moving soon," Jason said. "Just had a meeting with Nelson, Gallagher, and the chief."

"Moving where?" Kate asked.

"Amarillo," Carrie said.

Kate cracked up. "Shit, that's more of a wasteland than this place."

"You're more chipper than I expected," Carrie said. "How are you feeling?"

"Sad, but okay," she said. "I'm glad we're leaving. I could use a change of scenery."

"Me too," Kyle said. "Been watching the news about San Antonio?"

"I caught a glimpse, but that's all," Jason said. "Bad?"

"Insane," Kyle said, Kate leaning on him. "They blew up the river channel in several places. Flooded the whole downtown area."

"Oh no!" Carrie said. "Didn't see that. What about the Alamo?"

"It'll survive," Jason said. "That river used to flood all the time, before they built the concrete channels."

Eric walked over with Kim and Paco, who strained to get next to Dingo.

"Hey, guys," Kim said. "What's going on?"

"They're moving the still into that toy hauler," Carrie said. "Making it mobile. How are you guys feeling about the move?"

"Okay," Kim said. "Probably won't be the last time."

"Probably not," Carrie said.

"Mommy, I'm hungry," Chelsea said.

"You just ate a half hour ago," Carrie said.

"I know," she said, tugging on her mom's shirt.

"Go get an otter pop," Carrie said. "Just one. Bring it over and I'll open it for you, okay sweetie?"

"Okay, mommy." She skipped over to the coach and went inside.

"How are you feeling?" Kate asked. "You're showing more."

"My back hurts," Carrie said. "This one is gonna be bigger, I think."

"Want to sit down on the picnic table and start working up a shopping list?" Jason asked. "Might save us time in the meeting."

"Sure," Kyle said. Eric nodded in agreement.

"I'll go grab a pad and pencil," Carrie said. "Need to check on Chelsea anyway."

She walked to the coach, coming out in a few seconds, Chelsea hot on her heels with an otter pop in her hand. "Here you go." She set the pad and pen down.

"Thanks, baby," Jason said. They sat and worked through the tow vehicles they'd need.

Kim and Kate sat on chairs next to Carrie and Chelsea, under the shade of the coach awning.

"How's Kyle doing with this?" Carrie whispered as they looked at the men.

Kate looked at her teary-eyed. "He's been perfect. So thoughtful and sweet. It tore him apart. Maybe even worse than it hit me."

"Must have been so hard," Kim said.

"You and Eric are trying too, aren't you?" Kate asked.

"Yes," she said. "Probably a stupid idea, but I think about it constantly."

"Eric's okay with it?" Carrie asked.

"Yeah," Kim said. "He wants it. Even with all of this."

"Maybe pregnant women shouldn't be going on battles anymore," Carrie said.

Kate tried to keep from sobbing.

"Sorry, I didn't mean that the way it came out."

"No, Carrie, you're right. I was so stubborn. Now I feel so guilty."

"Don't feel guilty," Kim said. "Women have been pregnant through times like this for thousands of years, and they did everything right to the delivery time. You might have miscarried even without the battle. Never forget that. It happens all the time."

"She's right," Carrie said. "Don't feel guilty. Really."

"My head understands," Kate said. "My heart doesn't yet. It's broken."

"This too shall pass," Kim said. "We're going to see more death and destruction. You two know that, right? We'll be lucky to come through this mess alive, but that doesn't mean we should give up. We have to be strong."

"Mommy, this scares me."

Carrie shot a glance to the other women. "Don't worry, honey, we'll be fine."

"Maybe we should change the subject," Kate said.

The others nodded.

"You see how Curt and Don are so attentive to Amanda and Sydney?" Kim asked. "Easy to see where that's going."

"It's already there with Curt and Amanda," Carrie whispered. "These rigs don't deaden sound much."

Kate smiled. "Good for them. They deserve each other."

"Hell, they were made for each other," Carrie said.

"What about Don and Sydney?" Kim asked.

"Sydney worships him, but she's trying to hide it," Kate whispered.

"He's following her around like a puppy dog," Kim said. "It's fun to watch."

"Apparently they moved in together," Carrie said.

"Life goes on," Kate said. "Seeing them helps. With the miscarriage, that is."

"Mommy, what's a miscarriage?"

"Never mind, honey," Carrie said.

Jason walked over to them with a piece of paper in his hand. "Hey, honey, could you check the dealership in Fort Stockton for these?"

She looked at the list of Jeeps and Pick-up trucks. "Sure, honey," she said.

"Thanks," Jason said. "Now we can get on the weapons."

He walked back to the others at the picnic table.

"Well, duty calls," Carrie said. "I'm gonna go get my iPad. Want to come in with me? I'll crank up some coffee."

"Sure," Kate said. "Nice to have somebody to talk to."

"Yeah, I'll join you too," Kim said.

They went into the coach.

{ 16 }

Pleasant Dreams

Commissioner Holly and Jerry Sutton sat in the dark room.

"How much longer are these jerks gonna hold us?" Jerry asked.

"Not so loud," Holly whispered, eyes darting around.

"We don't even know anything," Jerry whispered.

"Yeah, and if they find that out, we're done," Holly said. "Keep that in mind."

"We're not going to live through this anyway," Jerry said. "You know that, right?"

"Never give up hope," Holly said.

"What, you expect Kip to ride to the rescue?"

Holly chuckled. "All he cares about now is his college buddy and that hot Latina that he fooled into being with him."

"You seemed to be on Nelson's side too," Jerry said.

"Nelson's a reactionary, but compared to these guys? Good Lord."

The door opened. Two militia thugs held it for an Islamist cleric, who carried in two manila folders. He was a tall, angular man, about sixty, with a long beard and a bad smell.

"Hello, friends," he said cheerfully.

"You again?" Holly asked. "How long are you gonna hold us here?"

"That depends on you," he said. "I have something that both of you will be interested in."

He handed one manila folder to Holly, the other to Jerry.

"Not interested," Holly said, tossing the packet on the floor in front of his cot.

"Pick that up or this nice man here will knee-cap you," the cleric spat. "Insolence won't help you."

Holly stared at him with hate-filled eyes, then reached for the folder.

Jerry opened his packet and poured out the contents onto his cot. His eyes got wide. "My sister? My mom and dad? My fiancé?"

"And your last few girlfriends, and your college roommate," the cleric said.

Holly felt the panic rise, and dumped the pictures out, rifling through them. "Okay, what do you want?"

The cleric chuckled. "We have people watching all of your loved ones right this second. If you guys don't agree to our request, all of them will be dead within the hour."

"I already told you that Franklin won't return my calls. Neither will Attorney General Blake. I've already tried. You were in the room with me, remember?"

"We no longer care about Franklin or the Attorney General," the cleric said.

Holly and Jerry shot a glance at each other. "We don't have any other contacts."

"Washington DC is going through a transition," the cleric said. "The two men you mentioned are no longer important. We found out why about an hour ago."

"Are you gonna tell us?" Holly asked.

"No reason we can't," the cleric said, a look of glee on his face.

"Well?" Holly asked.

"President Simpson and his entire Administration have been arrested."

"No way," Jerry said.

The cleric laughed. "I don't care if you believe me or not. Now we are moving on to what would've been your second task for us."

"And that is what?" Holly asked.

"We're going to let you go. You'll rejoin your friends. Jerry, I want you to re-connect with Kip Hendrix."

"Why?" Jerry asked.

"You might not be asked to do anything," the cleric said. "We want you in place as a trusted adviser just in case."

Holly rolled his eyes. "You want me to get back with Kip again too?"

"Well, yes, but more importantly we want you to reconnect with Police Chief Ramsey and Governor Nelson," the cleric said. "Same thing. Do nothing unless we contact you with instructions. If we do contact you with instructions and you don't carry them out, all the people in the manila folder will be wiped out, along with anybody they're with at the time we arrive. Do I make myself clear?"

Holly looked at Jerry, who was on the verge of tears.

"You can't help each other," the cleric said. "Do we have an agreement, or should I send a text right now?"

"No!" Jerry said. "I'll do it."

"Good," the cleric said. He looked at Holly. "And you?"

Holly looked down, then nodded yes.

"Great," the cleric said. "One more thing, and then we'll be done for now. You'll be released in two days."

"Why two days?" Jerry asked.

"You'll need a couple days to heal," the cleric said. He nodded to one of the militia men, who went to the door and opened it. A doctor came in pushing a small cart. There were things on the top, under a clean white cloth.

"What's that?" Holly asked.

"We're installing RFID chips," the cleric said. "They'll help us to know where you are at all times."

"You're chipping us like dogs?" Holly asked.

The cleric chuckled. "Funny you should say it that way." He nodded at the doctor, who rolled the cart next to Holly, then uncovered the top.

"I suggest you don't struggle with this part," the cleric said. "If you do, we'll just do it with no anesthetic."

"Arm, please," the doctor said. Holly sighed and stuck out his left arm, turning it so his inner elbow was exposed. The doctor tied a rubber strip on Holly's upper arm, then searched for a good vein. When he found it, he cleaned the area with a sterile swab, and injected him.

"What is that?" Holly asked.

"Demerol," the doctor said.

Holly felt the pleasure race through him, trying to fight it. "I'm twelve step."

The cleric laughed. "That's the least of your worries now."

The doctor moved over to Jerry and did the same procedure, then stepped back and watched them as the drug took hold.

"It's not really clean enough to do this here," the doctor whispered. "We should've taken them someplace else."

"Don't worry about it," the cleric said. "We put these into our men in the field with no anesthetic. These two are lucky. They'll be fine."

The doctor shrugged. "Looks like they're ready." He picked up an insertion tool, loaded a chip, and then walked towards Holly.

"Make sure you put the right one in," the cleric said.

"I know. I'm not an idiot." He turned Holly's arm so he could reach the back of his triceps and inserted the tool deep into the muscle, then worked a lever on the handle to inject the RFID capsule.

"There's one," the cleric said as the doctor withdrew the tool and tossed it on the cart. He cleaned and bandaged the wound, then turned to Jerry and followed the same procedure. Then he cleaned his hands, and looked at the cleric.

"They're gonna sleep for a couple of hours. They'll be in pretty bad pain when they wake up. I'll be back to give them some more pain meds."

"Thanks," the cleric said, watching as the doctor pushed the cart out of the cell. He turned back to Holly and Jerry. "How do you feel?"

Both men looked back at him with groggy eyes.

"Good, pleasant dreams," he said, turning for the door. He walked out, the two militia men following, one pulling the door shut behind them.

{ 17 }

Mock Venice

Lita was sitting next to Richardson on the roof.

"Quiet now," she said.

"Yep, and getting dark. Surprised the others can nap."

"We've had a busy few days," Lita said. "You tired?"

"A little," Richardson said. "I slept really good last night, though."

"Me too," she said, looking into his eyes. "We should be off on a honeymoon someplace."

"I know," Richardson said. "I'll make it up to you. I promise."

"This wasn't your fault," she said. "Not even a little bit."

"I know, but still," he said, brushing her hair out of her eyes. "I'm glad we did it instead of waiting."

"Me too," Lita said.

"The water quit rising," Richardson said. "Looks pretty stable now. Lots of current, though. It's gonna be tricky."

"Hey, anything happening?" Brendan asked, stretching next to Hannah.

"Not yet," Richardson said. "You get any sleep?"

"A little," Brendan said. "Hasn't been a sniper shot for a while. Chuck's guys must have nailed all of them."

"That'll make it safer for us to fight down there," Richardson said.

"Hey, honey," Hannah said, stretching against him. "You woke up."

"Yeah," Brendan said. "Look at Juan Carlos. He's out. Madison too."

"No I'm not, dude," Juan Carlos said. "Just resting my eyes."

Richardson felt his phone buzz. He pulled it out and looked at it.

"Jefferson?" Juan Carlos asked.

Madison's eyes opened. "Oh, no, is it time already?"

"Don't know, sweetie," Juan Carlos said. "Don't worry about it."

"Okay," she said, watching as Richardson made the call. He muttered a few comments, then took the phone away from his ear.

"Well?" Lita asked.

"Half an hour to forty-five minutes," he said, punching in a text.

"That to Chuck?" Brendan asked.

"Yeah," Richardson said. "We need to find a place on the water line. We'll probably have to swim to the boat."

"Shit, this is really happening," Hannah said, eyes filled with fear.

"Let's go down to the third floor," Brendan said, peeking over the side. "That'll put us about six feet above the water."

"Roger that," Richardson said. "You girls stay put. We'll be back in a few minutes. Okay?"

"Yeah," Lita said.

"Don't get hurt," Madison said.

"I won't," Juan Carlos said as he got up, following Brendan and Richardson to the door. They picked up their rifles and went into the stairwell.

"What about the SMAW?" Brendan asked.

"Maybe we ought to leave that with the girls," Juan Carlos said.

"Don't worry about it now," Richardson said. "We'll be back up there in a few minutes."

They rushed down the flights of stairs, stopping at the door that said Third Floor. Richardson tried it. It opened into a sterile-looking hallway.

"Wonder what's on this floor?" Brendan asked as they walked down the hall.

"Looks medical to me," Juan Carlos said. "Yeah, look. Ophthalmologists."

"Yep," Richardson said. "Let's check the windows at the end of this hall."

They rushed down and looked out at the water below, lapping against the side of the building across the street, the current swirling as it went past the front of the building.

"This is a good place to get out," Juan Carlos said. "Between buildings. It's not visible from either of the enemy lines."

"That's what I was hoping," Richardson said. He picked up a chair from a waiting room a few yards before the window and rushed it over. "This is gonna be tough to break." He picked the metal-legged chair up and swung it with all his might. The window cracked but didn't break through.

"This is gonna be a bitch," Brendan said. "Think we should shoot it out?"

"No, we don't want that much noise," Juan Carlos said. "Hit it again, boss."

Richardson nodded and swung it again, this time breaking through in one spot.

"Good, look for something smaller that we can break this out with," Richardson said.

"I know," Brendan said, rushing down the hall. He took a fire extinguisher out of its box on the wall, then rushed it to the window.

"That ought to do," Richardson said, watching as Brendan jammed the end into the glass, clearing out the loose shards all the way to the bottom of the window frame.

"Perfect, dude," Juan Carlos said. "That'll be enough.

"Yeah," Richardson said. "Let's get back to the roof."

They rushed back to the stairs, meeting Chuck and Carol just ahead of the roof door.

"Got people coming?" Richardson asked.

"Sure do," Chuck said. "They ought to be in place within the next fifteen minutes. You find a place to get out?"

"Yeah, end of the hall on the third floor," Richardson said. "We had to break out the window."

They came back on the roof.

"You found a good place?" Lita asked. "I thought I heard breaking safety glass."

"Yep, that was us," Richardson said. "We're set."

"What about the SMAW?" Brendan asked.

"The extractor is fixed now," Juan Carlos said. "Maybe we ought to leave it here."

"Yeah," Richardson said. "Who was using it when the mobile home park got attacked?"

"I was," Hannah said. "I only got off one shot, but I hit a chopper."

"It shouldn't jam on you this time, little lady," Chuck said.

"What now?" Madison asked.

"We wait," Juan Carlos said. "When we hear the choppers, we'll go down." He sat next to Madison and pulled her close.

"I'm scared," Madison said. "You'd better not get killed. I'm too young to be a widow."

"Tell me about it," Hannah said.

They sat quietly as night set in hard, and then they could hear the choppers approaching.

"Hand me one of those night-vision goggles, sweetie," Chuck said. Carol took one out and then slid the bag over to him. He put one on, then got up and looked at the enemy line to the left.

"Look like they hear it?" Richardson asked.

"Oh, yeah, they hear it," Chuck said. "They're scrambling around, looking for a better place to watch."

"The choppers are coming fast," Carol said. "I can see them, coming in from the north."

Chuck turned in that direction. "Yep, I see them. Shit, we got somebody with a stinger down there, looking for a good place to shoot from."

Richardson smiled. "Sounds like a good job for the BMG."

"I'll get on that, and blast him as soon as the choppers get close enough," Chuck said. "You guys need to get ready to go. Girls, grab your rifles."

Lita shook her head yes, glancing at Hannah, who picked up the SMAW and pulled the box of grenades closer to the façade.

"What do you want me to do?" Madison asked.

"Be ready to reload," Juan Carlos said. "Don't try to stand up. Those crutches will put you too far above the façade."

"Yeah, he's right," Lita said. "You know how to reload the M-16s, right?"

"Yes," Madison said.

The choppers were getting closer. Carol took another look with the night-vision goggles. "There's three, boats hanging under them, and a fourth behind them."

"That's probably the other crews," Richardson said. "They'll get right down on the water, I suspect."

"I'd better man that BMG," Chuck said, rushing over to the spot Richardson had set it up. He flipped up the lens caps on the scope and took aim, getting the stinger in his sights. "I'm gonna shoot the weapon first." He squeezed off a shot, an ear-splitting blast echoing between the buildings. The stinger missile launcher shattered in the enemy fighter's hands, and then Chuck fired once more, sending the man flying from the van he was standing on.

"Might as well open up on them now," Chuck said. "Send out the text."

"I'll do it, honey," Carol said. "You keep that big gun working."

"You got it," he said, firing quickly but carefully as Carol sent the text. Suddenly the roofs were covered with people, rushing to the edges with their rifles and pouring fire on the panicked Islamists below.

"This is like shooting fish in a barrel," Chuck shouted as he fired. Lita and Hannah joined in.

"See you soon," Richardson said. "C'mon, guys, let's go. Our boat will be in the water in a couple minutes."

"Be careful," Madison said to Juan Carlos. He winked at her, then turned to leave.

"Don't get killed," Lita shouted. Hannah just looked at Brendan, unable to say anything. He smiled at her and then followed Richardson and Juan Carlos through the door.

"Hope those boats are all ready to go," Juan Carlos said as they raced down the stairs.

"Me too," Brendan said. They bolted through the door to the third floor and ran down to the broken window.

"Should we just jump in?" Juan Carlos asked.

"Yeah," Richardson said. "Hold on tight to your rifles."

"Roger that," Brendan said. They jumped into the swirling water below as the choppers lowered the boats on winches.

"Here they come," Juan Carlos said, dog-paddling to the other two. They watched as the boat came down to about ten feet above the water and dropped. It sent up a big splash around all sides, then settled, rolling in the wake. All three paddled to the boat, Brendan climbing over the transom in the back, using the bottom of one of the outboards as a step. Then he reached down and helped the others as the second boat dropped. Men were sliding down a rope from the fourth chopper and getting into the water. The third boat came down with a splash, settling quickly.

"Hello, baby," Juan Carlos said as he got into the passenger seat.

"Hey, these have the new side guns with grenade launchers," Brendan said. "Bitchen."

A few rifle shots hit the side of the boat.

"Watch out!" cried Richardson as he got behind the gun shield on the starboard side. He turned the gun towards the source of the fire and pulled the trigger, lead flying into the open-air mezzanine of a hotel as the Islamists screamed.

"Get the motor running, man," Brendan said, getting behind his gun.

Juan Carlos cranked the engines and they started with a raspy two-cycle snarl. "Nice!"

They heard the other boats fire up, as bullets bounced off them from the other line of enemy fighters.

"Get us over to Flores Street," Richardson said. "Let's ruin their day."

"Hell yeah," Brendan said. Juan Carlos pushed the throttle lever forward, the engines roaring as the boat jumped on a plane.

"Remember the outboards," Richardson said. "They're vulnerable."

"Got it, dude," Juan Carlos shouted as they raced between the buildings, turning left from College Street to North St. Mary's, then right when they got to Commerce. "This is like frigging Venice."

"Stay sharp," Richardson shouted. "See the enemy, on Flores Street to the right?"

"Yeah, I'll get you closer," Juan Carlos shouted.

Brendan and Richardson both fired grenades, sending vans in the line flying into the air as the Islamists ran for their lives.

"Nail those assholes," Juan Carlos said.

"Get that big gun working," Richardson said.

"On it," Juan Carlos said. "I want to clear that building to the right."

He made a sweeping right turn onto Flores Street as Brendan opened up with the port gun, Islamists and militia men diving for cover. There was a large semi-trailer sitting along the side of the street, just feet above the lapping water.

"Perfect," Juan Carlos shouted, firing his big gun several times, all the grenades hitting, lifting the heavy trailer several feet into the air. It came down and rolled into a large group of fleeing Islamists, both Brendan and Richardson peppering the scene with lead and more grenades. Something big blew, turning the area into a sea of fire. People on the rooftops cheered as they fired their rifles into the breaking enemy lines.

"Damn, man," Brendan said. "What a mess. Who's gonna clean that up?"

Richardson shook his head. "Go down Flores Street further, but remember the engines are exposed."

"I'll give anybody who tries to fire on us a nice haircut," Brendan said, watching the area as the boat roared down the street.

"There's another clump of enemy fighters, see?" Juan Carlos said. "Down by Houston street."

"Let's go get 'em," Brendan said, firing several grenades into the crowd of Islamists as Juan Carlos turned towards them. He fired the big gun at another semi-truck, blowing it up, enemy fighters screaming as they ran for cover.

"Whoa, dude," Juan Carlos said. "Where to now?"

"Looks like we got deep enough water all the way down to Pecan Street, and there's enemy fighters down there. Let's go get them, and then turn around and go back past Commerce to clean that up."

"Got it, dude," Juan Carlos shouted, big grin on his face as he fired his big gun again, hitting another semi-trailer. There were secondary explosions and a bright flash.

"Damn," Brendan said. "I think we just hit some of their willie pete rounds."

"Looks that way," Richardson said. "Let's light that whole area up. We don't want them firing that crap at the rooftops."

"Roger that," Juan Carlos said, firing several more rounds from his gun as the others joined in. The whole area became a sea of fire, burning Islamists diving into the water, only to be cut up by .50 cal rounds from Brendan's gun.

"I think we've taken care of this area," Richardson shouted. "Let's go to the other side of Commerce and remove these creeps from City Hall."

"On it, dude," Juan Carlos shouted, turning the boat around in the intersection and pouring on the speed. "Keep your eyes open for enemy fighters on the side."

"Roger that," Richardson said, at the ready on his gun.

"Wonder how it's going on the other side?" Brendan asked.

"We'll go join them after we finish here, if it's still going."

"There's two boats over there," Juan Carlos shouted over the engine noise. "Maybe they ought to be helping us."

"Yeah, there's two boats, but neither of them are us," Brendan said.

Richardson chuckled. "Oh, crap, look over there. See it? GAZ Tigr with a pretty big weapon."

Juan Carlos fired several times at the vehicle before Richardson had finished speaking, all of them hitting. Richardson joined in, the armored vehicle blowing up as nearby Islamists ran up to fire on their boat. Brendan and Richardson flung lead at them as Juan Carlos sped up, getting past them and turning left on Commerce.

"Hey, we running away?" Brendan asked.

"No, dude, but they're gonna hit the engines from that angle," Juan Carlos said. "I'll move back up with our bow facing them and we'll let them have it."

Suddenly a lot more rifle fire started up, from the rooftop across the street from the group of Islamists, causing them to flee.

"Texas citizens ROCK!" Juan Carlos shouted, turning the boat around, hitting the area with his big gun, blowing their cover up. Brendan and Richardson both joined in.

"That got them," Richardson said. "Let's get to City Hall. I see another one of those semi-truck trailers sitting there."

"I can hit it from here," Juan Carlos said, firing several grenades, all but one striking the trailer broadside. Men scurried out, trying to carry boxes of ammo. Richardson saw them first and opened up with the machine gun. The others joined him, Juan Carlos sending several more grenades into the middle of them.

"We're gonna have to reload pretty soon," Brendan said.

"Yeah," Richardson said. "Think it's deep enough for us at Dolorosa Street?"

"I think so, boss," Juan Carlos said, turning left onto that street and going slowly down. "Shit, it's a lot more shallow here. I'm gonna turn left after those buildings and get back on Commerce. We can reload there."

"Got it," Richardson said. "Sounds like it might be over anyway."

"I still want to reload," Brendan said.

"Yeah, me too," Richardson said. Juan Carlos slowed the boat down, turning right on Soledad.

"This okay?" Juan Carlos asked.

"Yeah," Richardson said, looking around the area. "I think our side is controlling the rooftops around here."

"How the hell did all those citizens sneak in?" Brendan asked.

Juan Carlos laughed as he reloaded the big gun. "Hey, dude, I'll bet they swam in. Held their breath and went under water when they were close to the enemy."

Richardson laughed. "Shit, you're probably right. Somebody on the enemy side is gonna get their ass handed to them for this one."

"Should we go back there, or go check on the other side?" Juan Carlos asked.

"Let's go check on the other side," Richardson said. "All those snipers on the roofs along Flores and Main Street will start up again if the enemy regroups."

"We need ground forces to finish this," Brendan said. "We have a limited reach."

"True, but we probably turned the tide on them," Richardson said. "I know we blew up a lot of their ammo and mortar rounds."

"That's for sure," Brendan said. "I'm reloaded. They put a lot of ammo in the boat."

"Yeah, I'm done too," Richardson said. "Let's go, but keep your eyes open. There might still be enemy snipers here and there."

"Roger that," Juan Carlos said. He pushed the throttle lever forward and they cruised down Soledad street.

{ 18 }

Cleared for the Journey

Moe and Clancy watched as people slowly converged on the clubhouse in the dusk. It was almost time for the meeting. The video and audio was already set up.

"Gonna be okay leaving here for a while?" Clancy asked.

"Yeah," Moe said. "We'll be back, if we don't get killed."

Clancy chuckled. "Wow, that's a comforting statement."

"Sorry," Moe said. "I calls 'em as I sees 'em."

"Get a line on a place in Amarillo?"

"Yep," Moe said. "It's a long-ass drive. At least five hours."

"Yeah, I know," Clancy said. "Had a friend who lived there. Visited her a lot."

"I remember," Moe said. "What ever happened to that lassie, anyway?"

"She got tired of having a long-distance relationship," Clancy said. "I kinda did too, but it had some advantages."

Moe laughed. "Yeah, to the commitment phobic like you, I could see that."

"Shut up," Clancy said, looking at him with a twinkle in his eyes.

"What are you two jaw-boning about?" Junior asked, walking up hand in hand with Rachel.

"Oh, nothing," Clancy said. "Ancient history. Old girlfriend in Amarillo."

Kelly and Brenda walked up with Cindy and a couple other bikers.

"This gonna be a long meeting?" Kelly asked.

"I have no idea," Moe said. "That'll probably be up to us, although Nelson and the others will be on."

"They might be busy because of the San Antonio business," Brenda said.

"True," Junior said, "I've been trying to get news on that. Nada. I hope that isn't a bad sign."

"You and me both," Kelly said.

Eric and Kim walked up, nodding to Kelly and the others. "Any coffee in there?" Kim asked.

"Sure is, help yourself," Moe said.

"Little late for coffee, isn't it?" Eric asked.

"I'm sleepy," she said. "This is gonna be important, I think."

The room filled up quickly. Moe got up on stage to start the video and audio feeds as people found seats. The screen came on, showing Brian sitting at a conference table, eyes glued to his computer. The door opened and Governor Nelson walked in, with Gallagher and Ramsey by his side, all of them smiling.

"We're on," Moe said.

Brian looked up and nodded. Then a second window opened up, showing Director Wallis, also smiling.

"Something good must have happened," Junior said.

Brian gave a thumbs up to Nelson, and the camera focused on him, Ramsey, and Gallagher.

"Greetings," Nelson said. "Thanks for coming."

"Welcome," Junior said.

"We've got great news," Nelson said. "The enemy just lost in San Antonio. Big time."

There was applause in the room.

"How?" Junior asked.

Gallagher chuckled. "In the city center, DPS Patrol Boats and citizens made the difference."

"Yeah, I'm proud of our boat crews, that's for sure," Wallis said.

"How the hell did boats make any difference?" Jason asked.

"The Islamists blocked up the river and broke the channel," Ramsey said. "It flooded the entire city center. We dropped three patrol boats into it with choppers. They made a real mess of the enemy positions."

"Yeah, and by the time the boats got started, the Army National Guard showed up," Gallagher said. "They were aided by thousands of armed citizens all over town. It was a rout – even bigger than what you guys did the other night."

"Wow," Kyle said. Kate hugged him, smiling.

"Those patrol boats knocked out mortar positions that the enemy was going to use against the troops coming in from outside San Antonio," Gallagher said. "We probably would've won anyway, but it kept a whole lot of people from getting killed."

"Glad the Army National Guard got into it this time," Curt said. "You must have learned how to weed out the bad guys."

"We did," Nelson said. "This doesn't leave the room. Everybody understand?"

The people in the clubhouse murmured agreement, many saying yes or nodding.

"What is it?" Junior asked.

"All enemy personnel have those RFID chips in their triceps," Gallagher said. "We used x-rays to find them. On some you can still see the damn scars. Keep that in mind with anybody new you meet."

"How many bad guys did you find?" Cindy asked.

"About a third of the force," Gallagher said. "Similar numbers in the Air National Guard, too."

"Holy shit," Curt said. Amanda looked up at him, shaking her head.

"This was planned out for a long time, wasn't it?" she asked.

"We think at least two years," Ramsey said.

Nelson stood up to get everybody's attention. "One thing to keep in mind, folks. Don't get over-confident. There are at least a hundred thousand enemy fighters spread all over Texas, and a lot more in other parts of the Southwest. This isn't even close to over."

"He's right," Wallis said. "We could still lose this."

"Yeah, I agree," Dirk said, glancing at Chance and Francis. Sherry was next to Francis, looking terrified by the whole thing.

"So what now?" Sydney asked.

"We'd like to get you into position for the attack on the Santa Fe depot," Gallagher said. "Before the enemy decides they need to pick up and move again."

"So we'll be leaving soon, then?" Brenda asked.

"Yeah, we suggest you get on the road tomorrow," Gallagher said. "We're sending three fuel trucks your way for the tanks and the flatbed trucks. Should be there about noon tomorrow. We suggest you be ready to go shortly thereafter."

The room exploded in murmurs.

"I think that's doable," Junior said. "Most of us have been getting ready. We need a few things, though."

"Yeah," Jason said. "Tow vehicles are the most important thing now."

"Got your text," Ramsey said. "The assets you requested will be at the big dealership in Fort Stockton tomorrow by 10:00 AM. Just sign for them. We've got the fifth-wheel and tow bar setups being installed right now."

"Excellent!" Curt said. "We'll be ready."

"You guys find a place to stay?" Nelson asked.

"We've already got that set up," Moe said. "Used my connections with the RV Park Owner's Association. I know the owner. She's trustworthy."

"Perfect," Nelson said. "I'd suggest that everybody gets a good night's sleep. Tomorrow will be a long day."

"We've been working the social media side of this already," Don said. "We're getting great response from Amarillo and Lubbock."

"Good," Gallagher said. "We'll need all the help we can get when we move into New Mexico."

"Okay, everybody know what to do?" Nelson asked.

"I think so," Moe said, looking out over the crowd.

"Yeah," Junior said.

"We'll end this now, then," Nelson said. "Good bye and good luck."

Brian nodded and closed the meeting, the screens in the clubhouse returning to the sign-in page.

"Well, there we go," Moe said. "Clancy and I will be up early to help with loading the tanks onto the flatbed trucks. Any who can help will be appreciated."

"What time?" Dirk asked.

"Six," Moe said.

"Amanda, you got room in that bobtail for some supplies?" Clancy asked.

"Sure, now that we've put the still into the third toy-hauler," she said. "We're gonna run short on drivers, though."

"We'll have enough, but we'll have to divide it up," Moe said. "More of you will be driving alone this time."

"Yeah," Jason said. "We have enough drivers, but with only five people to spare, based on my calculations a little while ago."

"Good, then let's end this and get some shut-eye," Moe said. He switched off the equipment. "I'm gonna unhook this stuff. Maybe it'll fit in that bobtail too."

"Sure," Amanda said.

"Let me know if I can help with the loading," Sydney said.

"You'll be busy with your love-nest, won't you?" Amanda asked.

Sydney smirked. "We've already got that covered, and remember I'm not the only one with a *love nest.*"

Amanda giggled. "Fair enough. Maybe you'd better go break yours in."

Sydney shot an embarrassed glance at Don and walked to the front table to grab her laptop.

"I think you embarrassed her," Curt said.

"I know, I'm bad," Amanda said. "C'mon. We have things to do before we go to sleep."

"Coming dear," Curt said, drawing a chuckle from Don.

The room was nearly empty now, Moe and Clancy up on stage undoing their audio-video setup.

"Got anybody to watch this place for you while you're gone?" Don asked.

"No, not really," Moe said. "We'll just lock her up and hope for the best."

"That's what I did with my house back in Deadwood," he said. "I have no idea if it's still standing or not."

"You ready to go, Don?" Sydney asked.

"Any time you are," he said.

"Good," Sydney said.

Don picked up his laptop and they walked out the door, making their way to the trailer in the darkness.

"You think the trailer will tow okay?" Sydney asked.

"Sure. Glad I got the trailer hitch put on the SUV."

"Me too," she said. "One less thing tomorrow. Amanda is probably gonna need some help. How are Chloe and Alyssa taking this?"

"Talked to them a couple hours ago," Don said. "They're fine with it. Probably be worse if everybody wasn't going."

"Alyssa's sweet on one of the guys," Sydney said, watching Don unlock the trailer door.

"Really?" Don asked. "I hadn't noticed."

"I don't think she wanted *me* to notice," Sydney said. Don held the door open as she walked in, then followed her. They set their laptops on the table. Don pulled the door closed and hit the light switch over the counter.

"Want to fire up the laptops?" Don asked.

"No, I've got something else in mind," Sydney said, a twinkle in her eye.

"Oh, really?" Don asked, heartrate quickening.

"Why don't you stow the stuff we've got laying around in the salon while I go take care of some stuff in the bedroom?"

"Okay, honey," Don said. She went through the bedroom door and pulled it shut. Don looked at it for a long moment, then picked up items and put them into cupboards and drawers. He had a warm feeling as he looked around their little home. Pride and comfort. Would it last? Would they be dead before the week was out? His anticipation of Sydney's love pushed the worry into the background.

"You about done?" Sydney called from the bedroom.

"Couple more minutes," Don said.

"Make it quick," she said. "We need our sleep."

Don stuffed the remaining loose stuff away and then went to the bedroom door, breath coming faster.

"Turn off the lights out there," Sydney said.

"Will do," he said, rushing back to the light switch and turning it off. He came back to the door. "You decent?"

"You care?" she asked, her voice coy. Don slid the door open. She was already under the covers. He undressed quickly and slid in next to her. She was warm and soft, turning her head back towards him. "You can wait a little while longer, can't you?"

"Yes," he said, feelings of love building in him. She turned onto her back, locking eyes with him for several minutes. He petted her hair. "I love you."

"I know," she said. "Go to sleep." Her eyes closed, Don watching her beautiful face as her breathing changed, feeling the closeness that was gone from him since his beloved wife had died. He finally fell asleep, spinning into a world of battles and terror and loss that he'd been living with, every night since the horror at Deadwood.

{ 19 }

Old Friends

Kip Hendrix paced in the console room, going stir crazy.

"You okay, honey?" Maria asked, walking in from the living room.

"Cabin fever," he said. "Sorry. I'll get over it."

"Maybe we should see about joining Governor Nelson," she said.

"I don't think they want us there," Hendrix said. "I think they want to keep this site open for now."

"Maybe we could get a field trip," she said.

Hendrix's phone rang. He pulled it out, his eyes getting wide. "Jerry Sutton." He took the call and put the phone to his ear.

"Kip. Thank God."

"Jerry, where are you? Where have you been?"

"Holly and I were captured by the enemy," he said. "We just escaped, when they evacuated the site."

"Where are you now?" Hendrix asked.

"San Marcos," Jerry said. "I think the enemy fled after a battle in San Antonio."

"You need somebody to pick you up?" Hendrix asked.

"Yeah, we don't have a car. We're in an industrial park near the San Marcos Airport."

"Okay," Hendrix said. "You guys safe where you are?"

"I think so," Jerry said.

"Okay, sit tight. I need to talk to Ramsey. I'll get back with you."

"Thanks, Kip." Jerry ended the call.

"Was that really Jerry Sutton?" Maria asked.

"Yeah," Hendrix said. "Get the console fired up. Let's chat with Nelson and Ramsey."

"Will do," she said, taking the seat in front of it and inputting her code.

"Want a cup of coffee?" he asked.

"Sure, honey," she said. "This will be ready in a couple minutes."

"Thanks," he said, walking into the kitchen. He made two coffees and brought them out. "Here you go. We on?"

"Brian responded, said he'd have to round them up. I told them it was about Jerry Sutton. He got a lot more serious after I mentioned him."

"I'll bet," Hendrix said, pulling a chair next to her and sitting. "At least this got rid of my cabin fever for a while."

She glanced over at him, a wicked grin on her face. "There are other things we can do, you know."

He looked at her with loving eyes and smiled. "Again? Yeah, I'm game."

Brian came back on the screen. "They'll be here in a minute."

"Great, thanks, Brian," Hendrix said.

"Coffee tastes good," Maria said.

"Yeah, it does," Hendrix said. "Have any decorating ideas for the house?"

"It'll be months before it's ready," she said.

"I don't know," Hendrix said. "They're building fast. I was shocked when I saw the progress this morning."

"You didn't go outside, did you?"

"No, I used the video cameras," Hendrix said, "although it was tempting, now that we have the door fixed."

"Kip, what's up?" Nelson asked, walking into the conference room with Ramsey and Gallagher.

"Hey, boss," Hendrix said. "Brian told you that I got a call from Jerry Sutton, right?"

"Yes," Nelson said. "Fill us in."

"Well, not too much to tell. He said that he and Holly got captured by the enemy, who fled the area after the San Antonio battle. They were being held at an industrial park near the San Marcos Airport."

"The enemy just left them there?" Ramsey asked.

"Sounds a little fishy," Gallagher said. "I think they would've either taken them or gutted them."

Hendrix sighed. "I know, I had a similar thought. What should we do?"

"We don't bring them here," Ramsey said. "Wonder if they have chips?"

Hendrix was silent for a moment. "We should check. That would tell us a lot."

Gallagher chuckled. "He's right, Governor. If they have chips, we'll know we can't trust them, and we'll know that the enemy thinks we're still clueless. We could exploit that."

"I'm surprised they don't get it, after all of the people we've taken out of the military," Ramsey said. "Hard to contain something as big as that."

"We've been extremely careful," Gallagher said.

"We got a base near there we can take them to?" Ramsey asked. "With x-ray equipment?"

"Yeah, close by, too," Gallagher said. "We've got a few buildings at the airport. Not the most secure in the world, but secure enough."

"We could bring them here," Hendrix said. "To our bunker."

"Absolutely not," Nelson said. "You guys are too important to risk, and we don't want them anywhere near our systems."

“Let’s think about this a little,” Gallagher said. “Do we want to make them think we don’t know about the RFID chips? Just in case they have them?”

“There’s a good question,” Hendrix said. “Might be in our interest to hide the fact from them.”

“That’s all well and good, but *we* need to know,” Ramsey said.

“I agree,” Nelson said. “Where can we bring them where they can be walked through a body scan, like the setup we have here at the Capitol building?”

“Do we dare bring them *here?*” Ramsey asked. “We could put them into the place we had Landry.”

“What if they use the chips for targeting?” Nelson asked.

“It’s not like the enemy doesn’t know where the Capitol Bunkers are,” Gallagher said. “I’m changing my mind on this. We should bring them here. We’ve got the bunker very well hardened. Nothing short of a direct hit from a nuke is gonna reach us.”

“Aren’t there other places where you could walk them through a scanner?” Hendrix asked.

“We’ve got the setup in Fort Worth,” Gallagher said. “We’re holding all those bad guys there. Army National Guard and Air National Guard.”

“You’ve already got a lot of beacons there, unless you’ve removed the chips from all those traitors,” Ramsey said. “So that part doesn’t matter.”

“Yes,” Gallagher said. “You’re right. I’m still against taking them there, though, in case the enemy doesn’t know we’ve used the RFID chips to weed out their plants in the National Guard. It would be hard to hide that from Sutton and Holly. We don’t have a good setup where we could keep them in the dark.”

Nelson sat silently for a moment, thinking. “I don’t want them taken to the base in Fort Worth. Let’s bring them here. If they have no RFID chips, we let them back in with us and watch them like a hawk.

If they do have RFID chips, we very quietly stash them in the room we put Landry. We'll have to decide how we handle things beyond that."

"It's slightly risky, but I'm good with it," Ramsey said.

"What do you think, Kip?" Nelson asked.

Hendrix sighed. "I don't like it, but it's the best choice at this point."

"Okay, then it's settled," Nelson said. "Gallagher, think you can get an armored car detail together?"

"Sure," Gallagher said. "Kip, why don't you call Jerry and give him my cell number. I'll talk to him and make the arrangements."

"Okay, will do," Hendrix said.

"Anything else?" Nelson asked.

"How much longer do you want us to stay down here in the bunker?" Hendrix asked.

"Going a little stir-crazy, I'll bet," Nelson said. "A little while longer. We're not sure it's safe enough outside yet, and we want to keep that operation up and running just in case."

"No problem," Hendrix said.

"Okay, we'll talk soon," Nelson said. He nodded to Brian, who ended the meeting. Hendrix took a deep breath and got out of his chair.

"Worried?" Maria asked.

"A little," Hendrix said. "I'm glad they're doing full-body scans. If they've got chips, they obviously know about it. Ought to be interesting when they're led through the scanner. They might try to bolt."

"If they have any other devices the scanner will pick them up, right?"

"You mean like weapons or explosives?" Hendrix asked.

"Yes," Maria said. "Remember the underwear bomber? The shoe bomber?"

"Yeah, I remember," Hendrix said. "That's why I'm glad it's a full scan, although I can't picture either of those guys as suicide bombers."

"You better call Jerry back," Maria said.

"I'll do that now," Hendrix said. He picked up his phone and hit the contact. It rang twice.

"Kip," Jerry said. "What's happening?"

"I'm texting you Gallagher's cell number," Hendrix said. "He'll pick you up and take you to the Capitol building."

"Great, thanks so much," Jerry said, sounding relieved. "Holly wants to talk to you."

"Put him on," Hendrix said. He waited for a second.

"Kip," Holly said, sounding on the verge of tears.

"Holly, how are you? You don't sound so good."

"I thought we were dead," Holly said. "Still can't believe they let us go. You still close to Nelson?"

"I am," Hendrix said. "I was really worried about you guys. So glad you survived."

"We almost didn't," Holly said. "Any big changes since we've been away?"

"Not really," Hendrix said. "The battle continues, and it's not a lock that we're gonna win. That's not much of a change from last time we talked."

"No, it's not," Holly said.

"You got much info for us on the enemy?"

"They were pretty careful about talking to us," Holly said. "We probably don't know any more about them than you guys do, but I'll describe all of the conversations in detail."

"Good," Hendrix said.

"I'd better go," Holly said. "Jerry's anxious to call for our ride."

"Understand. Take care."

"You too, old friend," Holly said. The call ended.

"Well?" Maria asked.

"Jerry just wants to come in from the cold and be safe. I think Holly is hiding something."

{ 20 }

Waiting Rooms

Richardson, Juan Carlos, and Brendan sprinted up the stairs to the roof, bolting out the door.

"Oh, thank God," Lita said, rushing to Richardson. "We were so worried, especially when that big explosion went off."

"Yeah, I could see it in the air, and I was sitting down here," Madison said, Juan Carlos getting down next to her. He kissed her tenderly.

Hannah held Brendan tight, sobbing. "It's okay, honey," Brendan said. "We're safe."

"Until next time," she said. "Oh, hell, I don't even care now. I just want you to hold me."

Chuck and Carol came back on the roof.

"Good, thought I heard you guys," Chuck said. "Where's the boat?"

"Tied up by that third-floor window," Juan Carlos said.

"You guys were amazing," Carol said. "Same with the guys on the other side."

Richardson's phone rang. He looked at it. "Jefferson."

"Answer it," Lita said.

Richardson nodded and put the phone to his ear. "Hey, boss."

“Congratulations,” he said. “Heard about what you did. San Antonio is out of danger.”

“Good, the Army National Guard must have showed up for once,” Richardson said.

Jefferson chuckled. “Yep, they did.”

“What are we doing now?” Richardson asked.

“We’re sending a trailer and tow vehicle there, with a crew to help you get your boat out of the water. Same with the other two boats.”

“What then?”

“You guys will go back to R and R, or maybe I should say honeymoon.”

“That would be nice,” Richardson said. “Are we trailering the boat ourselves?”

“Probably the best bet, assuming your car is under water.”

“It is,” Richardson said. “There’s six of us, remember.”

“I know,” Jefferson said. “We’ll be sending a crew cab dually, but that will be a little tight. I’ll try to arrange another vehicle.”

“Great,” Richardson said. “How soon, and where are we going?”

“In the morning,” he said. “You guys have someplace to stay?”

Richardson laughed. “We’re on the roof of a building right now. It’s not a hotel.”

“Not the greatest,” Jefferson said. “Try to get some sleep however you can. We’re gonna suggest you head on to Houston. We’ll have a place where you can put the boat. You’ll have a few days to find apartments.”

“I hope Houston will be less exciting than San Antonio has been.”

Jefferson laughed. “Me too. I’ll call you when the trailers and vehicles have arrived. Take care of yourselves.”

“Will do,” Richardson said. He set his phone down.

“Well?” Lita asked.

“They’re sending us a trailer and tow vehicle in the morning,” Richardson said. “Until then, we wait.”

"Where we going, dude?" Juan Carlos asked.

"Houston," Richardson said. "Don't know much beyond that, other than we'll have a few days to get set up there."

"We have to sleep on the roof, don't we?" Madison asked.

"We can go down to another floor that's cleaner and warmer," Brendan said. "Maybe the elevator is working."

"It's not," Chuck said. "Water got to it down in the basement. Sorry."

"Where's the best place to sleep?" Hannah asked.

"Probably any floor other than the third," Chuck said, "since you guys busted the window down there."

"All those damn flights of stairs," Madison said, eyes weary.

"I can get you guys some sleeping bags," Chuck said. "On the house."

"You could charge them to DPS," Richardson said.

"Yeah, that's right, we can do that," Chuck said. "Which floor do you want?"

"Why don't you take the fourth floor?" Carol asked. "It's another medical floor. There's waiting rooms down there. Some of them are outside of the office doors. There's couches and chairs."

"Sounds like a plan," Juan Carlos said. "Maybe we should get a head start, honey."

Madison nodded.

"What about the guns and ammo?" Brendan asked.

"We'll get it once we're settled," Richardson said. "Take a weapon with you, though. Everybody. Just in case we have enemies who know how to swim."

"Help me up," Madison said.

"Okay, sweetie," Juan Carlos said, standing up next to her. He helped Madison to her feet and led her to the stairwell. They disappeared inside as the others gathered up weapons.

"I wish we still had our hotel rooms," Lita said.

Richardson chuckled. "They're gonna need a few screen doors. They got blown up, remember?"

"Yeah, I remember," she said, looking at him. "All that matters now is that we've made it through this. Six hours ago I thought one or both of us would be dead by now."

"I know, sweetie," he said. "I'm sorry."

Hannah helped Brendan carry the SMAW and grenades. They made it to the fourth floor after a few minutes, arriving at the door just as Madison and Juan Carlos got there.

"You two got down here pretty fast," Hannah said.

"I'm stronger now," Madison said. "Thank God."

"Yes, you are," Juan Carlos said. "That's good."

They went into the hallway. There was a waiting room with two couches and several chairs about half way down, and another similar space about five yards past that.

"Perfect," Richardson said.

"Still gonna be hard to sleep much here," Lita said.

"Oh, I don't know," Madison said. "I'm so damn tired after this craziness."

"Me too," Hannah said. "Once I get comfy, I'll be out for a while."

Chuck and Carol came in with blankets.

"These ought to help some," Chuck said. "Probably easier than sleeping bags. Just leave them when you take off tomorrow."

"Thanks so much," Richardson said. "For everything."

"Thank you," Chuck said.

"Yes," Carol said. "You guys were amazing."

{ 21 }

The Line-Up

Sydney woke up looking at Don as he snored softly. She petted his head, eyes tearing. *I love him so.*

There was a loud mechanical clank outside, jarring Don awake. He saw Sydney staring at him and smiled.

"Good morning," he said.

"Yes, it is," she said. "Sounds like they made good on getting the tanks loaded at six."

"That's what that was, eh?"

"I think so," she said. "Haven't gotten out of bed yet."

"Well I have to," he said, climbing out. "Cold!" He went quickly into the bathroom. Sydney stretched, happiness flowing over her. *He's mine.*

"It's even colder in the bathroom," Don said, shivering as he got back under the covers. Sydney snuggled up against him.

"Wow, you *are* cold," she said, pushing against him tighter.

Don looked at her, his hand roaming on her warm soft curves. "You mind?"

She smiled and moved more tightly against him. "No, I like it."

They petted each other like two high school kids in love. Sydney felt herself getting out of control. She stopped and looked into his eyes, feeling sheltered and warm and safe.

"Enough?" he asked softly.

"Enough for now," she said. "We've got a lot to do today. Up and at 'em."

Don groaned, but then laughed. "Okay, okay."

They dressed, then got bowls of cereal and sat at the dinette, looking at each other more than their food.

"Happy?" Don asked.

"What do you think?"

"Yes," Don said.

"Perceptive," she said. "How much do we have to do on the trailer?"

"Stow what we got out this morning," Don said. "Hitch her up. That's about it. I did a lot yesterday while you were helping Amanda lock down the still equipment in the toy hauler."

"Great," she said. "Your SUV gonna handle it okay?"

"Yeah, I think so," he said. "Used to hate driving that beast around. Too long and too wide for small parking lots. Now I'm glad I've got it."

She giggled. "Yeah, all those people who used to make fun of SUVs are probably eating their words now."

"Happened before," Don said. "Remember that big storm that went all the way up the east coast, about ten years ago?"

"Yeah, I *do* remember that, and I remember the stories about SUVs too. Resulted in a surge in sales even though gas prices were still way high."

"Yep," Don said. "You go ahead on to Amanda's place. I'll finish up here and join you in a little while, okay?"

"Okay honey," Sydney said, getting up from the dinette. She grabbed a few things and went out the door.

Don puttered around for a few minutes, then heard a knock on the door. He opened it. It was Alyssa and Chloe.

"Hi, Dad," Alyssa said.

"Hi Mr. D," Chloe said.

"Where's Sydney?" Alyssa asked.

"She left a few minutes ago," Don said. "Went to help Amanda. How are you two doing?"

"Good," Chloe said.

"You need any help?" Alyssa asked.

"Tell you what. You two could guide me while I back the SUV up. Might as well get it hitched."

"Sure," Chloe said.

"Yeah," Alyssa said.

"Good, I'll go get her fired up." He went out the door, the two girls following.

"Think Francis needs any help?" Don asked.

"He's all ready," Alyssa said. "Dirk and Chance helped. So did we."

"Good," Don said. "You guys can ride in the SUV if you want. Up to you."

"I think we're gonna ride with the guys," Chloe said.

"The guys?" Don asked, glancing at them.

"The one's we've been hanging with, from Gray's group," Alyssa said.

"Your daughter has a boyfriend," Chloe said.

"Shut up," Alyssa said, face turning red.

"It's okay to have a boyfriend," Don said. "Just be careful."

"Chloe has one too," Alyssa said. "Don't you?"

"We're just friends," Chloe said, her face now red.

"Yeah. Uh huh."

They looked at each other and giggled.

"Just make sure your car stays with the main group, okay?" Don said. "Call me if anything goes wrong and I'll come get you."

"I know, dad," Alyssa said. "Go ahead and back up."

Don nodded and got behind the wheel of his big SUV. He drove it into position and backed it up, following directions from the two girls.

"That's good, dad," Alyssa shouted.

Don shut off the engine and walked back to them. "Perfect, thanks!"

"Don't mention it," Chloe said.

The two girls walked towards the area where Gray's group was camped, Don watching them until they were out of sight. *Find out which vehicle they're in.*

Don finished hitching up the trailer and walked over to Amanda's bobtail. There were several people loading stuff in the back. Don joined in while Sydney helped Amanda in the toy hauler.

"Your trailer ready to go?" Curt asked as he walked up.

"Yep," Don said. "Already hitched up."

"Good," Curt said. "We'll need some drivers to go into town with us. Interested?"

"Oh, to pick up the new tow vehicles," Don said. "Sure, I'm game."

"Great. We're going in about an hour."

"Perfect," Don said. He walked over to the back of the third toy hauler, where the women were locking down the still. "You two need any help?"

"Yeah," Amanda said. "There's some more raw material in those big plastic containers. They have handles but they're heavy. Watch your back when you lift them."

"Will do," Don said. He walked over to them, trying to pick up two but then setting one down. He carried the first one to the back of the toy hauler and set it on the tailgate, then went to get the others.

"Got you busy, I see," Jason said, walking from his coach. "Your trailer ready to go?"

"Yep, already hitched up," Don said, breath laboring. "You?"

"Carrie's stowing the rest of the stuff now. I'm gonna get the Jeep hitched up."

"Need somebody to watch for you?"

"Nope, not with these telescoping tow bars. I just have to be straight and within a range."

"Okay," Don said, lifting another plastic container.

Curt cleared space in the back of his toy-hauler and drove the Barracuda up the ramp, parking it and connecting straps from its frame to the floor of his rig.

"Well, there we go," Curt said, walking down the ramp. "Want to give me a hand lifting the tailgate?"

"Sure," Don said. He set down the last of the white plastic containers by the back of the mobile still and trotted over. They closed up the back, Curt fastening the big latches as Don held the door in place.

"That's it. This puppy is ready."

"You fired that gun on the back yet?" Don asked, nodding at the machine gun pointing backwards from the roof.

Curt chuckled. "Nope, not yet, and I hope I don't have to on this trip."

"We won't be very inconspicuous," Jason said. "Jeeps and trucks with grenade launchers or machine guns. Reminds me of a Mad Max movie."

"Shut up, pencil neck," Curt said. "You don't like my handiwork?"

"I like it a lot," Jason said. "If the world ever settles back down we'll have to remove all this stuff."

"Yeah, I know," Curt said.

"Shit, if we win this war, a lot of this stuff will end up in a museum," Don said.

"Think so?" Jason asked.

"Hell yes," Don said. "These are wild times. Some of us might end up being famous."

Jason laughed. "I could just see an exhibit for Curt. It'll say something like *Shut up, pencil neck.*"

Jason and Don cracked up. Curt eyed them, smiling. "Yeah, what you just said.

"Boys, don't get out of control," Carrie said. "Chelsea is listening."

"Oh, yeah, sorry," Don said.

Eric and Kim walked over with Junior and Rachel.

"Hey, brother," Jason said.

"Hey," Eric said.

"You guys all rigged up?"

"Yeah," Eric said.

Junior smiled. "Me too. Got the old Brave ready to go. Kelly was just finishing up when we left."

"Wonder how Moe's taking this?" Rachel asked.

"Probably hard," Junior said. "This place is his pride and joy."

"Yeah, I gathered that," Kim said. "Nice guy, that Moe. Clancy too."

"Yeah, good people," Eric said. "You need any help over here?"

"We could use a few more drivers later," Curt said. "When we go pick up the tow vehicles from town."

"You think it's safe over there?" Kim asked.

"Should be," Curt said.

"Nowhere is a hundred percent safe," Jason said. "We'd best keep that in mind all the time. We need to stay sharp on the road."

"He's right," Eric said. "We should plan out how to space the vehicles with weapons. We should have some at the front and some at the back of our caravan."

"Yeah, seriously," Junior said. "Wish I had one of those machine guns mounted on the old Brave."

"Ran outta time," Curt said. "Maybe we can get that done when we're in Amarillo."

"Love it," Junior said.

"You'd let him put a big gun on the roof of our home?" Rachel asked.

"Sure, why not?" Junior said. "What if somebody comes up behind us?"

Rachel was silent for a moment. "Even with a gun, we'll be a sitting duck in that motor home if anybody shows up."

"She's got a point," Eric said. "We'll be vulnerable."

"Gets right back to what I was saying," Jason said. "Nowhere is a hundred percent safe. Not while this war is going on."

Kelly and Brenda walked over.

"You guys done?" Junior asked.

"Yeah," Kelly said. "The fuel trucks are coming. Saw them on I-10 before I walked up here. They ought to be going through the gate any minute now."

"Can those flatbeds keep up with the group?" Don asked.

"Probably," Junior said. "Might be a problem if we didn't have a bunch of RVs. We won't be doing eighty."

"True," Jason said. "Our rig feels pretty good at about sixty-eight."

"Same here," Junior said.

"I like to go a tad slower while towing my trailer," Kelly said.

A loud truck horn tooted from the gate.

"There's the fuel trucks," Kelly said. "Wonder if they need a hand?"

"Let's go down there," Junior said.

They took off.

"Our trip into town is gonna be the long pole in the tent," Curt said. "Maybe we ought to take off now. See if they're ready a little early."

"I'm game," Don said.

"Yeah, I'll go too," Eric said.

"And me," Kim said. "I can drive."

"I can go," Jason said. "We still need a couple more."

"I'm available," Kyle said, stepping out of his truck. "How we getting down there?"

"Want to pile in the back of my bobtail?" Amanda asked.

"Sure, that'll work," Curt said.

"We got enough drivers?" Jason asked.

"We need seven," Curt said. "So one more."

"I'll go," Sydney said. "I can drive anything."

"There we go," Curt said. "Let's saddle up. Sure there's not too much stuff in the back of that bobtail?"

"Yeah, I'm sure," Amanda said. "Moe's gonna stuff a bunch of food and his audio-visual stuff in the back, but we aren't doing that until we take off. Gonna have to ice a bunch of the food. No sense in having it melt for two hours before we split."

"Let's go, then," Curt said. "I'll call the guy on the way."

"Ride in the cab with me," Amanda said.

Curt nodded. Everybody piled in, Kyle joining Curt and Amanda in the cab, the rest getting into the back.

"Should we pull down the back door?" Don asked after he helped Sydney in.

"Yeah, it unlatches from the inside," Sydney said. "I can help."

"Okay," Don said, reaching up to the heavy canvas handle. Jason got up to help. They closed and latched it, then Sydney went to the front and knocked on the wall.

"What's that, your secret sign?" Don asked.

"Of course," Sydney said. "Rode back here more than once. You know what we deliver, right?"

They all chuckled and sat down as Amanda drove to the front gate.

"I can't quite picture you running moonshine," Don said as Sydney sat next to him.

"I grew up with it," she said.

"Yeah, funny that you were doing that business right next to a whole family of police officers."

"I don't think my dad liked it much," Jason said. "But he loved your old man."

"I know, the feeling was mutual," Sydney said. "He's gonna be really upset when he finds out what happened."

"You haven't talked to him since all this started?"

"No, he's at a remote location in Montana, and since we've been involved in all this, I'd just as soon keep it that way."

"They can't hack our cellphones anymore," Eric said.

Sydney laughed. "You think papá would own a cellphone? Hell, he bitches and moans that there's no phone booths around anymore."

"He thinks cell phones are too expensive?" Don asked. Both Eric and Jason snickered.

"What? I missing the joke?" Don asked.

Sydney sighed. "I guess you're going to find out about the family sooner or later."

"Maybe now's the time," Eric said.

"Shut up," she said.

"Sorry, you know I love the old guy," Eric said.

"Anybody going to fill me in?" Don asked.

"My dad is kind of a conspiracy nut," Sydney said.

"Kind of?" Jason grinned.

"Hey," she said. "Anyway, he believes the stuff about cellphones causing brain cancer."

Don chuckled. "Well he's not the only person I know who believes that."

"He thinks 911 was an inside job," Eric said. "Also thinks that the mob killed JFK, and that JFK and his brother killed Marilyn Monroe."

"He must be having a field day with what's going on right now," Don said.

Sydney smirked. "He saw it coming from a couple years out. I'm actually amazed at how close to correct he was."

"You don't think he knows about this?" Jason asked.

"He knew about the terror attacks. That's why they decided to stay up there. I doubt that he knows all this stuff about the government, the Islamists, and the UN."

"Truth is stranger than fiction," Eric said.

"We're slowing down, making a left," Jason said. "Probably be there in a couple minutes. The RV Park isn't far from town."

"*Town* is stretching it a little for this burg," Eric said. "The population of our park rivals the place."

"Be nice," Jason said. "Probably good people living here. Small towns are like that."

"Yeah," Don said. "Deadwood is small, but we had a nice town there until the enemy came along and ruined it." His eyes teared up.

"You're really hurting over that, aren't you honey?" Sydney asked, pushing his hair out of his eyes.

"I lost people," he said. "Close people. I won't get over it. Not for a long long time. Maybe never."

"You want to go back there?"

"I don't know, sweetie," Don said. "I just want to be where you are at this point. If it's there, fine. If it's here or in Dripping Springs, fine."

"We just stopped," Eric said, standing up. The vibration of the engine ceased, and they heard people getting out of the cab.

"Let's open the door," Sydney said, getting up. She undid the latch on the inside, then Jason and Eric pushed the door open. They squinted in the morning light.

"Big dealership for a little town," Eric said as he jumped out.

Don jumped out and helped Sydney down.

"I can get in and out by myself," she whispered as the others got out.

"Yeah, but this way I get to touch you," he said. She rolled her eyes, and they walked to the office, catching up to Amanda, Curt, and Kyle.

"What are we getting, anyway?" Sydney asked.

"Mostly pickup trucks," Jason said. "Several of them with fifth-wheel hitches."

"How about roll bars?" Curt asked.

"Most of them will have roll bars," Eric said. "We planned ahead."

"Can we run the 3D printers while we're driving?" Amanda asked.

"Could, but I wouldn't bother," Curt said. "We've already got several sets ready for the truck mounts. I'd rather not risk the vibration and movement messing with the material as it's coming out of the printer nozzles."

"Here early," the man behind the counter said. "Was just about to call you. Everything's ready to go."

"Fantastic," Jason said.

"Yeah, that's great," Kyle said.

"Who's signing?" the man asked.

"I will," Jason said. "How long is this gonna take?"

"Few minutes," the man said. "The keys are lined up here, the trucks in the back section of the lot. Go ahead and get them lined up by the gate if you want."

"How do we know which is which?" Sydney asked.

"Key fobs," the man said.

"Oh," Sydney said. "Duh."

Jason started signing paperwork as the others grabbed keys and went back outside.

"You guys are gonna see some action, I take it," the man said. "I'm Frank, by the way."

"Jason."

"Heard about what you guys did a few nights ago. I wanted to join in, but my wife talked me out of it. She's pregnant."

"Hey, you're helping here," Jason said. "We all do our part."

"Think there's gonna be action around here?"

"Possible," Jason said.

"You guys coming back?"

"I have no idea," Jason said.

"Where are you going?" Frank asked.

"Rather not say," Jason said. "Sorry."

"Oh," he said. "Yeah, I understand. You don't know me."

"It's nothing personal," Jason said. "This all?"

"Yep. Here's your copies." He tore pages off each of the multi-page forms.

"Thanks," Jason said.

"Welcome," Frank said. "I'll get the gate opened for you guys. Be careful. Godspeed."

Jason nodded and left with the papers in hand, heading onto the back lot. As he approached Eric tossed him keys.

"It's the one on the end," Eric said. "Red."

"Great, thanks," Jason said.

"The gate's opening," Curt said, watching.

"I'll drive the bobtail home," Amanda said, walking out to it. The others got behind the wheels of the trucks and drove through the gate in a long caravan, arriving back at camp ten minutes later.

"Back already," Moe said, rushing out to the gate. "We're almost done fueling up the flatbeds and the tanks."

"Perfect," Jason said, following the other trucks through the gate. "We'll get these delivered and then come back up to make plans. We need to make sure we've got the armed vehicles in the right places."

"Roger that," Moe said. He saw Amanda drive through, following the last truck. He waved her over.

"Ready to load the food and the audio-visual stuff?" Moe asked.

"Yeah, where do you want me?"

"Back up to the side door, around the far side of the clubhouse," Moe said. "I'll send the teenagers over to load and pack ice. Talked to them earlier."

"Okay," she said.

The flatbed trucks with M-1 tanks queued up on the access road.

"Which way we going?" asked the driver of the first flatbed. Clancy walked over.

"We're taking 329 up to I-20, and going through Midland so we're further away from the New Mexico border. You aren't leaving until we are though, right?"

"You want us to wait?" the man asked.

"Yeah, in case you get hijacked," Moe said, hearing the conversation. "You can pull out onto the access road now, though."

"Okay," the man said. "We'll do that."

"Good," Moe said. "We're going to work out the order of vehicles, so we have the armed ones strategically placed."

"Okay, brother, makes sense," the man said. He drove forward onto the access road, pulling up far enough for the others to fit behind him. More vehicles began lining up at the gate.

Jason and Eric walked over to Moe and Clancy. "Ready to go finish the order of vehicles?"

"Yeah," Moe said.

"Those flatbed drivers aren't taking off ahead of us, I hope," Eric said.

"No, I told them not to. They're on the access road to make room for the other vehicles to queue up."

"Good," Jason said. "They were hijacked once, and they can be hijacked again."

"Exactly," Clancy said. "Let's go work this out."

"Dirk and Chance over here yet?" Jason asked.

"No, but they'll be here in a few minutes, with Cindy and Kelly," Moe said.

They walked into the clubhouse.

{ 22 }

Scanner

Jerry and Holly watched out the windows of the armored personnel carrier as it drove into the parking lot of the Capitol building, parking in the back.

"Lots of people out and around," Holly said.

The driver looked back at him and smiled. "Yeah, things are almost back to normal in this area. Two officers will be over to escort you in a few minutes."

"We can't just walk in ourselves?" Jerry asked.

"Nope, we're following protocol for everybody entering or leaving the facility," the driver said.

"No problem, officer," Holly said.

They waited nervously. Two National Guard officers approached the vehicle after a few minutes.

"There they are," the driver said. Their doors unlocked with a clunk, and both men got out.

"Commissioner Holly?" the first officer asked.

"Yes, and this is Jerry Sutton," Holly said.

"This way, please," he said, leading them towards the front of the Capitol. There was a line of people at the door.

"Metal detectors?" Holly asked.

"Looks like it," Jerry said. "No, those are body scanners, like some of the airports have."

Holly glanced at him, feeling sweat break out on his forehead in the warm Austin sun.

"When did this go in?" Holly asked the officer next to him.

"Just before the Governor's Office moved in," he said. "You know what happened to the Governor's Mansion?"

"Yes, we saw that on the news before we were captured," Jerry said. They moved up slowly in line, Jerry's heart pumping a little faster with each step. He looked at Holly, who shot him a *calm down* glance.

Holly got up to the front of the line and walked into the scanner.

"Stand with your arms extended, please," the operator said.

"Yeah, been through the drill," Holly said, standing in the correct manner as the operator looked at the screen.

"Okay, thank you. Stand over in the white square until you're picked up, please."

Holly nodded and walked to the spot, watching as Jerry went through the scanner.

"Well, that wasn't so bad," Jerry muttered as he joined Holly in the white square next to him.

"That remains to be seen," Holly muttered under his breath.

"How long do we stand here?" Jerry asked.

"Until somebody gets us, I suspect."

The two officers that brought them to the door appeared. "Okay, let's go downstairs," said the first one.

"Lead the way," Holly said. They got into the elevator and rode it down to the bunker level. When the elevator doors opened, they saw people rushing around from one room to another in front of the vault doors. The officers led them past that, down a longer corridor, then down a second set of stairs.

"Why are you taking us here?" Jerry asked.

"For a meeting," the officer said, ushering them to the heavy metal door.

"This is the old bunker," Holly said. "It's not hardened like the main bunker."

"Yeah, I thought this one got retired," Jerry said. "Why are you bringing us down here?"

"Orders," the first officer said, holding the door open for them. They walked into the room, which contained a conference table and a second door in back. There was a TV screen on the wall opposite of the door.

"We're in quarantine, aren't we?" Holly asked.

"Sorry, I don't have that information," the officer said as he left, shutting the door behind him.

"Dammit," Holly said, sitting down at the table.

Jerry went to the door and tried it. "We're locked in."

"They saw the devices with the scanner," Holly said.

"Think so?" Jerry asked.

"What else could it be?" Holly said. "Our families are gonna die."

"Shit," Jerry said, sitting next to Holly, resting his head in his hands.

There was a beep, and the TV screen came on. Nelson, Ramsey, and Gallagher's faces appeared.

"Welcome home, gentlemen," Nelson said.

Holly and Jerry stared at the screen, then looked at each other.

"What's going to happen to us?" Holly asked.

"That depends on you," Gallagher said.

"What does that mean?" Jerry asked, trembling.

"We know you've been chipped," Ramsey said. "It came out in the scan."

Jerry and Holly were silent for a moment. Then Holly looked them in the eye. "They forced us. I hope you believe that."

"How did they force you?" Ramsey asked.

Jerry started to cry. Holly glanced at him, his own eyes getting glassy, then looked back at them.

"After they held us for a while, they brought in pictures of our family," Holly said. "They said if we didn't cooperate, they'd kill all of them."

"What did they ask you to do?" Ramsey asked.

"Not much," Holly said. "We had to agree to taking the RFID chips. That was all for right now."

"For right now?" Nelson asked.

"Yes," he said. "They said we'd be released in a couple of days, then they told us to get back in with you guys and wait for instructions."

"What kind of instructions?" Ramsey asked.

"They didn't say," Holly said. "These people are nuts. It could be almost anything. You know that."

"Yeah, we know that," Gallagher said.

"You put those scanners out there to find RFID chips, didn't you?"

"We're not going to discuss that," Ramsey said.

"What are you going to do with us?" Jerry asked.

"We don't know yet," Ramsey said.

"Will you try to get our families?" Holly asked.

"Like I said, we don't know yet," Ramsey said. "Probably. The enemy has a long reach, though. Are your families in Texas?"

"Most of them," Holly said.

"All of mine are," Jerry said. "What did you mean about long reach?"

"They got to Landry's daughter at her school in Europe," Gallagher said.

"You sure we should be telling them anything at this point?" Ramsey asked.

Everyone was silent for a moment.

"Look," Nelson said. "Right now we don't know if we can trust you, so you will stay where you are. We'll try to recover your families. If they have people watching them already, that's going to be risky. Do you understand?"

"Yes," Holly said. Jerry nodded in agreement.

"We will send interviewers in to talk to you," Nelson continued. "We want to know every detail about your capture, captivity, and release. Understand?"

"Yes, Governor," Holly said. Jerry nodded yes.

"Okay," Ramsey said. "There are beds and a bathroom behind the door. Also some snacks and water, but we'll bring in meals too. You will be well taken care of while we investigate. The better your cooperation, the better your chances of surviving this mess. Do you understand?"

"Yes," Holly said.

"Good," Nelson said. "We'll talk later."

The screen went dark.

"Shit," Jerry said. "Should we have asked for lawyers?"

Holly looked at him like he was nuts.

{ 23 }

Trailering

Richardson's phone alarm went off.

"It's time."

Lita stretched. "I slept better than I expected to."

"Good," Richardson said. "We'd better wake the children."

Lita snickered and got off the waiting room couch. "Children?"

"I heard that," Juan Carlos said, walking over from the other waiting room.

"Sorry," Richardson said. "How'd you guys do last night?"

"I slept like a rock," he said. "I think Madison had a hard time getting comfortable."

"How about Brendan and Hannah?" Lita asked.

"Don't know, they found another place down the hall," Juan Carlos said.

"Oh, they wanted to be alone, huh?" Richardson asked.

"Shut up," Lita said. "Men."

"Hey," Madison said, moving towards them quickly on her crutches.

"Wow, you're moving around better," Lita said.

"I'm a lot stronger. I won't need crutches much longer. My foot doesn't hurt anymore."

"Follow the doctor's instructions," Juan Carlos said. "You could re-damage your foot if you don't."

"Yes, daddy," she said, rolling her eyes.

"Yes *husband,*" Juan Carlos said.

She giggled. "I like the sound of that."

"I'll go wake the other *children,*" Richardson said, walking down the hall.

Madison shot a quizzical look at Lita. She shrugged.

"It was a joke," Juan Carlos said.

"No gunshots for quite a few hours now," Madison said. "That's a good sign, isn't it?"

"I think so," Juan Carlos said. "When we take off in the boat, I want you girls behind armor the whole way, though, all right?"

"You don't have to ask me twice," Madison said. "I'm still pretty scared. Always expecting the other shoe to drop."

"I know, me too," Lita said.

Richardson walked back over. "They'll be over in a few minutes."

"I'm hungry," Lita said.

"Me too," Juan Carlos said. "Maybe there's a McDonalds we can pull the boat up to."

Richardson chuckled and shook his head.

"I wish there was," Brendan said, walking up with Hannah.

"Seriously," Hannah said.

"You two sleep okay?" Lita asked.

"Yeah," Hannah said. "After this one left me alone for a while."

"Shhhhhh," Brendan said. "You're not supposed to tell people that."

Richardson's phone rang. He answered it, then put it on speaker and set it on the counter he was standing next to. "Hear me?"

"Yeah," Jefferson said. "The trailer and truck are ready to go. We didn't get a second vehicle yet, though, I'm afraid."

"Maybe a couple of us should ride in the boat," Brendan said. "If some bad guys show up, we could use the weapons."

"You know, that's not a bad idea," Richardson said. "At least until we get away from here."

"Is that legal?" Hannah asked.

"Who cares," Brendan said. "Nobody's gonna pull us over for that."

Jefferson laughed. "Yeah, you're probably right about that. You shouldn't have trouble around San Antonio, at least. We destroyed the enemy there."

"What about the stretch between San Antonio and Houston?" Lita asked.

"We don't think it's as bad as it used to be," Jefferson said. "I'd keep your eyes open and your weapons ready, just in case."

"Where do we take the boat?" Richardson asked.

"I'm not sure yet," Jefferson said. "I'll let you know, but I don't want to wait around on you leaving. The water level is gonna start receding soon. We need the boat out of there before that happens."

"Where's the trailer?" Juan Carlos asked.

"In front of the Alamo," Jefferson said. "There's a crew there to help you and the other two boats get loaded. You'll probably get wet."

Juan Carlos chuckled. "So what else is new. I'm ready to go any time."

"Yeah, I think we're ready," Richardson said.

"Okay, call me if there's any problems," Jefferson said. "Talk to you soon."

The call ended.

"Well, let's get going," Lita said.

"Yeah," Madison said, getting back to her feet without help. She got on her crutches.

"Nicely done, sweetie," Juan Carlos said.

The group picked up their stuff and headed to the stairwell, going down to the third floor. The breeze from the broken window flowed down the hall as they walked towards it.

"Wonder if there's bad weather coming?" Hannah asked.

"Hope not," Madison said. "I'm going to be in the water, aren't I?"

"Probably," Juan Carlos said.

"I'll need to clean my wound out as soon as possible, then," Madison said, "Who knows what kind of garbage is in this water."

"Yeah, you definitely should clean it out," Lita said. "I'll help you."

They approached the window and looked out. The boat was still there, tied to the window frame.

"Shoot, we're all gonna have to swim, aren't we?" Hannah said, looking down. It was about twelve feet from the opening to the boat.

"We might be able to lift you down," Brendan said, looking over her shoulder. "I'll go in first and see how high I can reach from there."

"Yeah, do that," Richardson said.

"What about our cellphones?" Lita asked.

Brendan tossed his onto one of the seats in the boat. It bounced and landed on the deck. "Hand them over." The others gave their phones to Brendan and he tossed them.

"I don't know why we're bothering," Juan Carlos said. "We jumped into the water with them before. They didn't get messed up."

"True," Richardson said. "But why push it? We have to take the guns through the water too."

Brendan tossed the last of the phones into the boat.

"Okay, dude, go for it," Juan Carlos said.

Brendan nodded, held his weapon tight, and leapt into the water. He swam around the side and climbed up the back, using the port outboard as a step.

"Is the water cold?" Hannah asked.

"No, it's not bad," Brendan said.

"Then screw it," she said, jumping in. She paddled over to the back of the boat, and Brendan lifted her up.

"There's two," Richardson said. "Guess I'll jump in too." He went out the window. "Want to get wet, sweetie?"

"Do I have a choice?" Lita jumped in next to him. They swam to the back of the boat, Brendan helping them in.

"Okay, what's it gonna be, Madison?" Juan Carlos asked.

She sighed. "I'm afraid I'll fall if you try to lift me down," she said. "That boat moves around a lot. You guys won't be able to brace yourselves enough."

"Probably right," Juan Carlos said. "I'll jump in. You follow me, okay?"

"Okay," she said, nervous look on her face.

Juan Carlos jumped in, holding his weapon. He tossed his rifle into the bow of the boat and swam to the window. "Hand me down your crutches."

She laid on the floor and handed them down. Juan Carlos tossed them into the bow. "Okay, honey, come on in."

She nodded and slipped into the water, coming up next to him. "I thought you guys said it wasn't cold."

"Trust me, this isn't cold," Juan Carlos said, taking her arm. They swam to the stern together, Brendan and Richardson helping Madison out of the water. "I'll go get the rest of the guns, and the grenades."

He paddled back to the window, climbing up by the ledge, using the bow rope to steady himself. Brendon got back in the water and helped. They were done in a couple minutes, then climbed into the boat.

"Okay, pilot, get us out of here," Richardson said.

"Aye aye, Captain," Juan Carlos said. He got behind the wheel and fired up the engine. "Keep your eyes open. Some bad guys might have showed up overnight. Ladies, stay low, beneath the sides, okay?"

The women nodded and got down. Brendan untied the rope and pulled it free of the window frame, and Juan Carlos turned the boat around and cruised slowly down College street, up to where it ran into Losoya.

"Which way?" he asked.

"Either Crockett or Houston Street," Brendan said. "Wait, Crockett is one way."

Richardson laughed, shaking his head.

Brendan got a sheepish expression on his face. "Okay, I guess that doesn't matter." Juan Carlos drove to the right, picking up Crockett and then turning left on North Alamo Street.

"There they are," Richardson said, pointing to a group of men working on one of the other boats, still dripping from its trailer.

"Hey, guys," one of the crew said from the bank. "I'll back this down. Makes a good ramp here. You can just drive her on, and we'll get her winched up." He got into the cab of the big truck and backed up.

"Perfect," Juan Carlos said. He waited as the trailer sunk beneath the water, and drove the boat onto it, one of the other ground crew men hooking up the winch and cranking the boat up to the front chock.

"Okay, Charlie, take her out slow," the man in the water said as he stepped away. The truck moved forward, pulling the boat out of the water.

"That was easy," Madison said.

"Yep," Richardson said.

The ground crew man got out of the truck and walked over. "Looks like you guys got a little wet."

"We had to jump into the water to get into the boat," Brendan said. "Gonna be a squishy ride for a while."

"There's not enough room in that cab for all of you," the other ground crew member said. "It's got bucket seats in the front and a bench in the back."

"We're going to ride back here," Juan Carlos said as he hit the button to tilt the engines up.

"Yeah, if anybody bothers us on the road we can blast them," Brendan said.

"Not such a bad idea," the first ground crew man said. "There's still a lot of enemy fighters around once you get out of the city. I'd stay on the interstates as much as possible. They're being patrolled more."

"Roger that," Richardson said, getting out of the boat. "C'mon ladies, let's get out."

"Maybe I should stay in the boat," Madison said.

"No, you should get out and have Lita redo the dressing on your foot," Juan Carlos said.

"Yeah, you don't want to be in the wind when you're wet, either," Richardson said.

"Brendan and Juan Carlos will be," she said.

"Yeah, but they haven't just been in the hospital," Lita said. "C'mon."

Madison sighed. "Okay." Juan Carlos and Brendan helped the women out, Richardson giving them a hand on his side.

"If I see a mall with a clothing store I'll stop," Richardson said.

"Find one next to a fast food joint," Brendan said.

"Yeah, dude," Juan Carlos said.

"Let's get that foot cleaned out," Lita said. "You got your stuff?"

"Yeah, in my pocket," Madison said. "Peroxide and some gauze. The tape might be toast. It wasn't in plastic like the gauze."

"We'll make it work," Lita said, helping her over to the truck.

"You guys keep a good eye out up there," Richardson said. "We'll take off as soon as Lita's done."

"Sounds good," Brendan said.

{ 24 }

Open Road

The caravan was queued at the gate of the Fort Stockton RV Park, Moe and Clancy taking a last look before locking up the buildings.

"You need to lock the gate?" Kyle asked from his truck window. He was in the lead.

"Nah, it's not gonna slow anybody down," Moe said. "We might as well take off."

"Remember where to let each of the tank flatbeds in," Jason shouted from the door of his rig.

"Yeah, we got it," shouted Junior from beside his Brave, Rachel next to him, arm around his waist.

The group started to move slowly onto the access road, turning left, then left on Warnock Road.

Junior and Rachel stopped to let the first flatbed get in front of them.

"That thing spews out some smelly diesel," Rachel said, waving her hand in front of her as if to fan it away.

Junior cracked up. "Yeah, it does, but I'm glad we have these suckers."

They took the bridge over I-10 and got onto the eastbound ramp, merging onto the empty road.

"Where is everybody?" Rachel asked.

"Hunkered down, I reckon," Junior said, glancing at her as he settled into cruising speed. "This baby purrs like a kitten."

"I'll need to drive part of the way," Rachel said.

"You don't have to," Junior said.

"You'll get too tired," she said. "It's okay. I used to drive my brother's rig, and it was bigger than this one."

"Oh," Junior said. "Seems like so long ago since we picked you up."

"I know," she said. "I'm glad you did."

"You happy?"

"Do you even have to ask?"

"Yes, I want to make sure things go well," Junior said.

"You remember our talk, right? I'll never leave you. Ever."

"I know, sweetie, but happiness is important too, and I want to make sure we keep track of that."

"No worries," she said, shooting him a smirk.

"That's an interesting grin," Junior said. "What's funny?"

"I'm not sure if I should bring it up," she said.

"Oh, go ahead," Junior said.

"I'm still late. I don't think it was nerves about the battle."

Junior froze for a moment, then shot her a smile. "Oh, really now?"

"We need to get a test kit when we can stop for a little while," Rachel said.

Junior glanced at her again, a look of pride on his face. "Wow. I thought it would take longer, since we're both a little older."

She giggled. "It's been just about every night, you know."

"I know," Junior said, face turning red. "I can't get enough of you."

"That's easy to see. We should make plans to get hitched."

"Amarillo is a bigger town," Junior said. "We might be able to get hitched there without too much trouble."

"Well, it's bigger than Fort Stockton, anyway," she said. "I kinda liked Fort Stockton, though."

"It's not bad, but I miss the hill country. Dripping Springs, Wimberley, Fredericksburg. Those areas."

"Is that where you want us to settle when this is over?"

"Maybe," Junior said. "It's not just up to me. We have to make that decision together."

"I know," she said, "but I don't have any one place in particular that draws me. *You're* what draws me."

"I have a pretty big piece of land outside Dripping Springs. The house isn't much, but there's room to put a nice place there."

She laughed. "Hell, I could just live with you in this thing forever and be a happy woman."

"I love the Brave," he said. "Not a good place to raise a child, though."

"True," she said.

"Looks like the last of our group is on I-10," Junior said, looking in his side mirror.

"I hope we don't get attacked on the road."

Junior chuckled. "I wouldn't want to attack all these heavily armed vehicles. I do wish we had a gun on the Brave, though."

Rachel chuckled. "Sounds like you might get your wish, from what Curt was saying."

"Sounds like," Junior said.

"Think we're going to make any stops?"

"For gas," Junior said. "I know everybody gassed up before we left, but it's a five-hour drive."

Kyle and Kate were in the lead, watching the road unfold in front of them.

"How you doing, honey?" Kyle asked.

"Better. I think my hormones are evening out a little bit."

"Good," Kyle said.

"You want to try again, don't you?"

"Of course, honey, but maybe we should give it a little time."

"We'll have to," she said, "but I still want to try. Maybe there'll be a doctor I can talk to in Amarillo."

"That would be good," Kyle said.

"You think we'll be up there very long?"

"No," Kyle said. "I think they'll move us someplace else, provided we're successful in taking out that depot in Santa Fe."

"They'll still use us if we aren't successful, won't they?"

He didn't say anything.

"Hey, don't clam up on me," she said. "What are you thinking?"

"If we aren't successful we might not survive," Kyle said.

"Oh. Shit. I had to ask."

"Sorry," he said. "It's my protective nature."

"Oh, I know. Speaking of doctors, I'm gonna push on Carrie to see somebody. She's gone too long without pre-natal care."

"Jason's worried about that too," Kyle said. "We were just talking about it."

"Maybe we should stop working on a baby until the battles are over. That way I can fight alongside you and not have to worry."

"Let's not make that decision now," Kyle said. "We're both too emotional after what happened."

She sighed. "Okay, I see your point."

They settled into the drive, Kate nodding off for a while. Kyle kept an eye on the road ahead, also glancing in the mirror from time to time. The long line of vehicles behind them was both comforting and worrisome. His phone buzzed. He answered it.

"Kyle?" Jason asked.

"What's up?"

"Just heard from Eric. He's near the back of the line. There's more people behind us."

"Maybe they just don't want to attempt a pass," Kyle said. "It's a long caravan, and we aren't going that slow."

"Might be all it is, but I thought I'd give you a heads up."

"You can't see them?" Kyle asked.

"No, I'm right in front of a flatbed. They're wide and tall. Hard to see behind it."

"How many we talking about?" Kyle asked.

"Eric said about five. Dammit. Gotta go."

"What's the matter?"

"Eric just sent me a text," Jason said. "I'll get back with you."

"Okay, man," Kyle said.

"What was that all about?" Kate asked.

"Jason said Eric is seeing other vehicles following us. He's in the back section of the caravan."

"Shit," Kate said, eyes full of fear.

"Don't worry yet," Kyle said. "Could just be normal highway travelers. This is a long caravan to pass."

"How are fast we going?"

"Sixty-six," Kyle said.

"That's pretty slow. Shouldn't we have the eighty mile-per-hour crowd trying to pass us?"

"You'd think, but we aren't in normal times," Kyle said.

Jason called back. Kyle answered it.

"Hey Kyle."

"What's going on? You sound worried."

"Eric said there's over twenty vehicles behind us now."

{ 25 }

Three Leagues

Brian walked into Governor Nelson's office.

"I got the meeting set up for three-thirty," he said.

"Thanks, Brian. Kip was okay with coming over, right?"

Brian chuckled. "He was ecstatic. You were right. He's got cabin fever bad."

"You're sending the armored car, right?"

"Yep," Brian said. "You want him going through the scanner, I hope."

Nelson gave him a sidelong glance. "You don't think he's dirty, do you?"

"He's close to Holly and Sutton," Brian said.

"He's closer to me," Nelson said. "The rule is that everybody goes through, so he'll be no different. I'm sure he's okay, though."

"Sorry, sir," Brian said.

"Hey, if you're worried about something, I want to know about it," Nelson said. "I don't care who's involved. Comprende?"

Brian nodded, then left his office. A moment later Nelson's desk phone buzzed.

Nelson pushed the button on his speaker phone. "What's up, Brian?"

"Wallis is calling. You have time for him?"

"Yeah," Nelson said.

There was a click.

"Hi, Governor."

"Wallis, how are you?"

"I'm okay. You?"

"Same," Nelson said. "What's going on? You sound a little worried."

"My intel guys just talked to me. We have a problem."

"What kind of problem?"

"The enemy knows about Amarillo," Wallis said.

"What? How?"

"Over-zealous social media recruiting," Wallis said.

"Shit," Nelson said. "Was this a mistake or a plant?"

"We don't know," Wallis said. "We might want to re-route the group."

"What about Santa Fe?"

"We wait," Wallis said.

"We can't wait," Nelson said. "What if we use airstrikes?"

Wallis sighed. "We don't know what Washington would do."

"They might do nothing, after the coup," Nelson said.

"I suspect there are still enemy agents throughout the Federal Government, and we can't tell them what we know about the chips yet for that reason."

"Don't we have the US Airforce on our side?" Nelson asked.

"I wouldn't say they're on our side exactly. They're against the Islamists and the UN. They might play along with whoever takes over in DC just to preserve their position."

"What do you mean by play along?"

"They might bomb one of our cities in retaliation," Wallis said.

"Really? You think they'd do that?"

"All of North America is at risk in this war," Wallis said. "We aren't their priority. Life on this continent is. I have that from some pretty good sources."

"Dammit," Nelson said. "Okay, I get it. We have any data on what our guys would be up against if we just let it go?"

"They'd probably get hit by thousands of enemy soldiers as soon as they get settled," Wallis said.

"Why wouldn't the enemy just hit them on the road?"

"They might do that too, but my intel guys doubt it," Wallis said. "They'll want to surround them in one location so our people don't escape. Taking on those crazy vehicles of theirs might not be so easy, even if the enemy has some big numbers to throw at them. Remember how many off-road capable vehicles our guys have."

Nelson sat in his chair silently for a moment.

"You still there, Governor?"

"I'm thinking, Wallis."

"Sorry."

"Find out how big the problem is, and whatever else you can. Then be ready to discuss it with the Fort Stockton group at the three-thirty meeting."

"I thought that was about the gulf coast operations," Wallis said.

"This is more important, and all the folks we need to discuss it will be on the line. I'll have Ramsey get some of the key folks from Fort Stockton on the call."

"Okay, Governor. Talk to you soon."

Wallis ended the call. Nelson hit the phone button again.

"Brian, find Ramsey, and Gallagher if he's around. My office, ASAP. Oh, and send Kip in here too, as soon as he arrives."

"Yes sir," Brian said.

Nelson got up and walked to the wall opposite of his desk, looking at a big map of Texas and the surrounding states, his face grim.

"Hey, boss, what's up?" Ramsey asked.

Nelson turned around. "We have an issue. Just talked to Wallis."

"Oh, shit, what happened now?"

"Let's wait until the others arrive," Nelson said, turning back to the map.

"We've got too much going on in too many places, don't we?" Ramsey asked.

"You're reading my mind," Nelson said, staring at the map. "We've got enemy fighters still coming over the Mexican border. We've got problems brewing along the New Mexico border. We can't even get decent information on what's happening along the Texas-Louisiana border, and we know there are more sleeper cells out there like the group we just defeated in San Antonio."

"Yeah, I've been losing sleep over this stuff," Ramsey said.

"On the other hand, it's not all bad. We've got at least part of our National Guard back on line, and we know how to weed out enemy infiltrators."

Gallagher came in. "Hey, guys. Just saw an armored car dropping Kip and Maria off. They're going through the scanner now."

"Good," Nelson said.

"Is there some kind of emergency going on?" Gallagher asked. "I thought we were going to meet at three-thirty."

Kip Hendrix walked into the room.

"Kip, nice to see you," Nelson said, grinning. "Glad to be out of stir for a little while?"

"You don't know the half of it," Hendrix said. "I take it something new has happened."

"Yeah," Nelson said. "Ramsey, you get to the Fort Stockton folks?"

"Yeah," Ramsey said. "Gave them the conference call number. I'll send a text to Jason when it's time to get on."

"How many we gonna have?"

"I told them whoever they wanted to bring in," Ramsey said. "Hope that's okay."

"It's fine," Nelson said. "Send the text."

Ramsey nodded and pulled out his phone.

"Where's Maria?" Nelson asked.

"She went to our office to gather up stuff we've been needing back at the bunker."

"Good idea," Nelson said. "We could get attacked here just like we were in San Antonio. I'm not ready to call an *all clear*. Not by a longshot."

"I know," Hendrix said.

"They're getting on the call," Ramsey said.

"Good." Nelson got behind his desk. "Take a seat, guys." He pushed the button on his speaker phone. "Brian, we're ready to start. Come on in when you've got the meeting running."

"Will do, sir," Brian said over the speaker.

After a few seconds, there was hissing coming from the phone speaker.

"Who's on, please?" Brian asked as he walked into the office.

"Jason and Carrie," Jason said.

"Curt."

"Kyle and Kate."

"Junior and Rachel."

"Kelly and Brenda."

"Dirk and Chance."

"Eric and Kim."

"Don and Sydney."

"Wallis is on."

"Okay, everybody hear us?" Nelson asked.

"Yep," Junior said. "Hey, Governor."

"Hi, Junior," Nelson said. "I've got Ramsey, Gallagher, Brian, and Hendrix in the room."

“Something bad happen?” Kelly asked.

“We have reason to believe that the enemy knows you’re moving to Amarillo.”

“Dammit,” Kyle said. “How?”

“Social media, it appears,” Wallis said. “Any of you put that out there?”

“Not that I know of,” Don said.

“We can’t rule that out, honey,” Sydney said. “We’ve got connections with many people now. There have been recurring conversations. Maybe somebody on our team doesn’t understand the danger.”

“Well, talk to them,” Ramsey said. “Sooner rather than later.”

“So what do we do now?” Kate asked. “Turn around?”

“We’ll tell you what we know,” Nelson said. “You’ll have to decide if you want to keep going or not.”

“We’re listening,” Junior said.

“Wallis, what’d you find out?” Nelson asked.

“We’re seeing a group massing on the New Mexico border,” Wallis said. “It’s a few thousand men.”

“Where?” Kelly asked.

“Glenrio,” Wallis said.

“Shit, that’s on I-40, just over an hour from Amarillo,” Jason said.

“Yeah,” Wallis said. “We think they’ll wait until you’re settled, and then attack.”

“How are they gonna get over the border?” Kyle asked. “Don’t you have I-40 under control?”

“We’ve got the usual roadblocks up, yes,” Ramsey said. “If a thousand men stream through there, they’ll steamroll the roadblocks with ease.”

“Are any of them already in Texas?” Eric asked.

“We haven’t seen any of this particular group coming across the border yet,” Wallis said. “Why?”

"We have a growing number of vehicles following us," Eric said. "I've been watching them."

"Uh oh," Ramsey said. "How many?"

"A shitload," Eric said.

"Honey," Kim said.

"Sorry," Eric said. "From what I can tell, at least sixty. Maybe more."

"Why didn't you guys call us about that?" Ramsey asked.

"We were getting ready to do just that," Jason said. "Eric and I were talking when the Chief's text came in."

"We're coming up to the big curve at Midland," Eric said. "I'll be able to see what's behind us a whole lot better then."

"I'll go in the back and look out the window," Kim said.

"Get out the binoculars," Eric said. "You know where they are, right?"

"Yeah, in the cupboard above the dinette."

"Good, maybe you can tell if these are Islamists or citizens," Jason said.

"That would be good," Ramsey said. "You got anybody with a gun in the back?"

"Yeah, we've got a pickup truck with a .50 cal and a bunch of bikers back there," Curt said.

"There's a tank flatbed right behind me," Eric said.

"How far are you from the curve?" Nelson asked.

"It's about half a mile in front of me," Kyle said. "I'm first in line. We have a really long caravan. Eric is at least a third of a mile behind me."

"Wow," Gallagher said. "If those are armed citizens on our side, we might not have to change plans. You guys might be able to draw the enemy in and spank them real good."

"That's a little risky, isn't it?" Ramsey asked.

"Depends on the numbers," Curt said. "We're heavily armed now. We can repel a fairly decent-sized force. If we've got a bunch of extra fighters, we might do pretty well."

"I can get our social media warriors back on line and add to our advantage," Don said. "There's pretty good LTE here."

"Yeah, I'm seeing good signal on my phone," Carrie said.

"I'm in the curve," Kyle said. "Holy shit, I can't see the end of the line following us."

Gallagher chuckled. "Gotta love Texans."

"Seriously," Nelson said.

"Kim's in the back looking now," Eric said. "Hey, honey, after you look through the binoculars, snap some pictures with your cellphone."

"Okay, sweetie," said Kim's muffled voice. Gallagher and Ramsey looked at each other.

"The citizens are gonna win this for us, aren't they?" Hendrix asked.

"Starting to look that way," Wallis said.

Ramsey's phone dinged. He looked at it, eyes wide. "My God."

"Let's see," Nelson said. Ramsey passed him the phone. Nelson, Gallagher, and Hendrix gathered to look at the screen.

"Those look like your typical Texas patriots to me," Kim said. "Get the picture okay?"

"Yeah, we got it," Nelson said. "Thanks."

"I was trying to count by fives," Kim said. "Hard while we're moving. There are several hundred vehicles back there."

"What if they're some of these militia folks?" Gallagher asked. "Like Simon Orr."

"You guys need to chat with some of them," Ramsey said. "When's the next time you'll have to stop?"

"Some of us are going to need gas," Jason said. "Hey, honey, where's the next town we can stop for gas?"

"Looks like Lamesa," Carrie said. "That's about an hour and a half. Sound okay?

"Yeah," Jason said.

"Wallis, can you get planes in the air?" Gallagher asked. "Just in case?"

"Yeah, we've got some close by already," Wallis said. "I'll talk with the commander as soon as we get off this call."

"Perfect," Nelson said. "What else?"

"I think we're good," Wallis said. "Gallagher?"

"Yeah, let's stick with the plan unless there's some reason we can't count on all those extra people."

"Everybody else agree?" Nelson asked.

"I'm good with it," Curt said.

"Me too," Jason said.

"Me three," Junior said.

"Okay, then let's end this call," Nelson said. "Be careful, you guys. Don't hesitate to call if this turns out to be hinky."

"Will do, Governor," Jason said. "Thanks."

"I'll go make that call about air support," Wallis said. "Talk to you guys later."

Brian shut down the call. "You want me to stick around?"

"No, you can get back to what you were doing, but set up that call on the gulf issue for an hour from now, okay?"

"Yes sir," Brian said as he left.

Nelson and the others exchanged glances.

"Hope we're doing the right thing," Hendrix said.

"Me too," Ramsey said. "Believe me."

"What did you want to discuss about the gulf?" Ramsey asked.

"Two things," Nelson said. "First, on the drone purchases from Israel. I had everything okayed in the Texas Legislature, the deal was signed with the Israelis, and the cash ready to flow. Then poof. Gone. The Israelis backed out. They wouldn't say why directly, but I found out through another channel that the interim Federal Government warned them not to do it."

"Shit," Gallagher said. "Wonder why?"

"Somebody probably thinks we'll use them against the United States," Ramsey said.

"We don't want them for that," Nelson said. "At this point there's nobody in the Federal Government who I can talk to. Things are still in flux. Nobody knows who's reporting to who, people are still being arrested right out of their offices, and there's even been a few murders."

"Are you so sure you won't ever use the drones against the United States?" Hendrix asked.

Nelson froze, eyeing Hendrix. "What do you mean?"

"If the Federal Government is still backing the Islamists and the UN, some of the people we target might be representing the United States, or at least on their side."

"Dammit," Gallagher said. "He's right, you know. That probably means there's still dirty people running the Federal Government. They probably used Simpson as a fall guy. There may not be any attempt to weed out the bad guys."

"If the good guys in the Federal Government don't know about the RFID chips, how *could* they weed the bad guys out?" Ramsey said. "Son of a bitch."

"Kip, you surprised me again," Nelson said.

"Wonder if General Hogan has time to chat with us on this?" Gallagher asked. "He might know something."

"Good question," Nelson said. He stuck his head out the door. "Brian, see if you can raise General Hogan."

"Yes sir," Brian said.

"You said there were two things," Ramsey said.

"Yeah," Nelson said. "I got a letter from the chairman of the Joint Chiefs this morning."

"Oh, crap," Gallagher said. "What now?"

"He warned me that our little aircraft carriers had better not get further away from the Texas coast than the official territorial waters for the state."

"Shit," Gallagher said. "I'm almost afraid to ask. How far is that?"

"Three leagues," Nelson said.

"Son of a bitch," Gallagher said. "That's about nine miles. Even bush-league artillery can go that far."

"That's what I was afraid of," Nelson said.

"They're doing this for the same reason that they're restricting our ability to buy the drones," Hendrix said. "We're gonna get squeezed."

"Yeah, I think you're right," Gallagher said. "Those bastards."

"So much for our lockdown of the gulf coast, then," Ramsey said. "Wallis know about this?"

"No, not yet. I'll let him know later. I want him to focus on air support for the Fort Stockton group right now."

Brian came in. "Governor, General Hogan is on the line."

"Great, thanks," Nelson said. He got behind his desk and punched the button on the speakerphone. "General Hogan, how are you?"

"I've been better," he said. "I can only talk for a few minutes. What's on your mind?"

"I've got you on speaker. Gallagher, Ramsey, and Hendrix are in the room with me."

"Okay."

"How confident are you that the Federal Government has weeded out all the infiltrators after the coup?"

General Hogan laughed. "I've heard that it's all a sham. President Simpson got sacrificed. Most of the other foreign assets remain. One of them is Kip's buddy Franklin. He just got the Attorney General's slot."

"Attorney General?" Hendrix asked. "What happened to Blake?"

"You know that guy that's been causing the ruckus in California?"

"You mean Ivan the Butcher?" Ramsey asked.

Hogan chuckled. "Yeah, that guy. He staged a nice hit in one of the LA suburbs. Killed a whole bunch of UN thugs and quite a few Federal Government wonks too. Attorney General Blake got killed in that mess."

"Couldn't have happened to a nicer guy," Hendrix said, wicked grin on his face. "Too bad Franklin wasn't with him."

"Seriously," Hogan said. "Why are you asking?"

"The Feds stomped on a deal I had with the Israelis. We were going to buy several drones."

"Oh, yeah, I remember you talking about that," Hogan said.

"They also warned us in writing not to take our aircraft carriers further into the gulf than the Texas territorial waters."

"Shit, that's less than ten miles," Hogan said. "That makes them vulnerable."

"Exactly," Ramsey said.

"Your guy having any luck breaking the RFID chips?" Hendrix asked.

"It's taking longer than we expected," Hogan said. "That's all I can say now."

"But you *are* making progress?" Nelson asked.

"Yes. Be patient. When we're ready, you guys will get a heads up."

"All right," Nelson said. "I'll let you get back to it. Things going okay?"

"Yes and no," he said. "Talk to you later."

The call ended.

"Well that was rather cryptic," Gallagher said.

"Yep," Nelson said. "They're further along on the RFID chips than he's letting on."

"Yeah, I got the same impression," Hendrix said. "What now?"

"There's nothing we can do about the drones at this point," Nelson said. "I wonder how closely they're watching the aircraft carriers."

"I'm surprised they recognized what we're using those things for," Gallagher said. "Those old tubs don't look like much."

"The Feds probably found out about them from the damn Venezuelans," Nelson said.

Brian stuck his head in the doorway. "Governor Nelson, Wallis is back on the line."

"Thanks," Nelson said. He punched the button. "Hey, Wallis, any luck with the air support?"

"Yes sir, we've got assets assigned. One of them already flew over the column. He said there's about four hundred vehicles there, including some bigger vehicles."

"Bigger vehicles?" Nelson asked.

"Yeah, buses," Wallis said.

"Holy shit," Gallagher said. "Assuming an average of four people per vehicle, that's sixteen hundred people."

"Yep," Wallis said.

"If they're fighters from that last battle, we'll handle what we see across the border with ease." Ramsey said.

"Yeah, and if they're bad guys, it's a death sentence," Hendrix said.

{ 26 }

Re-Routed Again

Richardson was driving the big pickup truck, the weight of the patrol boat making the rig feel sluggish.

"Not much fun to drive?" Lita asked.

"Not really," he said. "Glad there isn't a lot of wind."

"Traffic is light on I-10, at least." Lita said.

"Now that we've gotten past I-410, anyway. The girls are still asleep, aren't they?"

Lita looked in the back seat, then back at Richardson. "Battle fatigue."

Richardson snickered. "Madison is close to getting off those crutches already, isn't she?"

"I'd rather see her on them for another week, but I don't know if she can stand it," Lita said. "Think we can get all the way to Houston today?"

"We've got about three hours to go," Richardson said. "Give or take. Should be doable."

"Wish Jefferson would call us with the destination. It's not like we can park our rig at a motel overnight."

Richardson chuckled. "Yes, that would be a problem. Too bad we don't have any camping gear."

"We could get some, you know," Lita said. "It would fit in the truck bed."

"That's a damn good idea," Richardson said. "See if there's a Walmart coming up."

"Okay," Lita said. "We could pick up some clothes there too."

"And some food," Richardson said.

"What about the parking lot?"

"We leave Juan Carlos and Brendan in the boat. They'll take care of anybody who comes along."

Lita chuckled. "That would make the local news."

"What's going on?" Hannah's groggy voice asked.

"Oh, nothing," Lita said as she searched on her phone. "We were thinking about stopping at a Walmart and getting some camping stuff, just in case we don't have a place to stash this boat."

"Where are we?" Hannah asked, sitting up straight.

"About half way between San Antonio and Seguin," Lita said.

"That's all?" Hannah asked.

"What's going on?" Madison asked.

"Oh, you're awake now too, huh," Lita said.

"Yeah," Madison said. "Is something wrong?"

"No, we just aren't as far along as I hoped," Hannah said.

"It took us a long time to get out of the San Antonio area," Richardson said, "and it's not like we can go eighty pulling this boat."

"Oh," Madison said. "Shit. We going to have to sleep in the car if we can't make it tonight?"

"We hope not," Lita said. "Haven't heard from Captain Jefferson yet."

"Why don't you call him?" Hannah asked.

"In a little while," Richardson said. "He's probably busy."

"Hear from the guys lately?" Madison asked.

"No, but I was about to text Brendan," Hannah said.

Madison pulled out her phone. "Good idea, I'll text Juan Carlos."

"I hope nothing's wrong down south," Lita said quietly.

"Me too, but they're trying to set up a new operation with a skeleton crew," Richardson said. "Why don't you see how far it is to Galveston? If Jefferson can't find us a place, we might have to go all the way down there."

"Shit. Okay, I'll check."

"How are the men doing back there?" Richardson asked.

"Bored," Hannah said.

"And hungry," Madison said.

"They're always hungry," quipped Richardson.

"Dammit," Lita said. "We're talking almost another hour past Houston. Wonder why? It's not that much further, really."

"The road, probably," Richardson said. "Can you see how long it will take to get to that next town?"

"Seguin," she said. "Okay."

"Juan Carlos needs a restroom break before too long," Madison said.

"We're about twenty minutes away from Seguin now," Lita said.

"Hear that?" Richardson asked.

"Texting him now," Madison said.

"You young people and you're texting," Lita said. "Why not just call him?"

"I called Brendan shortly after we took off," Hannah said. "Too much wind noise in that boat."

"Oh, yeah, that'd be a problem," Richardson said. "And it's worse now that we're moving full speed."

"He says he can hold it that long," Madison said, "but not much longer."

"There's a Walmart Super Center in the middle of town," Madison said. "Get off on Route 90. It's a few miles on surface streets. Then we can take Route 123 back to I-10."

"Okay," Richardson said. "I'm gonna call Jefferson before we get there. If I can raise him, we'll pick up some camping gear and some food. Agreed?"

"Where are we gonna camp?" Madison asked.

"I know some places," Richardson said. He hit Jefferson's contact and put the phone to his ear, listening to it ring, his face grim.

"He's not picking up, is he?" Lita asked.

Richardson put his phone away. "No, he's not."

"You aren't leaving him a message?" Lita asked.

"If he's been captured or killed, I don't want to let the enemy know about us," Richardson said.

"You don't think that happened, do you?" Hannah asked.

"Probably not. Maybe he's just on a conference call or something."

"Then you should've gotten a busy signal," Lita said.

"We're going to be in trouble again, aren't we?" Madison asked, eyes welling with tears.

"Don't get too scared yet," Lita said. "We'll be okay."

"Hope so," Hannah said.

"Maybe we should turn on the news," Madison said.

"We can do that," Richardson said.

"I'll find a news station," Lita said, reaching over to the radio. She switched it on and found a news station after a few minutes. "There."

"There's the sign for Route 90," Richardson said.

The weather report went on in the background as they all looked out the windows.

"Pretty around here," Hannah said.

"Yeah," Lita said. "We're getting into the Hill Country. It's just a little north of us."

"We are still trying to get information on the attack in Galveston. The city was bombed just two hours ago. We have eyewitness accounts of the attack, which say it was carried out by US Airforce jets flying at low altitude. We do not have confirmation on those reports at this

hour. There has been large loss of life in the southwestern section of Galveston, and the bridge to Virginia Point has been destroyed, cutting off the easiest route into the area. We are monitoring the situation and will provide additional reports as soon as possible."

"Oh, shit," Richardson said.

"No," Lita said.

"Well, that explains it, I guess," Madison said. "I'll text Juan Carlos."

"Yeah, do that," Richardson said. "Here's the off-ramp for Route 90. Guess we *are* gonna need that camping gear. We aren't going to Galveston tonight."

"We're going to be chased around until this is over," Hannah said, a note of resignation in her voice.

"We're lucky it happened before we got there," Lita said.

"Yep," Richardson said. "Why the hell would the US Airforce attack us?"

"I hope Jefferson didn't get killed," Lita said.

"You and me both, honey," Richardson said.

They drove down the long ramp which turned into road 464.

"This isn't route 90," Hannah said, looking at the signs.

"It'll join up with route 90 at that Y up there," Lita said. She looked at Richardson. "See it, honey?"

"Yeah," he said. "We're going down the middle of a big city street. We're gonna attract a lot of attention."

"I know," Hannah said, "and it makes me nervous."

"How did the guys take the news?" Richardson asked.

"They're worried," Madison said. "How much further to the spot you know about. They're getting pretty fatigued back there."

"It's a little north of San Marcos," Richardson said. "I hope we can get there before dark. It's pretty rough."

"Can we tow this boat back there?"

"Yeah, I think so," Richardson said. "We should grab a flatbed at Walmart. We're gonna need quite a bit of stuff. We need to plan on being camped out a few days. We'll need a big ice chest, food, a Coleman stove, a lantern or two, sleeping bags, chairs, and pup tents."

"This is so scary," Madison said.

"Where's the Walmart?" Richardson asked.

"Turn right on South King Street," Lita said, looking at her phone. "It'll be on your left, a few blocks down."

"Got it," Richardson said. "You tracking it with your GPS?"

"Yeah, we're about a third of the way there."

"Good, give me plenty of warning before we get there."

"I will," Lita said.

Madison chuckled.

"What?" Hannah asked.

"Juan Carlos wants some of that pizza they sell," she said.

"That sounds pretty damn good to me too," Richardson said. "I feel like a drink, but that would be a bad idea."

"How secluded is this place?" Lita asked.

"Secluded enough to hunt in," Richardson said. "We should be fine. At least two people could sleep in the boat. Maybe we ought to buy a tarp."

"I need a change of clothes," Hannah said.

"We all need that," Madison said. "Getting a little ripe in here."

"I suppose that's true," Richardson said.

"How we gonna do this?" Lita asked.

"In shifts," Richardson said. "Can't leave the boat alone. We'll have to move quickly too."

"We're just a couple blocks away, honey," Lita said.

"Good," Richardson said. "Not much traffic."

"Wonder if that's good or bad?" Madison asked.

"Mid-afternoon," Richardson said. "It's before people get off work. Probably has a lot to do with it. There's our street."

He made the right turn, going down the access road. "That's a huge Walmart."

"A superstore," Lita said. "That's good."

"There's the driveway already," Richardson said. He made the left turn.

"Lots of people here," Hannah said. "We'll be parking a ways out."

"No problem," Richardson said. "There's a good spot, and it's not that far away." He turned into the spot, pulling over the dividing line to take both spaces. He shut down the engine and took a deep breath.

"You okay, honey?" Lita asked.

"I'm worried about my boss," Richardson said.

Juan Carlos and Brendan appeared next to the cab, opening the doors for their women.

"Wow, look at your hair," Madison said, smiling at Juan Carlos as she got on her crutches.

"Yeah, it's a little windy out there," he said. "You guys mind if I high-tail it to the men's room?"

"Go for it," Richardson said. "Both of you. Bring back some pizza if you want."

"Can we go with them?" Madison asked.

"Sure, Lita and I will hang out here," Richardson said. "We need to make a shopping list."

"Already been working that on my phone," Lita said.

"I figured, saw you typing."

They watched as the two younger couples headed for the doors of the store.

"How's this?" Lita asked, showing Richardson his phone. He read the list and nodded yes.

"We might be camping for a while."

"Hope not," Lita said. "Wish we knew somebody with a big garage or something."

"I know, me too," Richardson said. "I'll ask the others when they get back. We could rent a closed space in a storage yard, I suppose. My uncle had one of those for his motor home. It was completely enclosed, like a big garage."

"Did it cost very much?"

"Don't remember, honey," Richardson said. "Geez, I'm so worried about Jefferson."

"I know, me too."

A middle aged couple walked up, looking at the boat.

"DPS?" the man asked.

"Yep," Richardson said.

"Were you guys at San Antonio?"

"Yep," Richardson said.

"Can I shake your hand?" the man asked.

"Sure," Richardson said, walking over to him. They shook.

"That was great what you guys did. Really got the enemy on the run."

"Unfortunately we got hit in Galveston, though."

"Yes, I heard about that on the way over here. You were probably headed in that direction, weren't you?"

"Can't talk about that, but I *do* have friends there. Can't raise them now. I'm pretty worried."

"I'll bet," the man said. "We'll leave you alone now. Good luck to you, sir."

"Thank you," Richardson said.

"Interesting," Lita said.

"I had a feeling we'd get some of that reaction."

"Gonna try Jefferson again?" Lita asked.

"In a little while," he said, scanning the parking lot.

"See something that worries you?"

He glanced at her, then went back to scanning. "No, but I'm nervous. Something isn't quite right. Can't put my finger on it."

"You're scaring me."

"Sorry," Richardson said. "Let's climb into the boat."

She nodded, and they climbed in using the trailer wheel fenders.

"You think it's safer in here?" she asked.

"The boat has armor," Richardson said. "It's also higher, so I can see further."

"People are noticing," Lita said. "I've seen two people taking pictures with their phones."

"I just saw one in this direction too," Richardson said. "They're probably posting it to social media as we speak. We need to get out of here."

"What about the shopping?"

"I've got an idea," Richardson said. "Let's go on to San Marcos. The camping spot is northwest of there, in a place called Purgatory Creek. We find a place, unhitch the boat, and then some of us go into a store there."

"San Marcos, huh," Lita said, looking at her phone. "There's another Walmart Supercenter there. Why don't you text the guys and have them buy enough pizza and drinks for all of us? We can eat on the way."

"You got it," Richardson said, pulling his phone out, keeping one eye on the parking lot while he typed.

"Purgatory Creek is only about half an hour from here," Lita said.

"Good. Brendan just texted me back. They'll be back in about five minutes."

"You tell them why we're leaving?" Lita asked.

"Yeah. It's gonna be a late night."

"I'd rather be tired than dead," Lita said.

Richardson laughed, still scanning the parking lot. "At least I'm not seeing bad guys. Looks like just plain folks. I'd probably take pictures too."

"If they just post pictures to their own Facebook wall, is it really dangerous for us?"

"Can be," Richardson said. "Hackers know how to find stuff in Facebook feeds. That's why you have to be careful posting about vacations."

"People go to their house and rip them off?"

"It's happened before. Here they come. That was fast."

"It was," Lita said. "Should we get out?"

"Not yet. Sit tight."

"Madison's getting around really well now," Lita said. "She's not having trouble keeping up."

"Good," Richardson said.

"Hey, boss," Brendan said. "You want to eat on the road?"

"I'll eat a piece while everybody gets settled," Richardson said. "Sorry about this."

"I'm glad you noticed it," Juan Carlos said. He had drinks in his hands.

They got situated again with food and drink, Brendan and Juan Carlos back in the boat, the others in the truck, Richardson back at the wheel. They drove out of the parking lot.

"Just take route 123," Lita said. "Turn left at Rattler Road. That will take you right out there."

"Perfect, I know about Rattler Road. Once we're there, I'll know how to get to the camping spot."

They made it out of Seguin in less than ten minutes, and then were cruising north on 123.

"Not much out here," Madison said, looking out onto the flat farmland.

"Deadsville," Hannah said.

"We're gonna hit the massive town of Geronimo in a few minutes," Lita said. "Something wrong?"

"Somebody's on our tail," Richardson said, glancing at the driver's side mirror.

"Oh no," Hannah said.

"Don't worry, if it's bad guys we'll smoke them," Richardson said. "Could be more hero-worshipers."

"Hero-worshipers?" Madison asked.

"I'll tell you about that later," Lita said. "I see them in this side mirror too. They're getting closer."

Suddenly there was crack of gunfire.

"Dammit," Richardson said, speeding up.

"What if they hit one of the guys?" Madison cried.

"Can't see them," Hannah said, looking out the back window.

The sound of automatic fire started.

"That's them," Richardson said. Then there was an explosion.

"Whoa," Lita said, looking at a big fireball in the passenger side mirror. "Blew them up."

"Hope they didn't have friends," Madison said.

"Should we stop?" Hannah asked.

"That would be a big negatory," Richardson said. "One of you text back there."

"I just got a text from Juan Carlos. He said they smoked the bad guys, but we lost one of the outboard engines."

"That's the least of my worries," Richardson said. "They're both okay, right?"

"Yeah, they're fine," Hannah said. "Just got a text from Brendan."

"Tell them to get their eyes off their phones and onto the road," Richardson said.

"I will," Madison said.

They rolled along for a while, then Richardson's eyes got big.

"What's the matter?" Lita asked.

"Looks like we got a cop coming," he said.

"Is he gonna try to stop us?" Hannah asked.

"Yep," Richardson said. "Just turned their red light on."

"Shit," Madison said. "How do we know they're real cops?"

"We have to assume," Richardson said as he slowed down, moving to the shoulder. He stopped and looked into the mirror as the squad car pulled up behind the boat. "That's DPS. We'll be fine. I've got my credentials."

He pulled out his wallet and waited for the officer to walk up to his window, the partner standing by the boat.

"Good afternoon," the officer said. "You DPS?"

"Yes sir," Richardson said, handing his card out the window. The officer looked at it for a moment, then handed it back to him. "Saw what you guys did back there."

"They shot at us," Richardson said.

"I figured," the officer said. "Where you headed?"

"San Marcos," Richardson said. "We *were* under orders to go to Houston."

"You got re-routed due to that attack in Galveston, I reckon," the officer said. "We won't keep you. Watch yourselves around San Marcos. There's been some trouble there lately."

"What kind of trouble?" Richardson asked.

"Murders and abductions. You guys will have a big target on your backs if you hang out around there with this boat."

"We're going to hide north of town," Richardson said.

"What's that boat packing?" the officer asked.

"She's got .50 cal machine guns and grenade launchers," Richardson said.

"Okay, I'll let you guys go. Good luck. Be careful, especially with the ladies. They've been targeted around here."

"Targeted?" Hannah asked.

"Yeah, little lady. Abductions and rapes. Don't go anywhere alone. Be armed if you can."

"Geez," Lita said. "Thanks for letting us know, officer."

"No problem. Take care."

"Thanks," Richardson said. He watched the officer join his partner and get back into their cruiser.

"Let's go," Lita said.

Richardson nodded and drove forward. "Find us a way to the western side of Purgatory Creek that doesn't take us right through the main part of San Marcos."

Lita nodded and worked her phone.

"I'll try Jefferson again," Richardson said, hitting the contact on his phone. He held it to his ear, then set it down, face still grim. "Nothing."

"What if somebody tries to hit us from the front instead of the back?" Madison asked.

"The boys will shoot right over the top of this vehicle," Richardson said. "The boat is a lot higher than the truck, and the guns will have a clean shot in any direction."

"I found a back-road route," Lita said. "It's not in the middle of nowhere, but it's a lot more sparse. Take a left on 1101, then take a right on Kohlenberg Road. It's a little out of the way."

"Then why go that way?" Hannah asked. "Won't it just take longer?"

"Crossing I-35 is the problem," Lita said. "You can take Kohlenberg to Conrads Lane to cross, then get on 1102, which turns into Hunter's Road."

"That's perfect," Richardson said. "I've gone in that way. Might be a little bit of a challenge because of the dirt road, but we'll make it. I used to go through a small residential area to get there."

"The road is 233, right?" Lita asked.

"Show me," Richardson said. Lita moved over and held the screen in front of his face. "Yeah, that's it. We're good. It'll be hard to notice us going that way."

"Route 1101 looks pretty small," Lita said. "We'll have to keep our eyes peeled."

"I'll leave the GPS on and follow it," she said. "Probably better plug in my phone, though."

"You have your power cord?" Richardson asked.

"Forgot that I stuffed it in my pocket before we left the rooms at the Riverwalk," Lita said, fishing it out. She plugged the cord into the USB port on the dash radio. "Glad this is a new vehicle."

"Seriously," Richardson said. "Wish it were four-wheel drive. Didn't expect to be taking it in the dirt, but it'll probably be okay."

"See anybody else behind us?" Hannah asked.

"Nope, and the traffic's thinned out," Richardson said.

"Hey," Lita said. "Take Franch Road instead of 1101. It'll shave off a little time. Then turn left onto 1101 from there. Franch is a slight left. It'll be easy to see. Only a couple miles away."

"Okay, sweetie," Richardson said. He watched the road ahead, still glancing nervously into his rear-view mirror every so often.

"There it is," Lita said. Richardson took the slight left.

"Farmland as far as the eye can see," Madison said, looking out her window.

Richardson's phone rang. He checked it. "Jefferson! I'll put it on speaker."

"Richardson? Where are you?"

"On my way to a hiding place. Already got attacked on the road once. Where are you?"

"We escaped, barely," Jefferson said. "I assume you know what happened in Galveston."

"Some," Richardson said.

"Listen. Unplug the radio beacon in the boat. It's under the dash. Can't miss it. It's a gray plastic box on a connector. Just unplug it."

"We're being tracked, aren't we?"

"Yeah, probably," Jefferson said.

"Hey, Madison, text Juan Carlos and let him know, okay?"

"Already on it," Madison said.

"I thought we got attacked because there were people taking pictures of us in Seguin and posting them on social media. That boat caused quite a stir in the parking lot."

"What were you doing in a Walmart parking lot?"

"We were gonna buy camping gear and food," Richardson said. "When we couldn't raise you guys."

"Where were you planning to camp out?"

"Purgatory Creek, where I used to camp as a teenager," Richardson said.

"You do that," Jefferson said. "I don't know what the next plans are. Might as well lay low."

"Somebody shot one of the outboards when we were attacked."

"Don't worry about that, Richardson," Jefferson said. "Oh, and charge the camping gear to the DPS. I assume you've still got to get some."

"Yeah, we're going to park the boat in the boonies and take the truck into San Marcos."

"Good," Jefferson said. "Make sure you leave somebody with the boat while you're gone."

"Oh, we will," Richardson said.

"Juan Carlos unplugged that beacon," Madison said.

"Excellent," Jefferson said.

"Who hit us in Galveston?" Richardson asked. "One of the news radio stations said it was the US Airforce."

"It was," Jefferson said.

"Why would they do that? I thought they were against the Feds."

"We don't know," Jefferson said. "I'm sure the Governor is trying to figure that out right now. My guess is that they didn't like the aircraft carriers. Both of them were sunk."

"Shit," Richardson said. He made the left turn on 1101. "How do we protect the gulf now?"

"From land," Jefferson said. "All of our boats got destroyed. That's the only reason they bombed Galveston. They screwed up and hit some civilian neighborhoods. Also took out the bridge. We don't think they did that on purpose."

"Dammit," Richardson said. "You think the Feds are gonna invade Texas? Force us back into the union?"

"I don't know," Jefferson said. "I'm worried about it. So's my leadership."

"Geez," Lita said.

"You guys lay low for now. Nothing you can do here. I gotta go. We're moving out again."

"Okay," Richardson said. "Glad you're not dead."

Jefferson chuckled. "That which doesn't kill us makes us stronger. Remember that."

The call ended. Richardson stuffed the phone back in his pocket and glanced at Lita, who looked terrified.

"Maybe we should just ditch this boat and disappear into the woodwork," Lita said.

"This boat will protect us on the road," Richardson said. "It's worth keeping, at least for now."

"This road is out in the middle of nowhere," Hannah said. "Think we'll get to camp before dark?"

"Yeah, we should," Lita said. "It's not that far. Even going out of the way, we ought to be at that residential area in few minutes."

"Good," Madison said. "I just want to hold onto Juan Carlos at this point."

"I hear you there," Hannah said.

"Some big sweeping curves on this road," Richardson said. "Little bumpy too."

"Maybe you should slow down a tad," Lita said. "It's probably bouncing the guys around quite a bit."

"You're right," Richardson said as he slowed down. "We've got plenty of time."

"How long will we be able to camp out here?" Madison asked. "Before people start to notice?"

"Probably quite a while," Richardson said. "Assuming it hasn't changed much since I was here last."

"How long ago?" Lita asked.

"Fifteen or twenty years, I reckon," Richardson said.

"We need a house with an RV garage," Hannah said. "My uncle had one of those."

"Where?" Lita asked.

"Up north," Hannah said. "He's getting up there in age. Had to stop using the RV. Really broke him up."

"Where up north?" Madison asked.

"Wichita Falls," Hannah said. "Long way from here, and it's in the middle of the city. People would notice if we drove there."

"Here comes our road, off to the right," Lita said.

"See it," Richardson said. He made the right turn. "I can see I-35 already."

"Since they were tracking us, I'm glad we're on these small roads. Glad we're making a lot of twists and turns."

"Seriously," Madison said. "This still makes me really nervous."

"Honey, Conrads Lane jogs after the freeway. You've got to turn right onto Goodwin and then left back onto Conrads."

"Okay," Richardson said. "Here's where people will notice us if they're going to." They drove over the bridge at I-35, everyone looking out the windows.

They came back to street level, cruising along Conrads Lane.

"Big housing development to our left," Hannah said.

"Yeah, we'll go past quite a few of those," Lita said. "I'm afraid 1102 isn't as sparse as 1101, but it's a lot better than going through town."

"It'll be fine," Richardson said. "Here's that jog you were talking about." He made the right turn on Goodwin, then a left back onto Conrads after about a block.

"Nobody's out on the street," Madison said. "Wonder why?"

"They might be hunkered down," Richardson said. "Remember what that DPS officer told us about San Marcos."

"That means the enemy might see us," Hannah said.

"Yep, we need to keep our eyes peeled," Richardson said. "Glad we have the guys back there."

"Slow down, honey, here comes 1102."

"Hunter's road. See it." Richardson turned right. "Look at that big storage yard."

"I don't think we want our guns somewhere that we can't use them," Madison said.

"Yeah," Richardson said.

"Wish we had an RV," Lita said. "It's going to be a pain not having a bathroom."

"We'll get something for that," Richardson said, "but you're right, an RV would be nice."

"Are the trees this dense where we're going?" Hannah asked.

"Yes," Richardson said. "We'll have plenty of cover."

"Good," Hannah said. "How much longer?"

"A few minutes," Lita said, watching her phone, cable still attached to the dash radio.

"Well, a few minutes to the end of the road," Richardson said. "There's a little bit of dirt road. Not too bad. Another ten minutes max, assuming we can find a good enough place."

"How do we know this rig won't get stuck out in the dirt?" Hannah asked.

"That's possible, so we'll have to be careful," Richardson said. "We got a truck with a dually rear end pulling a two-axle trailer, though. We can probably make it, if the terrain hasn't gotten a lot worse than it was."

"I'm not seeing people watching us, at least," Madison said.

"I know, me neither," Hannah said.

They rode silently for a few more minutes, through the sleepy residential streets. There were occasional cars, but nobody paid them any mind.

"Starting to see more people," Lita said. "We're getting close to 233 though. Street name is McCarty."

"Oh, yeah, that's the name I remember," Richardson said. "Looks different around here. More homes. And look up ahead. Is that a car dealership?"

"I see two of them. That's our street. Get ready to turn left."

Richardson nodded, making the turn on McCarty.

"You sure this is gonna be secluded enough?" Madison asked, looking at the houses as they drove by.

"Yeah, trust me," Richardson said. They watched out the window as they rolled down the thin street, oak trees getting more and more dense.

"I think this is the street coming up," Lita said. "Paso Del Robles."

"Yep," Richardson said. "I recognize it." He turned right onto the small street.

"The Oaks are so dense that you can't see the houses," Hannah said.

"That's good," Madison said.

"There's one more turn, to the right," Richardson said.

"You're talking about Arroyo Doble," Lita said. "It curves around then straightens out and runs to a dead end cul-de-sac."

"That's right," he said. "Hopefully the dirt road hasn't been taken out by a new house or something."

"There it is," Lita said. Richardson made the right turn, driving several blocks then following the curve of the road to the right.

"This is the last part," he said. "This road looks the same as it did last time I was here."

"It so pretty," Madison said. "I'd love to have a house somewhere like this."

"Your own little love nest," Hannah quipped.

"Yes, as a matter of fact," Madison said. "Wouldn't you like it?"

"Rather be closer to the city," she said. "I'm not a country girl."

"What's that left?" Madison asked as they passed another street.

"That's the road we were just on," Lita said. "It curves around."

"Didn't before," Richardson said. "There's probably been more development over there."

"Not much this direction," Lita said. "The end of the road is only another five hundred yards."

"Yep," Richardson said. "There's the end up ahead." He slowed down.

"It look the same?" Hannah asked.

"There's a mailbox near the road back," Richardson said nervously. "Must be a house back there now." He stopped at the end of the pavement, a rounded cul-de-sac with mailboxes at noon, three o'clock, and nine o'clock. A dirt road was just to the left of the noon position. "Shit, I wonder if that's still a road or just a driveway?"

"No clue," Lita said.

"Only one way to find out," Richardson said, slowly driving forward.

The road was uneven, with trees along either side, some of the branches a little too close to the highest parts of the boat.

"Well, if we can get back here, we'll be hard to see," Richardson said. They passed a driveway to the left, the rustic house barely visible about a hundred yards in.

"Good, that's the driveway," Richardson said. "Must be a lot of fun in the rain."

"Tell me about it," Lita said.

Suddenly there was frenzied barking by two large dogs.

"Dammit," Richardson said, slamming on the brakes. There was a large middle-aged Mexican man holding a shotgun, a small white woman with gray hair next to him.

"Who are you?" he yelled. "Dogs, shut up!" They whimpered and stopped barking.

"Hold your fire," Richardson yelled out the door. Then he got out and yelled to the back. "Don't shoot, guys. That's an order."

{ 27 }

Lend-Lease

The armored personnel carrier drove to the new gate of Kip Hendrix's residence and beeped the horn. Two soldiers rushed out and opened the gate, eyes darting around.

The house's studs were rising, some sections of the second floor already up.

"Can't believe how much progress they've made on the house," Maria said, checking out the window as the vehicle drove through the gate.

"Seriously," Hendrix said. "I'm surprised we didn't get called back."

"Maybe they want us here," Maria said. "To spread people out. You think the US Airforce really attacked Galveston?"

"I suspect we'll find out in a few minutes."

"Mr. Hendrix, stay put until we've gotten out and checked the elevator enclosure."

"Will do," Hendrix said. Maria shot a worried glance. "It'll be okay, honey."

The man left the vehicle and ducked into the black metal enclosure.

"I'll never get used to living like this," Maria said.

“It’ll pass,” Hendrix said. “Trust me. May take a while, but no war lasts forever.”

“All clear,” the man said. He opened the passenger door of the vehicle and helped the couple out, rushing them into the enclosure. Kip used his key to open the elevator.

“Take care,” the man said.

“You too,” Hendrix said. “Thanks for the ride.”

“You’re welcome, sir,” he said, leaving them as the elevator doors opened. They rode down to the basement, then went to the vault door. Hendrix put in the code and it opened before them.

“Home sweet home,” Hendrix said.

“Yeah,” Maria said. “Our little love nest.”

Hendrix chuckled as they went inside. Maria went to the console and closed the door. “Hey, honey, meeting notice. Want me to connect?”

“Yeah, go ahead. I’ll go fetch us some bottles of water.”

“Sounds good,” she said.

When Hendrix came back the meeting was already up. Brian was sitting at the conference table, a concerned expression on his face.

“Got home safe and sound, I see,” Brian said, trying to force a smile. “You hear what happened?”

“Yep,” Hendrix said. “Was it really the US Airforce?”

“I’ll let the governor address that,” Brian said. “Everybody will be on in a couple minutes. Good time for a short break if you just arrived home.”

“I think I’ll go powder my nose,” Maria said.

“Maybe I should hit the restroom, too,” Hendrix said, getting up. They were both back in front of the console monitor in a couple minutes.

“We’re back,” Hendrix said.

Gallagher walked into the conference room, followed by Ramsey. A new window opened on the screen, and Wallis's grim face appeared.

"Where's the governor?" he asked.

"He'll be here in a moment," Brian said.

"Anything happen with the Fort Stockton group since we left the Capitol?" Hendrix asked.

"Nope," Gallagher said. "Not that I've heard yet, anyway. Glad we ruled out an airstrike on the depot. We probably would've drawn a response."

"Maybe we'll draw another response with a ground assault on the depot in New Mexico," Hendrix said. "They seem to want us staying inside Texas."

"Something to worry about," Gallagher said. "As if we didn't have enough already."

Governor Nelson came into the room.

"You look happy," Ramsey said.

"The Israelis are convinced that the Federal Government is still dirty," he said. "We'll get our drones tomorrow."

"They aren't afraid of retaliation?"

"They are, but they think if Texas falls it will be a lot more dangerous for them, so they're taking the risk."

"How will we get them?" Ramsey asked. "Our port situation isn't so hot."

"They're flying them in," Nelson said. "From one of their ships, under the radar."

"How many?" Gallagher asked.

"Twenty-five," Nelson said.

"We can't afford that," Hendrix said.

"Let's just say we're getting a kind of lend-lease," Nelson said with a twinkle in his eye.

"Hope this stays a secret for a while," Wallis said. "You know the Air Force is gonna get wise eventually."

"I heard a rumor that the Air Force leadership is horrified at what happened," Gallagher said. "It's not the brass doing this. They've got dirty people, just like we had in the Air National Guard."

"And we can't tell them about the chips," Hendrix said. "Dammit."

"Let's get started," Nelson said. "By now you all know about the attack. The US Airforce took out those two junker aircraft carriers, and the port at Galveston."

"We lose all the choppers on those carriers?"

"No, thank God," Wallis said. "Most of the aircraft were out on sorties when the boats were attacked."

"Crew?" Hendrix asked.

"Mostly dead," Wallis said. "There were only about twenty men on each boat, though. We lost all the DPS patrol boats and some of our crews too."

"Dammit," Gallagher said.

"We're being squeezed, to insure we stay within our borders," Hendrix said, "That's pretty clear."

"Yes," Wallis said.

"How long can we survive without the ports?" Hendrix asked.

"We'll start seeing problems after about two months," Nelson said. "We do have some pressure relief valves. Not sure how long they'll last, though."

"What are they?" Ramsey asked.

"We've got friendlies in Oklahoma, Arkansas, and Louisiana who are moving supplies to us," Nelson said. "This doesn't leave the room, okay? That's one of the reasons I wanted the drones so badly. To protect supply convoys."

"Why are they squeezing us so hard now?" Hendrix asked.

"They're afraid we'll seal up New Mexico," Gallagher said. "Had a brief chat with General Hogan about that earlier. Those citizen groups he's working with have caused a lot of death and destruction. The enemy needs more men and materials. They can't count on California anymore. The worm is starting to turn there."

"Good," Hendrix said.

"Yeah, good, except it dumps more pressure on us," Gallagher said.

"What are we gonna do about the gulf now?" Hendrix asked.

"We've got more patrol boats in the manufacturing pipeline," Wallis said. "We're extremely short on crews now, though. It's a bad situation. We'll have to beef up our protection from shore to compensate."

"We have the stuff?" Ramsey asked.

"Gonna be tough," Gallagher said. "We're already moving assets around from one crisis to another. That battle in San Antonio was a great victory, but it forced us to take our eye off the strategic. We're back in reactive mode, and we don't have the weapons or men to cover everywhere they might pop up."

"Dammit," Hendrix said. "This will lead to more civilian deaths."

"What about the Fort Stockton group?" Hendrix asked. "They still gonna do the attack in Santa Fe, or would we see retaliation from the Feds on that too?"

"I'm more worried about the attack they've got coming at them," Wallis said. "The build-up on the New Mexico border is still going on."

"What are our folks gonna do next?" Hendrix asked.

"We don't know yet," Gallagher said.

"They're gonna stop in just a few minutes and talk to the people following their convoy," Ramsey said.

"How many people is it looking like now?" Hendrix asked.

"Could be as many as five thousand, based on the latest recon I got," Wallis said, "and get this. There's another huge group coming in."

"Good guys or bad guys?" Ramsey asked.

"Good guys, we think," Wallis said.

"From where?" Nelson asked.

"Dallas and Fort Worth," Wallis said. "It's a lot bigger than the other group, and they're heading right towards Amarillo on route 287."

Gallagher chuckled. "Their social media campaign is working. This could be huge, you know. Something we can replicate."

"They gonna make it in time?" Hendrix asked.

"That's the real question," Wallis said.

"Let's keep our fingers crossed," Nelson said.

"I think we ought to get good numbers and use them to adjust the arrival in Amarillo," Hendrix said.

"Yeah, Kip's right," Gallagher said. "We should work that right now, and get word to the group."

"Agreed," Nelson said. "I've got to work on other things at the moment. Can the rest of you stay on and work it?"

"Yep," Wallis said.

"Let's do it," Hendrix said.

{ 28 }

The Rodeo

Kyle watched the road as they pulled into Lamesa.

"We'll clog up the truck stops real good," he said.

"That's an understatement," Kate said. "Eric's gonna flag down some of the followers, right?"

"Yeah," Kyle said. "Hope he's careful. Hope they're good guys. I'm going in here." He drove his truck onto the big truck-stop lot and went to an open pump. Others flooded in, lining up. The truck stop across the street filled up too. Other cars stopped on the curbs to wait.

When Kyle got out of his truck, several people cheered. Kate went to the store to get coffee.

"We're with you guys, man!" yelled somebody from about ten stalls over. "Bitchen machine gun."

Kyle smiled and nodded to the man, then pumped gas. He looked around at the sea of vehicles lined up now, trailing way down the street as far as he could see.

"Damn, we're liable to run these guys right outta fuel," Kate said as she walked back over, two coffee cups in her hands. "Huge line at the coffee station in there too. I beat the rush."

"I think these folks are friendlies," Kyle said, taking one as he finished fueling up. "Thanks for the joe."

Jason, Eric, and Kim trotted over, Paco trying to keep up. "Hey, man, we're gonna have a quick meeting just outside of town, so stop there, okay?" Eric asked. "The locals say there's a huge flat spot that we can park on. They use it for parking when they have a rodeo over there. Should hold a lot of our rigs. There's good shoulder several miles on either side too."

"Who are they?" Kate asked. "You talk to them?"

"Yeah," Eric said. "A bunch of them fought with us in the last battle, but there's gobs more."

"There's a huge group on the way from the Dallas area too," Kim said. "Don called us. The social media thing is working."

"This RV park won't hold everybody," Jason said. "You guys know that, right?"

"We need to strategize," Kyle said. "We might want them outside of that area so we can draw in the enemy."

"Yeah, Junior came up with the same idea," Jason said. "I was on the phone with him and Kelly a little while ago."

"I'm full, so I'd better move out of the way," Kyle said. "See you down at that lot."

"Yeah, man," Jason said.

Kyle and Kate got into their truck and drove off the truck stop lot, heading down route 87 through town.

"This town is bigger than I expected," Kyle said, looking around. Look, the gas stations down here are full too. Wow."

"We're raising an army, aren't we?"

"Seems that way," Kyle said. "Hope I recognize the space they were talking about."

"It's thinning out now, so I don't think we'll have a problem," Kate said. "Probably desolate outside of town."

"Look, beyond that small clump of buildings to the right. See that huge patch of hard-pack there?"

"Yeah, I see it. Looks like the spot. Think the dirt's hard enough?"

"Only one way to find out," Kyle said. He turned onto the dirt hard-pack. The vehicle lurched as it dropped off the shoulder of the road but then settled on the surface. "Level as a pool table."

"I wouldn't go that far," Kate said, gripping her seat.

"I'm gonna pull all the way to the far end and park diagonally, heading back onto the highway."

"Sounds like a plan," Kate said. "Slow down a little."

He glanced over at her and chuckled.

"Really," she said. "The trailer is behind us. I don't want everything all over the floor."

"Good point," Kyle said, slowing way down. They rolled to the end, and he made a sweeping turn, heading to the highway. There was a farm house just across the small dirt road that bordered the space.

"Here comes more vehicles," Kate said, pointing.

"Yeah," Kyle said. "This must be it."

They both got out. A little old man with a shotgun trotted over from the house.

"What're you guys doing here? This is private property."

"We were just stopping for a brief meeting," Kyle said. "We'll be gone pretty soon."

He squinted, looking at the top of the truck's roll bar. "Holy crap, is that a machine gun?"

"Yeah," Kyle said.

"You're that group that took on the heathens north of Fort Stockton, ain't ya?"

"Yep," Kate said.

He grinned. "Stay as long as you like." He lowered the shotgun. "Pleasure to have you here. Name's Jake."

"Kyle and Kate," Kyle said. "Thanks."

Vehicles flooded onto the property, parking neatly in rows behind and beside Kyle and Kate's rig.

"Wow," Jake said. "Battle coming?"

"Sure is," Kyle said. "Not around here, though. We're headed north."

They watched in awe as the huge field filled up.

Jake chuckled. "Glad I gassed up today. You guys probably bought everything."

"We were thinking the same thing," Kate said.

"You're purty," Jake said. "Ever been on TV?"

Kate's face turned red. "I was a news person for a while," she said. "West of here, though."

"I knew it," he said. "I remember you. Thought you were great."

"Thanks," she said.

"Wow, my woman is a celeb." Kyle grinned.

Jason trotted over with Carrie and Chelsea, Kelly and Brenda hot on their heels, followed by Junior and Rachel, Don and Sydney, and Curt with Amanda.

"Can you believe this?" Brenda asked.

"After what happened in that last battle, yes," Curt said. "Texas has the best people in the world."

"You better believe it," Jake said.

"Who's this?" Amanda asked.

"Everybody, this is Jake. Jake, this is…"

"Stop!" Jake said. "No need. I know who you are, and you guys have bigger fish to fry. Mind if I listen in?"

"No problem," Jason said.

"You look familiar too," Jake said. "Shit, you're one of those Austin cops that whacked the Islamists when this stuff started."

Junior laughed. "We were all in on that. Well, most of us, anyway."

"I'll be damned," Jake said. "Need more people? Love to join, and I got a lot of friends just itching to strike back."

"Hell yeah," Kelly said. "Might be rough, though."

"I can take rough," Jake said. "The hardest part will be telling the wife."

Curt chuckled.

"Look at all the vehicles," Carrie said. "They're not going to fit on this land."

"There's another piece of land like this on the other side of my house," Jake said. "Feel free."

"I'll go direct them," Junior said.

"I'll help," Rachel said. They ran out to the street and pointed at the other spot.

Dirk, Chance, Francis, Sherry, and Cindy all showed up, followed by many people they didn't know.

"Want a bull horn?" Jake asked. "Got one at the house. Use it for the rodeo."

"That would be excellent," Jason said.

People gathered around tighter and tighter as vehicles continued to arrive and park, on the highway shoulder and in the new space past the house.

Moe and Clancy walked over. "We left the tanks on the shoulder, with crews to protect them," Moe said.

"I don't know of an RV Park anywhere that will hold this many people," Clancy said. "Geez."

"I just talked to Ramsey a few minutes ago," Jason said. "There's an even larger group on the way from the Dallas area, believe it or not."

"Holy shit," Dirk said. "What are we gonna do with them all?"

"They aren't ours to do anything with," Curt said. "They're coming to stop the enemy."

"Damn straight," yelled a large man with a blonde beard and a shaved head. "My name's Jax. What's the plan?"

"Here's the bullhorn," Jake said, handing it to Jason. He got into the back of Kyle's pickup, leaning against the roll bar and machine gun.

"Everybody hear me?" Jason asked through the bullhorn.

"Yeah," Jax said.

There were others saying yes in the crowd, which appeared to be over five hundred people, and growing fast.

"How many of you guys were at the battle north of Fort Stockton?" Jason asked.

About half of them raised their hands.

"Thanks for that!" Jason said. "I'm glad to see you here. Texas needs all of us now. Things have gotten worse. The Feds and Islamists are squeezing us, and trying to keep us from shutting down their men and materiel flowing through New Mexico."

"Yeah, we heard about Galveston," somebody yelled from the crowd.

"That's right," Jason said. "They're trying to choke off our supplies and fuel. They're also trying to keep the National Guard busy with attacks like we just saw in San Antonio."

"We kicked their asses there!" somebody yelled.

"Yes, we did, but it took our people away from the task at hand," Jason said. "They slowed us from taking out the supply line in New Mexico. We need to get out of reactive mode and attack."

"So what's the plan?" Jax yelled.

"There's a huge supply depot in Santa Fe, New Mexico. We're planning to take a team across the border to destroy it. There's a big problem, though."

"What's that?" somebody yelled.

"There's a huge force of Islamists massing on the New Mexico border," Jason said. "They've been watching the same social media you guys have. They know we were planning to set up a base in Amarillo. They're going to attack us there."

"So what do we do?" somebody next to Jax yelled.

"We want to draw them in and kill them all," Jason said. "Then we want to go take out that supply depot."

"We should consider doing both at the same time," Junior shouted.

"Junior, come on up here and use the bullhorn," Jason said.

"Okay." He scrambled up onto the truck bed and took the bullhorn. "Everybody hear me?"

"Yeah, pencil neck," Curt yelled. People in the crowd laughed.

"Okay," Junior said. "We should draw the fight and take a smaller group into Santa Fe to take out that depot. We've got enough people."

"This is enough people for something like that?" Jax asked.

Jason took back the bullhorn.

"There's another group on their way in from the Dallas area," he said. "It's bigger than this group. A lot bigger."

Jax laughed. "Bitchen. So what now?"

"We need to hide our numbers," Jason said. "I'll throw out a suggestion. Our core group goes ahead. Give us about three hour's lead. Then every hour after that, more people take off. Not huge numbers. That way it'll be harder for the Feds to see what's going on with their satellite imagery."

"Wouldn't they have already seen us showing up here?" asked Dirk.

"Yeah, that could be a problem," somebody else shouted.

"I got a suggestion," Jake said. "Let's set up the rodeo stuff. I can get a bunch of livestock here in no time, and the group can hang out on the bleachers for a while. We dole people out from here slowly. If they see that in their satellite pictures, it might fool them about the large movement of folks."

"Damn good idea," Jason said. "We'll get on social media and ask the folks coming from the Dallas area to spread out too."

"Sounds like a good plan," Curt yelled. "Let's do it."

Jake climbed onto the truck bed and took back the bullhorn. "Okay, everybody, let's work this. I'll enlist townspeople too. We'll get bleachers set up. Even do some real rodeo to keep you entertained, and we'll get a barbeque going as well to get you all fed. Sound like a plan?"

There was a huge cheer from the group.

Jason took back the bullhorn. "Okay, everybody, we'll keep in touch. We're gonna nail these cretins in two locations. Catch them with their pants down. Long live Texas!"

The people cheered as Jason, Junior, and Jake got off Kyle's truck.

"You really think you can pull that off, old man?" Junior asked.

"Damn straight," Jake said. "You really think you can take out that depot in Santa Fe? That's a long ways into New Mexico."

Junior grinned. "Same answer."

{ 29 }

Action in Purgatory

Richardson and the big Mexican man stared at each other.

"You have somebody in that boat?"

"Yeah. That's a DPS Patrol Boat," Richardson said. "It's got two .50 cal's on it, manned by two of my men. We're DPS agents."

"There's no lakes back there," the man said, looking Richardson up and down. The woman looked scared to death. "No rivers big enough to float a boat that big either. What are you doing back here?"

"We're being chased by the Islamists. We need a place to lay low for a while. I used to hunt back there. Know the terrain."

"Oh," the man said. "You got any credentials? There's been some real scumbags coming through here, doing home invasions and taking away women. Islamist bastards."

"I'm going to approach. Don't shoot, okay? I'm not here to hurt you guys."

"Come ahead," the man said. Jason walked over to him and pulled out his wallet, then fished out his DPS ID.

"Here you go," Richardson said, handing it to him.

The man took it and looked it over, then handed it back. "Checks out. What do you plan to do?"

"Camp out for a few days. I'm Richardson. This is Lita, my wife."

Lita nodded to him cautiously.

"I'm Roberto," the man said. "Good to meet you. This is my wife, Kris. Sorry, hard to know who to trust anymore."

"I know," Richardson said.

"The road is on my property but there's an easement that belongs to the Purgatory Creek folks. Probably a good place to hide out. Nobody's been back here for a while. Not since all the nonsense started."

"Okay," Richardson said. "Thanks so much. We're gonna unhook the boat back there, then take the truck back through here to make a supply run. We'll try to be back before dark so we don't bother you."

"Don't worry about it if you do," Roberto said. "How come you guys are so far from any of the waterways?"

"We were on our way to the Houston area, to become part of the Galveston operation," Richardson said, a grim look on his face. "My commanding officer told us to lie low with the boat somewhere, and I remembered this area."

"Shit, you were in on that battle in downtown San Antonio, weren't you?"

"Yup," Richardson said. "Us and two other boats."

"Where are they?"

"Don't know," Richardson said. "Hopefully still alive. We were attacked on the road."

"You were, huh," Roberto said. "How'd you survive that?"

"My guys in the boat blasted them with the .50 cals."

Roberto snickered. "Well, that ought to do it."

"Yep," Richardson said.

"Okay. Good luck to you guys. If you need anything, let us know."

"Much obliged," Richardson said, smiling. He and Lita got back into the truck.

"Everything's okay?" Madison asked.

"Yeah, he's a nice guy, but he's cautious. Don't blame him a bit."

"Me neither," Lita said.

Richardson drove down the skinny dirt road, following it as it curved into the hills. "This is gonna be fine. Can't see it from the end of the street at all."

"How far in do we have to go?" Hannah asked.

"Not much further," Richardson said. "I don't think we want to be inside the boundaries of the Purgatory Creek area. I'd rather be outside it at least a few hundred yards."

"Look at that place there," Lita said. "Large flat spot, mostly covered by trees. Think the boat will fit under there?"

Richardson smiled as he looked at it. "Perfect. There's enough room to turn this thing around and get us pointed back down the road. Gonna be hard to get here from Purgatory Creek, too. Look at that little ravine."

Lita smiled. "That's why there's the big turnaround. You can't driver further than that unless you have a Jeep or something."

"Yep," Richardson said, making the sweeping turn. He pulled forward on the road out until the boat was fully under the trees, and shut down the engine. "Honey, we're home."

Madison snickered. "Oh, brother. This ain't the Ritz."

"It'll do," Hannah said. "I'm just glad we'll get a breather."

They got out of the truck. Juan Carlos and Brendan were climbing out of the boat as they approached.

"It's pretty back here, dude," Juan Carlos said, looking around at the old oak trees and brush around them. He gave Madison a hug. "How you holding up, baby?"

"I'm glad we're finally here," she said. "I want to stay here with you while they go to the store."

"No problem," Richardson said.

"Want me to stay here too, boss?" Brendan asked.

"It'll be okay with Juan Carlos and Madison," Richardson said. "We'll have a lot to carry."

"Teach her how to work the guns," Brendan said.

"Yeah, I can do that," Juan Carlos said. "Piece of cake."

"I'm game," Madison said. "Now I need to hobble off to the bushes."

"Me too," Brendan said.

"Yeah," Richardson said. "Never got to at the last stop."

"Oh, honey," Lita said.

"No worries," he said. "I can go a long time if I don't have beer or coffee."

"TMI." Hannah laughed.

They walked off to do their business while Hannah and Lita watched the road nervously. Everybody was back in a couple minutes.

Suddenly the big dogs started barking again.

"Geez, what are those?" Lita asked. "Rottweilers?"

"Sounds like Rotts to me, dude," Juan Carlos said. "Something's wrong. That Mexican guy shut them up real fast last time, remember? They're still barking."

There was a shotgun blast.

"Shit, grab the M60s and the M-16s," Richardson said.

"Roger that," Brendan said.

"Lita, remember what I showed you on those guns? Get in the boat. If somebody rushes back here, light them up."

"Got it," she said to Richardson as he checked the magazine on his M60.

The barking of the dogs became more frenzied, and there was automatic fire from a small-caliber weapon.

"Hear that?" Juan Carlos said as they ran. "AKs. Lay you ten to one."

They got to the back of Roberto's property. "Look, they're trying to surround the place."

There was another shotgun blast, and then more automatic fire.

"Well, we know Roberto is still kicking," Richardson whispered. "I'll take one M-60 on the far side of the house. Brendan, take the other M60 and hit this side. Juan Carlos, come up behind the house in the middle."

"You got it, chief," Brendan said. Juan Carlos nodded, and they crept forward.

Richardson ran behind the house and around to the front of the other side. He had a clear shot, so he opened up with the M60, causing screams in Arabic. Several of the Islamists fell where they stood. Several others ran right into Brendan. He opened fire, killing all but two of them. Then Roberto got a clean shot and fired the shotgun, knocking one of the remaining men about four feet backwards. Richardson blasted the last guy, and then there was the roar of an engine.

"Look out!" Juan Carlos yelled, firing full auto with his M-16 at the truck rushing towards Brendan. He dived out of the way, and then the front of the truck exploded.

"What the hell?" Brendan asked, turning to see Hannah holding the SMAW.

"Yes!" Juan Carlos yelled. "Nice frigging shot!"

"Saved me," Brendan said. "Thanks, sweetie."

"Don't mention it, honey," Hannah said.

"Let's go down the road a piece and see if there's more," Richardson said.

"Wait!" Roberto shouted. "I'll let the dogs out. No need to get shot."

"Good idea," Richardson said.

"Get up here by me," Roberto said. "So they don't kill you guys."

They all ran to the porch of the huge house. Then Roberto rushed around back and opened a gate. The dogs flew out, barking as they ran.

"Thanks, guys," Roberto said.

"Yes, thanks so much," Kris said. "They would've killed us. There were too many."

There were screams in Arabic and the snarling of dogs, then a cracking noise.

"Ouch!" Juan Carlos said.

Somebody else yelled, running for his life.

"Look, see him?" Juan Carlos said. "Should I nail him?"

"Save your ammo," Roberto said. "The dogs will take him."

There were snarls again, and screams as the big dogs ripped the Islamist's throat open.

After a few seconds the dogs trotted back over, blood around their mouths and chest.

"C'mon, let me introduce you guys," Roberto said. He brought the dogs over to Richardson, Hannah, Juan Carlos, and Brendan, letting them sniff each of them. Then one of the dogs froze and growled.

"Honey?" Lita called.

"Over here," Richardson said. "Madison with you?"

"Yeah," she said.

"I'll bring the dogs over," Roberto said, getting off the porch and walking with them. He introduced them to the dogs, and they all went back up to the porch.

"What the hell were you guys shooting?" Roberto asked.

Richardson held up his weapon. "M60 Machine gun."

"Wow," he said, "Never seen one of those up close."

"I'm sorry we brought these people at you. We'll have the DPS pay for any damage to the house."

"Hey, no problem," Roberto said. "Gave me a chance to kill these heathens. Not a bad day."

"Roberto!" Kris said. "That sounds downright barbaric. You aren't like that."

"I am when somebody attacks my homeland, or my house."

"Glad they came before we left for the Walmart," Lita said.

"Seriously," Juan Carlos said.

"What were you gonna get at the store?" Kris asked.

"Camping gear, so we could stay out here a few days," Richardson said.

"This place is almost four thousand square feet, and we've got extra bedrooms," Kris said. "Why don't you guys bunk here for a few days?"

"We wouldn't want to impose," Lita said.

"Nonsense, you'd be doing us a favor," Roberto said.

"Hey, if we do that, maybe we ought to pull the boat up here," Brendan said. "It's armored and it's got a hell of a lot of firepower. If anybody shows up to avenge the cretins, they won't live long."

"That's a good idea," Richardson said.

"I'm game, as long as we can get it far enough out of sight," Roberto said. "Don't want it visible from the road."

"How about alongside the house there?" Juan Carlos asked, pointing to a space. "Looks protected enough, but still open enough to move the turrets."

"That'll work," Roberto said.

"You know there's a good chance somebody else will show, right?" Lita said.

"Maybe, maybe not," Richardson said. "I don't know how they followed us. We took out the beacon."

"Yeah, we got hack-proof cellphones too," Madison said.

"We'll have to keep somebody on watch all night," Richardson said.

"No we won't," Roberto said. "The dogs will let us know if anybody's around. Trust me. Especially now. Their blood will be up for days. Always like that after a kill."

"Let's go get the boat," Richardson said.

Lita nodded, and they walked back.

"You folks hungry?" Kris asked.

"Just had pizza a little while ago," Hannah said.

"What's that thing you have there?" Roberto asked, looking at the SMAW. "Looks like a little bazooka."

"It is," Brendan said. "It's called a SMAW. Handy for taking out vehicles."

"We've got better than that on the boat," Juan Carlos said. "Two .50 cal machine guns with rocket launchers, and a big grenade launcher. Top notch stuff."

"I remember reading about those patrol boats," Roberto said. "I thought they only used those in the Rio Grande Valley and at Falcon Lake."

"They were," Brendan said. "We were on Falcon Lake when that submarine weapon went off. Barely made it to shore."

"Really?" Roberto asked. "I'll bet you have plenty of good stories to tell."

"Yeah, we do," Juan Carlos said.

Madison rolled her eyes.

"What?" he asked.

"Oh, nothing," Madison said. "I long for the simple, peaceful life."

"Here comes Richardson," Brendan said. "We'd better guide him while he backs up."

"Yeah, I'll help," Roberto said.

The men left the porch and helped Richardson get the boat in the right place. Then he killed the engine and got out. "This is perfect."

"We gonna unhook her?" Juan Carlos asked.

"Yeah, might as well," Richardson said.

The dogs growled again. Roberto froze.

"Oh, shit," Richardson said. "Juan Carlos and Brendan, in the boat."

"Girls, get in the house," Juan Carlos yelled.

"Hell no," Hannah said, reloading the SMAW.

"Give me Brendan's M60," Lita said.

Richardson nodded to Brendan, and he handed it over to her. "Don't get killed."

"Not part of the plan," Lita said. They all sought cover as Brendan and Juan Carlos got behind the port and starboard guns.

"What about the big gun?" Brendan asked.

"Let's see what's coming first," Richardson said. "That might start a damn fire back here."

Brendan chuckled. "Yeah, you might be right about that."

A pickup truck drove up the road fast, men in the bed holding onto the roof of the cab until the driver saw the house. Then the truck stopped and the men opened fire with AK-47s, bullets bouncing off the armor plating of the boat. Brendan brought the big gun to bear and pulled the trigger, .50 cal bullets cutting clean through the men in the cab and hitting the legs of the men standing behind the cab.

"There's another truck behind them," Brendan yelled. "Get on the damn big gun."

"Roger that," Juan Carlos said, getting into the pilot seat and pulling down the sight. He aimed and fired, blowing the second truck sky high. Then there was a pop and a whistle, and the woods behind the house exploded in flames.

"Oh, shit, they've got a mortar set up!" Brendan shouted.

{ 30 }

Accommodations

Jason got off the phone as Carrie was driving the motor home.

"Is Don's team making progress on the folks from the Dallas area?" she asked.

"Yeah," Jason said.

"Mommy, I'm hungry," Chelsea said from her seat on the couch.

"Give her a breakfast bar, okay sweetie?" Carrie asked.

"Sure." He got up and went to the pantry, Dingo sauntering over. "I know, boy, you're sick of all this traveling. So am I." He grabbed a bar and handed it to Chelsea.

"Daddy, you have to open it for me," she said.

"Oh, yeah," Jason said. He took it and tore it open, then handed it back to her.

"I want something to drink too," she said.

"Your water is right next to you."

"I don't want water," she said.

"Give her a box drink," Carrie said. "In the door of the fridge."

"Okay," Jason said. He took off the strap so he could open the fridge door, grabbed a drink, and turned towards the front. "You want a soda or something, Carrie?"

"Sure," she said.

He grabbed two sodas and then closed the fridge and re-strapped it.

"Finish the bar first," Jason told Chelsea. "I don't want this falling over on the couch. You have to hold it until it's empty, okay?"

"Yes, daddy," she said, mouth full of the bar. She finished it in a couple more bites, and then Jason put the straw in the box drink and handed it to her.

"Don't make a mess, honey," Jason said. "Don't squeeze the box too hard."

"Everybody knows that, daddy," she said. Carrie snickered as Jason got into the passenger seat. He opened the soda for her and put it into the cup holder on the center console.

"She takes after her mom," Jason quipped.

"Shut up," Carrie said, smile on her face.

"Mommy, don't say shut up," Chelsea said.

Jason shot Carrie a sidelong glance.

"You're right, sweetie," Carrie said. "I'm sorry."

"How're you holding up?" Jason asked.

"Usual pregnancy soreness," she said. "My back doesn't do as well on these long traveling days."

"Want me to drive?"

"No, it's really not any easier on my back if I just sit. Maybe it's even a little worse, because I slouch more."

"Okay, but let me know," he said.

"You think we're gonna survive this?"

"What? The attack in Amarillo or the attack on the depot?"

"Which are you gonna do? We're doing them at the same time, right?"

"We can't send our entire core group on the raid," Jason said. "We'll have to split up."

"Try to be on the team that stays where I am," Carrie said.

"Not sure I'll be able to do that. Hell, every couple is gonna want to do that."

"Every couple doesn't have a toddler and a bun in the oven," she said.

"Okay, you have a point there, I guess."

"Damn right I do," Carrie said. "What happens after this mess? We gonna have something like this to do over and over?"

"We're at war, honey," Jason said. "If we don't win, it'll be hell for our kids. You know that."

She sighed. "Yeah, I know that, I'm just tired. How far are we from Lubbock?"

"Just a sec," he said, pulling out his phone. He brought up the GPS app. "Really close. We're almost to Woodrow."

"Good," she said. "How far from Lubbock to Amarillo?"

"If we can stay on I-27, just under two hours."

"Shit, then we're gonna need gas again," she said.

"Yeah, but we can get it at Kress. We won't have to fight with the crowds in Lubbock."

"Well, that's something," Carrie said. "You're worried. What aren't you telling me?"

"The US Airforce," Jason said. "They can't weed out the bad guys like we've been doing. I'm afraid they're gonna hit us, either during the raid on the depot or even while we're in Amarillo."

"They could hit us on the road, too," Carrie said.

"They could, but it wouldn't be as easy. I think they'll wait if they're gonna do it."

"What happened with them?" Carrie asked. "I thought they were on our side."

"Remember what happened in the DPS? Those traitors who told the enemy where our trailers were?"

"Yeah," Carrie said. "I understand that, but it seemed like they were okay before."

"They might still be," Jason said. "Some of them attacked Galveston. We know that, but we don't know how widespread the problem is. Gallagher told Ramsey that the Airforce brass was pissed about it. They might have already locked those traitors up."

"Hope so," Carrie said. "We'll see, I guess."

Further back in the convoy, Don was driving his SUV and pulling the trailer, Sydney by his side. She was busy on social media.

"I'm surprised you still have a signal," Don said.

"I'm surprised too, but I read they've been building out the infrastructure into the remaining dead spots," she said. "At least in Texas. It's a different story in other parts of the southwest."

"Helps us out now."

"It does," Sydney said. "I'm surprised the enemy hasn't started hacking away at the infrastructure."

"Maybe they need it themselves," Don said.

"That's probably it," she said. "I'll bet it has something to do with those RFID chips."

"Think so?" Don asked.

"Yeah, I read an article about that technology a few years ago."

"Why would you be reading about that?" Don asked.

"Inventory control," she said. "The article was well written and easy to understand, even for somebody like me who isn't an IT person. Wish I could remember the name of the author. Frank something. Might be interesting to read now that we know the enemy is using similar technology."

Don snickered. "So you were thinking of putting RFID chips on your moonshine jugs?"

"Yeah, as a matter of fact. Those jugs are expensive. We charge if they aren't returned. It'd be nice if we knew in a flash how many we had and where the outstanding ones were."

"You can track outside of your own facility with these chips?"

"Yeah, that was what the article was about," Sydney said. "It was for multi-national corporations, so they could keep track of inventory world-wide over the internet."

"Oh," Don said.

"Frank *Johnson*," Sydney said. "I think that was the name. Maybe I'll google him when we're on a break someplace. The article was available on the web. That's how I got it before."

"You better hold off on that," Don said. "Remember what Ramsey and Nelson said. We don't want the enemy seeing us research their RFID setup on the internet."

"Shit, you're right," Sydney said. "I'll lay off."

"I wish that guy working for General Hogan would figure this out," Don said. "It'd be nice to know where all these creeps are at any given time."

"Wouldn't they just dig the chips out if we cracked them?"

"Easier said than done," Don said. "The ones we've seen so far were buried deep. It's dangerous to dig them out if you're not in a hospital. Good chances of infection."

"How do you know that?"

"Eric told me," Don said. "He's the person who dug them out after the last battle."

"You go back a long time with him, don't you?"

"Not nearly as far back as you do," Don said.

"We were kids when we were together," she said.

"I know, he told me all about it," Don said. "Well not *all* about it."

Sydney rolled her eyes. "Oh, please. How did you meet him?"

"He showed up near Deadwood after he crossed the border into Texas. Helped us fight."

"That's in the middle of nowhere, isn't it?"

"Kinda sorta," Don said. "He couldn't get past any of the border checkpoints from Louisiana, so he found a spot where he could drive across in the forest. Good thing he did. He helped us figure out that the enemy was coming over that way too. We would've lost a lot more people if not for him."

"I can't wait until we stop for a while. So tired of this."

"I can't wait until I get back into bed with you," Don said, shooting her a smile.

"Don!" she said.

"What? We're alone."

"I'm just teasing you," she said. "I've been itching for that too. Even if we don't do anything but cuddle."

"I know," Don said. "Maybe tonight."

"We'll see," Sydney said. "I think this is a dangerous time."

"Don't get into a bad mindset," Don said. "That doesn't help either of us."

"You're right," she said, watching him drive. "I love you so much."

"And I adore you," he said.

The phone rang. Don picked it up off the center console and looked at it.

"Moe," he said. "Here, put it on speaker."

"Okay," she said, taking it from his hand.

"Hey, Moe, hear us okay?" Sydney said.

"Yeah," Moe said. "Hold the line for a moment. I'm trying to patch in Jason, Kelly, Junior, Kyle, Curt, Cindy, Chance, and Dirk. Clancy's already on."

"Okay," Sydney said, shooting a worried glance at Don.

"Don't get worried yet, baby," Don said.

"Sorry, can't help it."

They waited as the phone beeped several times.

"Okay, I think everybody's on. You all hear okay?"

Several people said yes.

"Okay, here's the deal. I talked to the owner of the RV Park we're going to in Amarillo. Told him we had a whole lot more people coming."

"They can't handle that many, can they?" Curt asked.

"The park we're going to can handle a hundred and fifty coaches," Moe said. "They're pretty empty right now, and they're closing up until we get there."

"That's more than I expected," Jason said.

"Yeah, seriously," Dirk said, "but it's still nowhere near enough."

"There's two other big parks nearby. Almost walking distance. The biggest one is about half full, but it has a huge surge capacity."

"Surge capacity?" Junior asked.

"Yeah, they put on music festivals every few months. They've got about six- hundred RV spaces with hookups, and room for another several hundred tent campers."

"That's still not enough," Kelly said.

"Not finished yet," Moe said. "They've also got a huge flat area behind the park. He said we could put at least eight hundred tents back there, and he's got water and bathrooms on that end of his park. There's also a less level area behind that which could hold several hundred more in a pinch."

"Okay, so we're talking about fifteen hundred spaces, then," Kate said.

"Yep, and then there's the third place. It's more expensive, and it's got quite a few full-timers, but they still have another three-hundred spaces available."

"So roughly eighteen hundred," Kate said. "It's a good start."

"The surrounding area is pretty flat too, so we can expand out."

Junior chuckled. "It's gonna look like the Rio Grande Valley when the snowbirds show up."

"Yep," Moe said. "It's gonna be nuts."

"We'll be a big target for the enemy," Chance said. "Might be a problem."

"Yeah, I was thinking the same thing," Jason said. "Remember what the US Airforce did in Galveston."

"Shit," Curt said. "Maybe we ought to have some people stay in Lubbock, and some of the other towns in the area. There's a lot of small towns showing up on the map."

"Lake Meredith is pretty close by, too," Brenda said. "There used to be a lot of big camping spots there."

"Few of the small towns around there have RV Parks big enough to make a dent," Moe said. "Clancy and I have been looking into it. I could see Lubbock and the lake."

"What's your suggestion?" Jason asked.

"Maybe we should see if Nelson will cover reservations for all the places still open in Amarillo," Moe said. "What do you think, Jason? Could you run it up the chain?"

"Sure, I'll call Ramsey," Jason said. "I share Chance's concern, though. We don't want to expose ourselves any more than possible."

Junior chuckled. "Guys, we're gonna have many thousands of people showing up, from what I'm seeing on social media. No matter where we go, we'll be visible to the enemy."

"Yeah, Junior's right," Curt said. "I say we go ahead and reserve the spaces we can, and play it by ear. Don't think I like the idea of our forces being too far away. We could die waiting for them to arrive if there's a problem. My cellphone early warning tools aren't worth much anymore. They got wise."

"Anybody object to making the arrangements?" Moe asked.

Nobody said anything.

"Okay, I'm gonna do it," Moe said. "Work the money, Jason, okay?"

"You got it," Jason said.

"Take care, folks," Junior said. "See you there."

A few people said goodbye and the call ended.

Don looked at Sydney. "Scared?"

"Yeah, but I've been scared since I joined up with this crazy outfit. It is what it is."

{ 31 }

B-1 Bombers

Maria's phone rang. She looked at it, and glanced over at Hendrix, on the couch next to her.

"Shit, it's my mom." She put the phone to her ear and got up, walking into the console room.

Hendrix turned down the TV and listened as the conversation on Maria's end got more and more heated. Maria ended the call and came back into the living room, tears running down her cheeks.

"You okay?" Hendrix asked, getting up to hug her.

"Mom found out we're married," Maria said.

"It was bound to happen eventually," Hendrix said, hands caressing her back. "How?"

"Some reporters saw us together when we went to the Capitol," she said. "They thought our body language looked a little strange, so they did a records search and found out about the marriage. I'm so sorry."

Hendrix pulled back from her and lifted her chin so she was looking at him. "I'm proud we're married, and I want everybody to know about it."

"I know, honey," she said. "It makes it more difficult for you, though."

"No it doesn't," Hendrix said. "Don't worry about it."

"Celia screwed my mom's boyfriend again," Maria said. "My family is so messed up."

"Celia needs help," Hendrix said. "She's mentally ill. You know that."

"Frankly, my mom's not much better," Maria said. "She said she's going to kick Celia out of her house again."

"Do we need to take her in?"

"Absolutely not," Maria said. "I won't have her here. No way, no how."

"Well, I'll support you any way you want me too," Hendrix said.

"I know, honey," Maria said. She kissed him gently. "Look at the family you've married into."

"Don't worry about it," Hendrix said.

"What if she shows up?"

"Do you think they know where we are?" Hendrix asked.

"I didn't tell her, but Celia may figure it out."

"Then we'll deal with it," Hendrix said. "Don't worry about it now."

"I'll try not to," she said.

"Good. Want a drink? Might settle you down."

"I'd rather have you," she said. "Let's go in the bedroom for a little while."

"I like that idea." Hendrix smiled.

They broke their embrace and were walking towards the hallway when the console beeped.

Hendrix laughed. "Shit."

Maria giggled. "So much for that idea. I'll go log on."

"Okay," Hendrix said, following her into the console room.

Maria got the meeting up while Hendrix pulled the second chair next to her. They watched the monitor as Ramsey, Gallagher, and Nelson walked into the conference room, Brian at the laptop again. A second window opened showing Wallis's face.

"Thanks for coming, everybody," Nelson said. "We've got a possible emergency brewing. I wanted the team to know about it right away."

"Wonderful," Hendrix said.

"Go ahead, Wallis," Nelson said.

"Yes sir. I got an encrypted message from the leadership of the US Airforce."

"Uh oh," Gallagher said.

"What's going on?" Hendrix asked.

"Half a dozen bombers flew out about half an hour ago, without authorization."

"Without authorization from whom?" Ramsey asked. "The folks that ordered the bombing of Galveston?"

"I wish," Wallis said. "No, they think it's the people who *were* involved with that bombing. Something tipped them off that the brass was close to exposing them."

"Does the brass know about the RFID chips?" Gallagher asked.

"Don't know, and I didn't mention that," Wallis said.

"Son of a bitch," Gallagher said. "What did they take?"

"B-1 Bombers," Wallis said, grim look on his face.

"Well, at least they didn't take off with any of the stealth bombers," Ramsey said.

"These are just as bad," Wallis said. "All they have to do is fly low, and that's easy over Texas."

Nelson's forehead was sweating. "What's the payload? Not nuclear, I hope."

"They aren't saying, Governor," Wallis said. "Probably conventional. The B-1 isn't their strategic platform anymore."

"What should we do?" Nelson asked.

"If the drones are ready, maybe we should get them in the air," Ramsey said.

"No," Wallis said. "The B-1 bombers will see them and shoot them down. We don't want that. They're not ready yet, anyway. We just got them a few hours ago. We have ground stations to set up and man."

"So, what do we do?" Gallagher asked. "Sit here with our thumbs up our butts until they run out of fuel?"

"Colorful," Wallis said. "I'm afraid that's all we can do at this point. I suggest we keep important personnel underground."

"Should we warn the Fort Stockton group?" Ramsey asked.

Nelson sighed. "Yeah. Not that there's anything we can do beyond that."

"I'm not giving up yet," Wallis said. "When we get off this call, I'm gonna call my contact and chat about putting some reliable people in the air to counter this."

"Don't mention the RFID chips," Nelson said.

"I won't," Wallis said. "Trust me on that."

"Okay," Nelson said. "Brian, send out a text to everybody on the list. Order them to get to an underground shelter as quickly as possible. Got it? Say it's an order from me."

"Will do, Governor," Brian said.

Wallis's eyes got big. "Just a sec." He left the screen.

"Shit, wonder what that's about?" Hendrix asked, feeling his heart beat quicker.

Wallis came back, sweat on his brow. "San Antonio is under bombardment."

"Oh no," Nelson said. "What are they hitting?"

"The National Guard troop encampment just outside of town," Wallis said.

"Son of a bitch," Gallagher said. "We've got anti-aircraft batteries there. I'm gonna make the call. Talk to you guys later." He got up and rushed out of the conference room.

"I'm ending the call now," Nelson said. "Stay underground. That's an order."

The monitor went dark. Maria looked at Hendrix.

"Don't worry, we're safe down here," Hendrix said. "They can't touch us."

"I know," she said. "I'm scared for Texas."

He took her hand. "Me too."

The monitor beeped again.

"Oh, crap, what now?" Hendrix asked.

Maria clicked on the monitor. "This is outside."

"President Pro Tempore Hendrix?" the man asked.

"I'm here," Hendrix said. "What is it?"

"There's a hysterical young woman at the gate," the man said. "She's insisting we let her in. Says she's your sister-in-law. It looks like she's off her meds. What do you want me to do?"

Hendrix and Maria looked at each other in shock.

{ 32 }

Amarillo

Kyle took the off-ramp onto Bell street in Amarillo. "We're gonna attract a lot of attention. Wait till those tank flatbeds roll through here."

"I don't think we can worry about that now," Kate said. "This is mostly residential. Nice looking homes."

"Yeah. Where do I turn?"

"Get on Westbound·I-40," Kate said. "All three parks are next to it, each further out of town."

"Shit, we're probably visible from the damn interstate, then. Which one is ours?"

"The first one we run into," she said. "It's just past South Soncy Road, on the right-hand side of I-40. The next one is on the left-hand side, about half a mile down."

"What's the name?"

"Amarillo Oasis," Kate said.

"Where's the third one?"

"Quarter of a mile past the second one, on the right-hand side of I-40."

"Damn, wish we weren't gonna be clustered so close together," Kyle said. "I've got a bad feeling about this."

"Look, that cop over there is looking us over," Kate said.

Kyle looked over, then cracked up. “He just gave me a thumb’s up sign. Must know who we are.”

Kate smiled. “Good. Now I can relax a little more.”

“I see I-40 down there already.”

“Yeah, this isn’t a huge town,” Kate said.

“The second group ought to be taking off soon,” Kyle said. “Hope we’re doing the right thing.”

“You think we’ll get attacked before we have enough people here?”

“Probably not,” Kyle said. “Remember what Jason told us a little while ago. None of the enemy fighters have come across the border into Texas yet. They’re still where they’ve been for the past several days. They can’t get here that fast.”

“I was looking at that earlier,” Kate said. “It’s just over an hour from Glenrio to Amarillo. That’s not much. If they left now, they could get here before the entire group arrives.”

“Thanks for that warm fuzzy feeling,” Kyle said, grinning at her.

“You don’t look very scared.”

“Somebody’s watching out for us,” Kyle said.

“Or we’ve been lucky, and you know what they say.”

“What’s that?”

Kate looked down the road. “Luck has a way of running out.”

“Don’t worry, honey,” Kyle said. “Here’s I-40.” He drove over the bridge, then took the frontage road to the on-ramp. “Not much traffic.”

“I’m glad,” Kate said. “It’s not too far, so stay in the right-hand lane.”

“Okay,” Kyle said. “Look at that mall to the left. It’s huge.”

“Yeah, this is more built-up than I expected. Guess the bulk of the town runs along I-40.”

“You didn’t look at the satellite view of the map?” Kyle asked.

“Too damn small,” Kate said. “There’s your off-ramp.”

"I see it," Kyle said, taking it onto the frontage road. "That must be it. Corny sign."

Kate laughed, looking at the sign. It had a picture of a camel wearing sunglasses. The letters it was standing on spelled out *Amarillo Oasis.* "Of course they're going to have a camel. It's an Oasis."

Kyle turned into the driveway, then busted up laughing. "No frigging way."

"What?"

"Look who that is," he said, nodding towards the small old man with white hair sticking out of his face and head.

"Oh, shit, is that Brushy?" she asked.

"Sure as hell is," Kyle said as he pulled up into the check-in lane. They got out of the truck as others pulled up.

"Well I'll be damned," Kyle said, rushing over. "We were wondering what happened to you."

Brushy laughed as he approached. "Kyle! Kate! Great to see you. I was hoping it was you when my sister told me there was a big group coming in from Fort Stockton."

"What happened?" Kate asked. "Where'd you go?"

"My sister got into a bad car accident," he said. "Had to rush home and take care of her. She owns this park."

"Oh," Kyle said. "She okay now?"

"Almost," he said. "I've been helping her run the place. Not like I can get mine started back up."

Kelly and Brenda parked and trotted over. "You've got to be kidding me," Kelly said. "Brushy?"

"Kelly!" Brushy said. "Brenda! Damn, you're a sight for sore eyes."

"Likewise," Kelly said.

"You guys lose anybody?" Brushy asked.

"Gray," Brenda said, choking up.

"Oh no," Brushy said. "How?"

"Killed by a sniper after a battle," Kelly said. "It was a hard loss. We also lost Fritz, Earl, Jackson, and…" Kelly broke down. Brushy looked at him helplessly.

"Nate too," Brenda said softly.

"You guys have had a tough time," he said. "I don't remember Earl or Jackson, but I remember Fritz and Nate. Good guys."

"Yes, they were," Kyle said.

The rest of the vehicles were lining up, overflowing the check-in area.

"Why don't you guys go find spaces so we don't get too clogged up," Brushy said. "We'll deal with the particulars later."

"Okay, Brushy," Kyle said. "Thanks."

They got back into the truck and drove into the park, the others following. It took nearly an hour for everybody to come through the gate and find a space.

Jason, Kyle, Kelly, Junior, Eric, Chance, Dirk, and Francis met by the clubhouse. Curt walked over too, with Amanda by his side. Moe, Cindy, and Clancy joined them a moment later. A few others straggled over as they talked.

"Can you believe that Brushy is here?" Junior asked.

"You guys know him?" Chance asked.

"Yeah, from an RV Park we spent the night in, early on," Jason said.

"Had a hell of a battle there," Curt said. "Almost got killed. After we left he got attacked again. They burned down his park."

"Junior and I stopped there," Kelly said. "It was in ruins, and we almost got killed."

"You guys weren't together by then?" Eric asked.

"No, we met up with Jason, Kyle, Curt, and the others later. Brushy joined us after his park was burned to the ground."

"He's one guy that won't let an attack ruin a good barbeque, I'll tell you that," Curt said.

Jason busted up. "Oh, yeah, forgot about that."

"What are we gonna do now?" Eric asked.

"I think we ought to go check out the clubhouse," Junior said. "They might have a pot of coffee going. I could use it."

"Seriously," Kelly said. "I'm gonna go get Brenda."

"Yeah, I'll pick up Rachel too," Junior said. "Meet you over there."

"Want to go over too, honey?" Amanda asked Curt.

"Yeah," he said. "Whenever you're ready."

"I'm gonna go get Don and Sydney, okay?"

"I'll go too," Curt said.

"Curt, stick around for a second," Jason said.

"It's fine, honey," Amanda said. "I'll go. Meet you at the clubhouse."

Curt walked over to Jason. "What's going on?"

"Just a sec," Jason said. "Hey, Kyle, come over here, okay? You too Dirk, Chance. Eric."

"What's going on?" Kyle asked.

"Ramsey called me right before we came in here. We might have a problem."

"You gonna tell us, pencil neck?" Curt asked.

"Yeah," Jason said. "There was some kind of blow-up in the US Airforce. Ramsey said some of the bad apples took off with half a dozen bombers. B-1s."

"Oh, shit," Eric said. "We know where they're going?"

"Two of them were bombing the outskirts of San Antonio right before he called," Jason said, grim look on his face. "They hit the camp where the National Guard men were. Luckily more than half of them were gone before it happened."

"Son of a bitch," Curt said. "We know what payload they're carrying?"

"Not for certain, no," Jason said. "Probably conventional. That's what they hit San Antonio with."

"I'm not hiding this from Amanda," Curt said.

"Carrie already knows," Jason said. "She's spreading the word quietly to the others."

"Afraid to let the park owners know?" Francis asked.

"I think we'd better go tell Brushy right now," Kyle said. "We don't want to hide it from him. He's a friend."

"I agree," Jason said.

"We should've told Kelly and Junior."

"Was going to, but they took off too quick," Jason said. "They probably know by now. Carrie was gonna tell Brenda and Rachel. They've gotten pretty close."

Brushy walked over. "You guys are in a huddle, and you don't look happy. Give me the bad news."

"We were on our way," Jason said. "There are six rogue B-1 Bombers on the loose over Texas."

"Wonderful," Brushy said. "Think they're coming here?"

"We have no idea," Jason said. "Two of them just hit the outskirts of San Antonio. They might only concentrate on the big cities."

"They know about us," Dirk said. "We're pretty high on their shit list."

"Here come the others," Curt said. "Let's go to the clubhouse."

"I was just coming to invite you over," Brushy said. "We got coffee made, and my sis made up a bunch of cobbler this morning."

"Let's go, then," Jason said.

Carrie, Kate, Kim, Brenda, Rachel, and Cindy walked over. Don was behind them with Sydney and Amanda. Sherry followed with Alyssa, Chloe, and the other teens. The rest of the people were behind them. They made their way to the clubhouse, following Brushy.

"This is never gonna end," Kim whispered to Eric. He put his arm around her shoulder. They walked through the large veranda into the clubhouse.

"Everybody, this is my sister Pat," Brushy said. He nodded to her, a woman in her mid-sixties with longish gray hair, about the same height as Brushy with a similar smile.

"Welcome, everybody," she said, beaming.

Brushy whispered in her ear, her eyes widening.

"Sorry," Jason said. "Hope we don't bring a problem to you guys."

She smiled through the fear. "I know about you guys. Brushy told me. I also heard about what you did north of Fort Stockton. I'm ready to join the fight. Don't worry about it."

People lined up to get coffee and cobbler, set up on a row of long tables against the paneled wall. The clubhouse was large and rustic, nicer looking than Moe's, but without the electronics he had. There was a small stage in the back wall, and an old flat screen TV on the wall next to it. The kitchen was to the right of the stage, through a double-wide door.

"Nice place," Moe said to Brushy and Pat. "Thanks for taking us on."

"It's a pleasure," Brushy said. "Hard to get these places out of your blood."

"You'll get your place back," Pat said. "Just you wait and see."

"I know," Brushy said. "Pisses me off that I lost my barbeque setup. It was one of the best in the state."

Pat snickered. "Oh, please. It was a bunch of fifty-five gallon drums. You can make another one just like it, you know."

"It was seasoned," Brushy said. "That takes years."

"I saw that there," Kelly said. "When we stopped by, after it got burned. Looked okay to me. You haven't been back there?"

"Nope," Brushy said. "It's really okay?"

"Looked like it," Kelly said.

“I don’t know, man,” Junior said. “We didn’t have time to do a good inspection. Going there was almost our undoing.”

“Why did you go, anyway?” Brushy asked. “I didn’t know you guys then.”

“We wanted a place to spend the night,” Kelly said.

“Oh,” Brushy said. “Sorry we weren’t open.”

Kelly and Junior looked at each other, then Brushy. All of them laughed, Pat shaking her head. “I can see why you all get along.”

There was a low rumble outside. Everybody froze.

“Dammit, what’s that?” Kelly asked, Brenda getting closer to him.

Jason, Kyle, and Curt ran to the door and looked to the west.

“No!” Carrie cried, coming up behind Jason with Chelsea in her arms. There were two B-1 Bombers flying low and fast towards the west.

Brushy rushed out. “They’re heading towards the Johnson place,” he said. “Lot of coaches there. Probably looks like a better target.”

“They’re gonna see the tanks here in no time,” Curt said as the bombers dropped a load on the RV Park, the fireball growing huge before their eyes, the ground rumbling.

“Everybody out!” Brushy yelled. “Run into the field behind the park, and keep going. Spread out!”

People flooded out of the clubhouse in a panic, racing towards the back of the park as the two bombers made a sweeping turn.

“They’re gonna make another run!” Brushy shouted.

To be continued in Bug Out! Texas Book 7.

Cast Of Characters

Texas Hill Country Group

Jason – Austin PD. Young man with family. Brave, trustworthy, great in a fight, loyal. Six foot four and handsome with thick sable hair. Considered to be a high-potential employee by Austin PD. Responsible. Mid 30s.

Carrie – Jason's wife. Strong, brave, witty, smart. Short dark hair and delicate, pretty face. Girl next-door type. Has calming effect on Jason and others. Good in a fight, brave to a fault. Pregnant. Mid 30s.

Chelsea – toddler, daughter of Jason and Carrie. Cute, rambunctious.

Kyle – Austin PD. Partner of Jason. Large man, built like a linebacker, with sandy blonde hair and a sly grin. Cheerful, funny, great in a fight, puts on front of being player, but really a romantic. Worships girlfriend Kate. Mid 30s.

Kate – strong, beautiful, emotional, witty. Former news reporter for a local Texas TV station. Fell hard for Kyle, carrying his baby. Temper. Early 30s.

Kelly – leader of Rednecks. Huge man with long brown hair and a beard. Tough, gruff, smart, great judge of character. Strategic thinker. Man's man. In love with Brenda. Mid 50s

Brenda – half-owner of Texas Mary's Bar and Grill in Dripping Springs. Voluptuous with bleach blonde hair and a slightly wild look. Deeply in love with Kelly. Extremely intelligent. Runs business side of Texas Mary's. Strong but worries about Kelly constantly. Good in a fight. Mid 50s.

Junior – Kelly's best friend. A tall rail of a man with a thick beard, usually wearing a battered cowboy hat. Funny, crazy, smarter than most people realize, good in a fight, strong, loyal to the death. In love with Rachel. Early 50s.

Rachel – picked up on the road. Black hair and brown eyes, short and thin, with a face of delicate beauty. Former drug abuser with difficult past. Lost only child to SIDS, which broke up her first marriage and led to the drug abuse. Leans on Junior, needs strong man in her life. Late 30s.

Curt – former police officer in Austin, and most recently San Antonio. Large man with a military haircut, clean shaven. Punched superior officer in San Antonio. Genius. Renaissance man. Understands many technical disciplines, creative, skilled. Has temper but with heart of gold. Likes to tease his friends. Would die for them. Skilled fighter who can turn the tide of a battle on his own. Sense of humor can be very crude but funny. Mid 40s.

Simon Orr – dangerous leader of militia movement, trying to take over Kelly's group. Large man wearing cowboy garb. Shadowy, cruel. Crossover character from original Bug Out! Series. Wants to become warlord. Playing against every side except his own. Mid 40s.

Sydney – one of the Merchant girls living outside of Fredericksburg, next to Jason's family homestead. Grew up with Jason and his brother Eric. Former teenage girlfriend of Eric. Beautiful, smart, funny, avid hunter and tracker, runs family moonshine business with her sister Amanda. Raven hair and stunning bright blue eyes. Mid 30s.

Amanda – Sydney's older sister. Raunchy, wild, aggressive, knows what she wants and goes for it hard. Beautiful, deep blue eyes like Sydney, hair bleached blond, contrasts with jet-black eyebrows. Tattoos. Smart, good negotiator, runs family moonshine business with Sydney, more technically savvy. Early 40s.

Gray – leader of the bikers, originally from southwest Texas. A large man with black hair and a black beard. Brave and resourceful, suspicious of strangers, but loyal once he's gained respect. Late 40s.

Cindy – Gray's wife. Nervous, small dainty blonde with tattoos and piercings. Pretty face ravaged by a hard life. Early 40s.

Moe – owner of the Fort Stockton RV Park. Overweight and balding with a gray and brown beard, shrewd and strong, strategic thinker, protective, kind. Mid 60s.

Clancy – Moe's nephew. Scraggly thin man with a wicked grin and long stringy brown hair. Works at the Fort Stockton RV Park. Smart as a whip with good intuition. Outdoorsman. Protective of the group, good with technology, good at organizing and getting things done. Mid-30s.

Brushy – owner of an RV Park overrun early in the story. He's been missing for a while. Small man with a huge beard and long hair, about sixty years old. Good in a fight, fearless, crazy, funny.

Pat – Brushy's sister, owner of the Amarillo Oasis RV Park. She's a couple years younger than Brushy, with a similar look. Short, robust, friendly, smart. Brave, angry at the invaders.

Jax – huge man with a blonde beard and a shaved head. Joined the group with a huge group of citizens. Gung ho, brave to a fault, cunning and loyal.

East Texas/Florida Group

Eric – Jason's brother. Over six feet tall with a trim but massive build. Was living in Florida before the war started. Private Investigator working elder fraud cases in retirement areas of central Florida. Brave, very athletic. Fast, good with guns and other weapons. Smart, charismatic. Loved by everybody. Loyal to a fault. Mid 30s.

Kim – Eric's girlfriend. Red-haired, freckled beauty with a slim build. Tough as nails but gentle, head over heels in love with Eric. Mid 30s.

Dirk – leader of Deadwood, Texas group. Medium sized man with a muscular build. Gruff, shrewd, brave, sentimental. Loves family and friends. Large man, muscular build. Late 50s, but a young late 50s.

Chance – best friend of Dirk. Short and chubby but quick, good in a fight. Wise cracks a lot. Good mixture of smarts and bravery, but cautious. Mid 40s.

Don – single dad widower with teenage daughter. Large man, average build with a conservative haircut. Kind and gentle, smart, protective. Lonely, misses wife. Brave but not really a fighter. Took in daughter's best friend when her family passed. Late 30s.

Francis – Don's older brother. Local political figure in Deadwood. Older man, spry for his age. Smart, good strategic thinker, understands the meaning of events better than rest of group, sage. Mid-60s.

Sherry – Francis's wife. Younger than him by ten years. Still pretty, trying hard to live during wartime but having trouble. Depression. Mid 50s.

Alyssa – Don's daughter. Pretty, a little self-centered. Misses mother. Terrified of enemy after attacks on Deadwood. 17 years old.

Chloe – Alyssa's best friend. Orphan taken in by Don after both parents killed. Mousey, kind, smart, helps Alyssa to cope. 17 years old.

Alex – Owner of the MidPoint 66 Café, who met the group during the I-40 battle. Older man, bald and heavy set, robust, funny.

Kitten – Daughter of Alex. Middle aged, chubby with light brown hair and a pretty face. Waitress at her father's Café.

Stanton Hunt – War Chief of the Mescalero Tribe. Brave man, thoughtful, severed in the Army for years, friends with General Hogan.

White Eagle – adviser and spokesperson for the Mescalero Tribe. Doesn't trust the white man. In favor of keeping an alliance with the Islamists. Dangerous man.

DPS Patrol Boaters Group

Juan Carlos – young, handsome Hispanic, full of vigor and enthusiasm. Skilled boat pilot, brave and cunning. Family in Texas since before the Alamo. Loves the state, patriot. Mid 20s.

Brendan – partner of Juan Carlos. Also young and handsome, ginger redhead. Loves to joke and tease, but can be serious. Good with weapons, natural fighter. Mid 20s.

Lieutenant Richardson – Leader of Juan Carlos and Brendan. Handsome man of average size and build with light brown hair. Tough, strong, thoughtful, loyal, brave. Headed for higher rank. Mid 30s.

Lita – girlfriend of Lieutenant Richardson. Beautiful Hispanic woman with model's figure and expressive eyes. Witty, smart, brave. Emotional, worships her man. Protective, mothering. Mid 30s.

Madison – girlfriend of Juan Carlos. Emotional but brave, beautiful with thick blonde hair and curvy figure, college girl forced to quit due to war. Head over heels for Juan Carlos. Mid 20s.

Hannah – best friend of Madison and girlfriend of Brendan. Dark haired beauty. Slim dancer's figure, athletic. Self-conscious, afraid to be hurt, passionate, very deeply in love with Brendan. Can rally in a fight if needed, surprisingly brave when pushed. Terrified of losing Brendan in the war. Mid 20s.

DPS Commissioner Wallace – overall head of DPS Organization. Strong, cunning, thinks several steps ahead of most others. Black man, large and imposing. Loves his men. Feeling is mutual. Early 60s.

Chuck – Gun shop owner in downtown San Antonio, Texas. Big man, brave, expert gunsmith. In love with Carol.

Roberto – owner of a property near Purgatory Creek. Large Mexican man, middle aged, with a good heart, brave but cautious.

Kris – small white woman with gray hair, middle aged, married to Roberto. Brave and strong, used to hardship from childhood. Generous and loving.

Gerald – Roberto's friend. Redneck always ready for a fight. Long gray hair, thin, always wearing a railroad cap. Brave to a fault.

Jay – Roberto's friend, and friends with Gerald. Lanky black-haired man in his early fifties. Sensitive but will fight hard when pushed.

Hector – Another friend of Roberto's. Overweight Mexican man in his mid-forties. A little crazy. Demolition expert. Always ready to bring dynamite to any party.

Harley – DPS Lieutenant, stationed at the new South Padre Island base. Good man with goofy sense of humor and an easygoing manner.

Leadership

Kip Hendrix – President Pro Tempore of the Texas Senate, and the leading liberal in that body. Large man, bald, with a wrinkled face but a dashing look. Has corrupt past, problems with sexual harassment, but down deep has a good heart. Trying to be better. Very complex person. Old friends with Governor, loves him even though they were estranged for many years. Multi-level thinker, good intuition, protective of those he loves, nasty enemy to have. Deeply in love with

Maria, although he viewed her as just another conquest at first. Early 50s.

Maria – secretary to Kip Hendrix. Hispanic beauty with curvy figure and a haunting face, well liked and respected by all around her. Knows how to get things done in Texas government. Fell hard for Kip Hendrix, now loyal to him above all else. Late 30s.

Governor Nelson – Charismatic conservative leader of Texas. Handsome in a rugged way. Patriotic, honest, strong, but opinionated. Old college buddy with Kip Hendrix. Strong bonds between them, even though they are political opposites. Thinks several steps ahead of others, takes risks when he knows he's right. Loved by the people of Texas, for the most part. Has solid-gold BS detector. Early 50s.

Brian – Governor Nelson's secretary and right-hand man. Black man. Cunning and loyal to the Governor. Protects him at all times. Much more important person than most people know. Mid 30s.

Commissioner Holly – ultra left-wing member of the Police Commission. Friends with Kip Hendrix. Tall and skinny with a goatee. Smart but far from open-minded. Constantly knocking heads with the Austin Police Department. Holding his nose to support Governor Nelson while the war is on. Mid 50s.

Jerry Sutton – aid to Kip Hendrix. Political operator. Clean shaven and pudgy. Tries to do a good job. Cares more about power than political philosophy. Early 30s.

Chief Ramsey – Austin Police Chief. Overweight but still burley, with the look of a redneck. Old friends with Governor Nelson. Didn't get along with Kip Hendrix in the past, but friends now, fighting a common enemy. Brave and loyal, strong leader, cares more about his cops than himself. Early 50s.

Major General Gallagher – head of Texas Army National Guard. Old-time soldier, tough and strong, unafraid. Loved by his men. Mid 60s.

Major General Landry – head of Texas Air National Guard. Cocky but cautious about using his resources, almost to a fault. Late 40s.

General Walker – US Army General, stationed in Texas until the war broke out. Near genius intelligence, charismatic, uncanny ability to turn a defeat into a victory. Feared by the enemy. Crossover character from original Bug Out! Series. Mid 50s.

General Hogan – US Army General, friend of General Walker. Black man, loved by his men, tough, no-nonsense. Strategic thinker, takes risks, understands people. Fine leader. Crossover character from original Bug Out! Series. Mid 50s.

Saladin – evil leader of the Islamist forces in the western states. He is not in Texas, but the Texas leadership is aware of him and his plans. Crossover character from original Bug Out! Series.

President Simpson – current President of the United States.

Major Josh Carlson – Second in command over the Texas Air National Guard. Right Hand Man of Major General Landry.

Celia – beautiful but troubled sister of Maria. Mental issues; depression and addiction.

Private Ken Brown – General Hogan's son. On special assignment to help the Fort Stockton team.

Private Jose Sanchez – on General Hogan's staff. Childhood friend of Private Brown. On special assignment to help the Fort Stockton team.

Captain Smith – near genius Texas Army National Guard officer with rank of Captain. Pilots effort to mass-produce Curt's gimbal system for vehicles. Designs adjustable mounts for mini-guns.

ABOUT THE AUTHOR

Robert G Boren is a writer from the South Bay section of Southern California. He writes Short Stories, Novels, and Serialized Fiction.

Made in the USA
Las Vegas, NV
19 July 2021